"*Our Calling. A White ...* ph A White Jr continues the story of Jeff who is now almost used to lucid dreaming and his frequent astral projections. However, that doesn't mean he is okay with what he sees when he is projecting. Things change when Jeff's lucid dreams take him to the South American jungle where he becomes privy to information Jeff is not meant to receive. Strange and dangerous drugs are being pumped into the United States and Jeff is the reluctant witness to it all. He doesn't want to be a part of it, but when matters are taken out of proportion, Jeff has no other option but to get involved. With lucid dreaming on his side, Jeff has the power to stop the mess before it is too late. Will he do something about it? Or will Jeff be a silent bystander?

Intriguing and complex, *Our Calling* picks up after *The Between State* instalment and Jeff is far more mature than he was; he has accepted his astral projection and lucid dreaming. Does it make him uncomfortable at times? Of course, it does. Does that stop him from working his butt off to stop the drugs from entering the USA? Joseph A. White Jr has created heaven for suspense readers who love a little tension and a lot of drama. The descriptions are fantastic, so much so that I felt like I was right in the middle of thick trees and standing among men with strange accents. Jeff journeys from a man who is excited yet timid of his lucid dreams to a man who is looking forward to solving a mystery. It is apparent that White did some deep research for this story and I loved every bit of it!"

—Rabia Tanveer for Readers' Favorite

"Who would have thought that we would encounter metaphysical activities like astral travel and lucid dreaming in the context of the drug trade? Joseph A White Jr. has the courage and fertile imagination to create such a narrative and make it work. *Our Calling* is the second book in *The Between State* series. It is replete with exciting and suspenseful moments that keep you on the edge of your seat. The book shows you the fun side of lucid dreaming and astral projection, albeit with some exaggeration, which keeps the plot interesting. You don't even need the backstory, as this book can be read as a standalone. I liked the way that some of the dialogue is presented in Spanish. It made the setting more relevant and also gave the characters some flavor. The twists and humorous rejoinders further sweetened the plot. I was impressed by the precision with which the scenes were narrated and the realistic integration of the metaphysical aspects, which made for a complicated plot. White did well to exclude unnecessary information and keep the narration concise while still managing to have a great ending and enough material for the next installment."
—Joshua Olokodana for Readers' Favorite

"At the heart of *Our Calling* lies a new kind of angle in the crime genre that crosses with the paranormal to deliver non-stop excitement. As the protagonist can enter the subconscious of another, the storyline supports the perspectives of different individuals that intensify the conflict. Joseph A. White Jr. balances his prose with sensory details and characters' thoughts while using a thriller as a backdrop to explore the psychology of drug dealers. The tension springs from the question of whether Jeff, with his psychic abilities, will be able to rescue Mindi on time. *Our Calling* feels like a cross between *The*

Cell and *Sicario*, a powerful mix that takes the cross-genre of paranormal and crime to new heights. It doesn't pretend to be a hardcore superhero type of story. It simply delivers a tale about an ordinary guy with extraordinary abilities and how it blends with his strengths and weaknesses as a human being. Highly recommended."

—Vincent Dublado for Readers' Favorite

"The book is well written with the dialogues adding to the story and the characters. White's concepts are clear from the beginning and do not confuse you. The characters' relationships are also made clear early on. We understand the relationship between Mindi and Jeff and that they meet through dreams and get to know each other through their mental connection. It is intriguing to read the idea of lucid dreaming presented here to create characters with metaphysical powers and a mystery to solve. White uses several languages in his narrative but always remembers to translate into English for understanding. The dream sequence is displayed vividly whenever the main character uses his mind to talk to other people. The dialogue is italicized so you understand that the dialogue is not being spoken aloud. The story also talks about the effect of drugs on humans and society in a subtle but powerful manner through small scenes with the characters. *Our Calling: A Lucid Dreaming Adventure* by Joseph A White Jr is recommended for audiences who love metaphysical powers and mystery."

—Manik Chaturmutha for Readers' Favorite

"The author vividly describes Jeff's and Mindi's experiences in their lucid dreams, enabling the reader to create mental images of the events. It made my entire reading experience feel as though I was experiencing the dreams with them. I also loved the natural chemistry between Jeff and Mindi. I marveled at their vulnerability and desire to do good. Jeff's previous heartbreak with Charlene made him question his subsequent relationship with Mindi. Not only does this reveal the uncertainties that young people have to contend with, but it also highlights their doubts and mistrust of their subsequent partners. The dialogue between each character was realistic, giving this novel a holistic aspect that is hard to find. I recommend this book to lovers of thrillers and mystery novels."

—Helen Huini for Readers' Favorite

"The mechanics of this universe are well realized – the protagonist can "leap" in and out of situations, and is able to direct himself away from a lucid dreaming episode by using an "escape word". Furthermore, he is able to commune with Mindi in a "gray room", an incorporeal space where they can compare notes about the dreams they are experiencing, and he conceives a sort of system for directing the dreams, a couple of "Quiet Modes", in which he is able to subliminally nudge the person he has "leapt" into, or simply remain a passive observer. Dialogue is on the whole believable, with a certain pithy quality, and there is a good grasp of pacing at the level of the scene. ... An interesting and clever story that plays with concepts such as lucid dreaming, time travel, and astral projection in a thriller-type plot."

—IndieReader Review

OUR CALLING

A LUCID-DREAMING ADVENTURE

JOSEPH A WHITE JR

AIA PUBLISHING

Our Calling
Joseph A White Jr
Copyright © 2022
Published by AIA Publishing, Australia
ABN: 32736122056
http://www.aiapublishing.com

ISBN: 978-1-922329-45-5

CHAPTER 1

For the second time that night, Jeff felt the familiar sensation of falling and floating in his gray-fog dream state. He'd just said good night to Mindi. Had she called him back? Was he going to see her again? They'd never before had two visits to the gray room in one night.

But it was not to be. When his vision cleared, Jeff stood in an open-sided building with a corrugated metal roof, seeing through the eyes of his host. The man's shirt clung to his skin in the hot, humid, still air that smelled of chemicals mingled with the earthy smell of the jungle. Sweat ran down his face and neck.

Tools, gloves, beer cans, soft drink bottles, and empty cigarette packs lay scattered across a nearby worktable made of scrap lumber. A young man, an *indígena*, barely old enough to shave, dressed in torn work pants and a faded green T-shirt, handed Jeff's host a small bundle—somewhat larger than a softball—wrapped in white cloth and shuffled out into the bright sunshine. Jeff guessed the bundle weighed a couple of pounds.

The man's calloused hands were the brown color of tarnished copper. He pressed the putty-like ball into a thick metal mold about the size of a fat paperback book. The mold had holes drilled in its sides and was lined with clean white cloth which folded over the top of the putty-like material. He placed a thick steel plate on top of the ductile mass, centered the ram of a hydraulic press on it, and pumped the press's handle. The ram pushed down, forcing a milky liquid through the holes and onto the dirt floor. When the press ceased moving and the liquid flow stopped, the man removed the steel plate along with the pins that held the corners of the mold together and took out the nearly solid pressed block. He placed it on a ceramic plate in a microwave oven, set the timer, and pushed *Start*. The microwave hummed. While the block spun on the turntable, the man took a crumpled pack of unfiltered cigarettes from his shirt pocket, lit one, and discarded the match. Jeff hated the taste of the cigarette smoke, but he endured, obligated to watch the scenario into which he'd been dropped.

The timer signaled the end of the microwave's cycle. The man retrieved the white brick and placed it on a balance scale, grunted in satisfaction, wrapped the block in plastic film and stacked it with dozens of others like it.

That's cocaine! Jeff shouted inside the man's mind.

The man heard him.

The startled host looked first at one, then the other of the two men working in the building. "*¿Quién dijo eso? ¡Yo sé qué es esto! Y . . . ¿quién de ustedes habla inglés?*" Who said that? I *know* what this is! And . . . who of you can speak English?

He looked from one worker to the other. Both returned his puzzled look. One shrugged and turned away. The other replied, "*¿De qué estás hablando?*" What are you talking about?

Jeff's host said, "*Alguien dijo en inglés que esto es cocaína.*" Someone just said in English that this is cocaine.

The other worker frowned at him. "*Estas escuchando cosas, amigo mío.*" You are hearing things, my friend.

Jeff felt no guilt for the confusion he'd created. Because of the heat, humidity, cigarette smoke, and discomfort of watching these people, he mistakenly called out his original escape words to force himself to end the dream. "Charlene, Charlene, Charlene."

It didn't work. He was still there. The humid air held him hostage.

"*¿Quién es Charlene? ¡Esto no es gracioso!*" his host said in anger. Who is Charlene? This is not funny!

Wrong escape word, Jeff thought, then used the correct one. *Ciao!* he shouted in his mind.

Before Jeff left, he felt the man's head jerk up and heard him say, "*¿Chao?*"

Jeff awoke and lay in his bed for a few minutes before he rose and documented the dream in a new notebook—his old one safely locked away.

The clock said 4:35 a.m. *This is crazy*, he thought to himself. *Was that the start of a new adventure?* "No!" he said aloud. He didn't want another "adventure!"

Then curiosity tempered his fit of pique. *Where was I? South America somewhere?* He wished he remembered more of his high school Spanish.

It was too late to go back to sleep for just an hour, so he made coffee and googled "cocaine manufacture" on his laptop. "Well, Jeffy ol' boy, it looks like you've been south of the border," he said quietly to himself.

He learned more than he thought he wanted to know while watching a documentary about drug labs in Colombia:

the laborious steps of turning coca leaves into cocaine using gasoline, acids, bases, and time-consuming, sweaty, arduous labor—and just as in his dream—he saw the bricks molded, dried, wrapped, and stacked.

When was that? Did I time travel or was that real-time?

He added a footnote to his journal entry that his senses—smell, touch, taste, and hearing—were more acute in that dream than ever before. He'd felt the oppressive heat and humidity and tasted that ugly cigarette smoke.

Mindi's smiling face looked out at him from the page cut from a *Vogue* magazine that he'd stuck on the refrigerator door. Jeff smiled at the picture and shook his head. "I can't wait to tell you about the crazy dream I had."

~

Earlier that day, Jeff had taken Mindi to the airport. When he returned home, he phoned his brother to wish him a happy birthday.

Mark answered with, "Hey, bro, good to hear from you."

Jeff began the verbal joust of close brothers. "Happy birthday, old man. What are you, twenty-eight? Twenty-nine?"

"You're senile at thirty-four if you can't remember," Mark said with a laugh.

"Even if I am," Jeff said, "I can still take you down, you whippersnapper."

They both laughed, then Mark asked, "How *are* you? And how's Charlene? When're you guys gonna tie the knot?" Jeff hesitated and Mark sensed it. "You're still a couple, right? She's a sweetheart."

"Well, that's just it, Mark. We're not together now." Anticipating the next question, he said, "No, nothing bad happened. I *did* ask her to marry me—last month. That's what ended it. She's not ready. We didn't fight or anything. We figured . . . Well, she figured, it was best that . . . with her career taking off . . . she doesn't want to settle down, and . . ."

When Jeff trailed off into silence, Mark said, "I'm sorry, bro. Are you okay? You are okay, aren't you?"

"Yeah, I'm alright. Thanks for asking. Well, matter of fact, after Charlene pulled the plug, I met a model who works for Charlene's agency, and we've gone out a couple times since Halloween." Jeff smiled, glad to be able to share this with Mark. "The problem, though, is that Mindi's, well, kind of geographically unacceptable. I put her on a plane back to LA a couple of hours ago. Coincidentally, she's Craig Howe's cousin. You remember Craig, at my work? We played golf when you were out here last year."

"Yeah, I remember Craig. Great sense of humor. He always has a joke. So tell me about her."

"She's fun to be with, a good listener, pretty, and really smart," Jeff replied. "If you want to see some of her work, her picture's on the makeup company's website, LaDormeur, and in the latest issue of Vogue. She's the brunette with big dark eyes."

"It sounds like you like her. I'll check the mag." Mark told Jeff that their dad and stepmother Christine were going on a cruise to the Caribbean, leaving just before Thanksgiving. They'd be gone through Christmas.

"What are you doing for Thanksgiving?" Jeff asked.

"Oh, my boss said whoever wanted to work on the holiday they'd pay double time, and I took him up on the offer. That's good scratch. What are you doing?"

"Oh, same as you. I'll catch up on some work, order a pizza."

They talked for a while to catch up, and just as the call ended, a text arrived from Mindi: *Just landed, waiting to deplane. Good flight, great view from the window seat—I love flying [smiley face]. Thank you for a wonderful vacation. I enjoyed spending time with the real-time Jeff but can't wait to see you in our gray room tonight. I'll listen for your shout-out. [hug, heart and kiss emoji].*

He texted back: *Glad u safe. Me too, see you tonight. [hug emoji].*

Jeff smiled. He'd met Mindi six months ago when he traveled back in time in his dreams, landed in her mind, and saw her world through her eyes. After a few visits, they discovered they could talk with each other telepathically when he was with her in her head. Their paranormal skills developed to a point where, with astral projection, they projected their images so they could see, hear, and interact with each other in a special psychic space they called their gray room, which Jeff figured was a space inside her mind. Their metaphysical friendship continued to evolve, even though two years separated their physical selves. When their timelines finally aligned six months later, and they met in the real world, their friendship evolved into the beginnings of a romantic relationship.

Jeff had been looking forward to that text that told him she was safe on the ground in LA, and he especially looked forward to visiting her in the gray room in his dreams. Could they meet that way in real-time though? He wasn't sure. Before when they'd met there, he'd traveled back in time.

There was only one way to find out.

He fell asleep around ten and—well practiced now—he soon became aware he was dreaming. As usual, he relaxed, floated briefly, then called, "Mindi, Mindi, Mindi." He was relieved when a doorway appeared and he saw their gray, overstuffed chairs waiting for them, and Mindi walking toward him.

They hugged.

"Well, it works in real-time." He spread his arms as he looked around, smiling.

"Yeah, I called for you, and here you are. Did you call for me?"

"I did."

"So what do we talk about?" Mindi said.

"Tell me about your flight."

"Let's see, I told you I had the window seat. I liked that. I haven't flown that much, so it's exciting—it's like looking at Google Earth." She looked at her hands as she fidgeted them in her lap. When she looked up, she said with shyness in her voice, "Could you come down for Thanksgiving? I'd love to cook for you, show off what Mom taught me. I won't be working at the restaurant like I did last year."

Jeff smiled at her as he searched her eyes. "I'd like that. I've got Thanksgiving and Friday off, and vacation days left. Yeah."

Mindi exhaled and a relieved look crossed her face. "Oh, good. I finish a photo shoot the Friday before, then a couple of meetings on Monday. I told Jeri I'd sub for her at the Denny's on Tuesday, so my holiday begins Wednesday." She tilted her head expectantly, as if it were his turn to share.

Jeff didn't move or speak. He just stared at her.

"Jeff." She moved her head forward and peered at him. "Are you still here?"

He snapped out of it. "I'm sorry. I just love watching your eyes dance."

She looked down at the floor, her expression embarrassed.

7

"I was afraid you'd frozen, like Shirley did before she disappeared."

"I'm sorry. I—"

Mindi cut in. "You know, I really didn't want to leave Seattle today."

"I felt the same." He relaxed. "So where would I stay?"

"Well, here . . . uh . . . there . . . uh . . . at my place." She laughed.

"Are you sure?"

"Of course! There's plenty of room."

"I don't want you to feel, uh, self-conscious, threatened, or anything."

She shook her head. "Jeff, you should know me by now. I can't imagine ever feeling threatened by you."

They'd dated every evening while she was in Seattle, and he'd returned her to Craig's home where she stayed the week. The subject of anything physical, beyond holding hands and chaste hugs, hadn't entered the picture. Jeff had remained a perfect gentleman.

"Yes, I do know you. That's why I need to respect your space."

Mindi smiled. "I wondered if you'd found something wrong with me. You never, well, made a pass at me. I wondered if . . ."

"Mindi, you *are* beautiful, charming, and . . ." His smile was warm, though he was ill at ease. He changed the subject. "I'll book a flight for Wednesday?"

"Sure. That's great. I'll have to go shopping to get stuff for dinner," she said, clapping her hands together with glee.

He saw she was excited at the prospect of his visit, and he certainly wanted to spend time with her. "I can help. I enjoy holiday crowds."

"Good." She sighed. "There's a meat market a few blocks down from me. Do you like turkey or ham?"

"What's *your* favorite? Mom cooked both on Turkey Day. Big family. You choose."

"I'll order a small turkey."

Jeff nodded. "Say, about Jeri. I haven't told you that I talked with her at your work, when I was down there, before I was sure you were a real person."

"You told me you went by the restaurant. What did you say to her?"

"When I asked her about you, she was guarded, said she didn't know you."

Mindi nodded. "Yeah, I remember she told me a 'good-looking guy' asked about me and then gave her a big tip. I shrugged it off. There're always guys trying to pick us up. That was you?"

"Yeah, I was playing detective, but I left the Sherlock Holmes hat and magnifying glass in the car," he said with a smile. "By the way she acted, though, I knew you were real. Please don't tell her I said that. Is she a friend?"

"Yes, she's helped me a lot."

"Good. It'd be fun to meet her now and see if she remembers me . . . You know, I don't think I ever asked if you had a car—how did I not ask that of an Angeleno? Should I take a cab or Uber to your place, or can you—or do you want to—pick me up?"

"I don't live in LA, but I'm in the county, so Angeleno fits. I like it. I'd love to pick you up. I've got my father's car, a Honda Civic. I don't drive it that much. I mostly take the bus. Text me your flight number. I'm looking forward to it."

Jeff felt warm inside. "Me too."

They embraced.

Mindi held him tightly. "I don't want the evening to end. But I've got an appointment with Dr. Singh tomorrow morning, and I'm still in my modeling class with a final just before the holiday, so I've got some studying to do."

Jeff frowned, puzzled.

"What did I say?"

He tipped his head sideways, shrugged, and looked around the room.

She laughed. "Oh, yeah, that's silly. We don't lose sleep when we're here like this."

"What are you going to tell your doctor about me? Will you tell her I'm really the guy in your dreams—that I'm real?"

"No. I'll play it cool and tell her I met one of my cousin's friends in Seattle, and we hit it off. She doesn't need the whole backstory, or we'll end up featured in her psych paper."

"I agree. It's enough that Charlene knows."

"I know. Charlene was so nice to me when we had lunch last week, so sweet and understanding, and she said she wouldn't tell anyone. Did she tell you she contacted Rick's doctor and then somehow managed to track down Carolyn? She didn't know he'd died."

"No. I'm not surprised she did that. I'm sure it was for closure."

Mindi nodded her understanding. "I really enjoyed our time together last week. I'm so glad we can still meet here. Let's do it again soon, okay?"

"Yes. Should we say our escape word together?"

She nodded, and they said, "Ciao."

But then instead of finding himself back in bed, alone in Seattle, Jeff returned to his gray-fog dream, felt the familiar sensation of falling, and landed in a jungle somewhere in the head of a man making cocaine. After causing some confusion for the man, he got out of that leap with another ciao and awoke in his own bed.

The dream and his subsequent research into the making of cocaine raised a lot of questions, and he felt grateful that he had someone he could talk to. He rushed through his workday, eager to see Mindi in their dream room.

~

When he arrived in the gray room that night, Mindi was already in her chair, wearing her pink hoodie and sweatpants, the only color in the vast gray space.

Jeff looked at her feet. "Are those bunny slippers?"

She stood up, put her arms around his neck, pulled him toward her, and gave him a kiss, then said with a giggle, "Yeah, I splurged a little. They're perfect for the outfit, don't cha think?" She spun around in a mock model's move, then stopped and said, "I can't wait to tell you about a dream I had last night after we left here."

Jeff grinned. "Me too. Mine's weird, but you share first." They sat down, their knees touching.

"Well, I now know how you felt when you landed in my head the first time."

Jeff inclined his head to the side. "What do you mean?"

"Yeah, I know. I was as puzzled as you look right now." Mindi told him that after they said ciao last night, she'd started falling in her dream. Initially, she'd been scared, but then remembered to relax, then floated.

"Was everything gray?" Jeff asked.

"Yes! At first I felt disoriented, but you'd told me there was no need to be afraid."

He nodded.

11

"Then I was standing and, well, seeing through someone else's eyes. It took a few moments to realize it was a young guy. He was stacking blocks into an old jeep." She motioned with her hands to indicate the size of the blocks.

"And?"

"It felt weird being inside someone else's mind. I'm glad I kinda knew what to expect."

"Okay . . . and . . . ?" Jeff prompted, eager for her to continue.

"Yeah, the blocks were white, wrapped in plastic . . ."

Jeff leaned forward, anxious, and serious now that she'd described the bricks of cocaine he'd packaged. "Tell me about the kid. Please."

Mindi tilted her head as if puzzled by his impatience. "Okay." She took a deep breath. "Well, I never saw more than his hands and arms, and a little of his jeans and boots. Everything was worn, like almost worn-out. His skin was brown. His hands were calloused, his nails dirty. He took off his straw hat, and I felt him wipe sweat from his forehead with his arm. Then he went back into the shed and picked up more bricks. Here's what made it really strange: there were some men in there, and as he walked inside, one of the men said something in Spanish that included the name Charlene. The other two guys, and my guy, just looked at him."

Jeff sat up straight and stared at her and said slowly, "Okay."

"Then I woke up. That's it. I felt confused. I wrote it all down."

Jeff hadn't moved. He looked at her in amazement.

"What?" she said, but didn't wait for an answer. "I know, right? That I should have a traveling dream like you do. Now I know what you must've gone through."

Jeff remained quiet for a moment as he processed what

she'd said. Then, with a subdued voice, he asked, "Was he, your kid, wearing a torn green T-shirt with a 2003 Superbowl logo?"

"Why?"

Jeff waved his hands as a signal for her to answer him.

"Okay. Yeah. It was green, but I don't know about the logo. Why?"

"Were there barrels, bags of chemicals, tables, and equipment? Three other guys?"

"Yeah. What're you getting at?"

"I was there. That was *my* dream. It was my guy, me, that said Charlene's name. Right after we left here, just like you did, I fell again and landed there. They heard me try to use her name as my escape word."

Mindi looked stunned, her mouth hanging open. "Jeff . . . ?"

"Uh-huh. I watched him mold those bricks. I'm sure it was cocaine. He molded them, cooked, wrapped, and stacked them. You, you . . ." He looked at Mindi.

She finished his sentence. ". . . packed them in the jeep. We were both there at the same time. Oh, Jeff. What? Why? And when was that? Did we time travel?"

"I don't know. . . Got no way of knowing."

She sat back and gave a laugh. "I won't tell doctor *that*, for sure."

Jeff shook his head. "Now we're *both* traveling . . . to God knows where, and I've taken you with me. Oh, Mindi, I'm sorry."

Mindi laughed nervously. "No, no. It's okay. It's something we can share."

"I'd rather go to Disneyland with you and ride Space Mountain, not to some jungle, sweltering at ninety degrees and ninety percent humidity," he said, returning the laughter.

"What do you mean?"

"Didn't you feel the heat and the mugginess? Couldn't you feel it when you loaded the bricks? You said the kid wiped sweat from his head."

"Yeah, he did, but I didn't feel the heat. Did you?"

"Yes, all my senses were in play."

"Not for me. I could only see and hear. And feel what he touched."

"If you do it often enough, it'll all happen for you too," he said with a sigh.

"Do I have a choice?"

"Always be prepared to escape. 'Ciao' worked—when I finally remembered it."

"Well, I guess it could be kinda fun—that is, until one of them has to go to the bathroom."

Jeff remembered one of his first leaps into her mind when he'd accompanied her to the bathroom at the restaurant. He had never told her.

"What do we do now? Could it get scary?" she asked.

"Not much we can do, I guess. Just learn to relax. The more you do it, the easier it gets. Scary? Well . . . it looks like those guys are at the headwaters of the cocaine trade. I looked it up; the governments of Columbia, Peru, Bolivia all cooperate with the US Drug Enforcement Agency, the DEA, and do military flyovers in helicopters. Then burn the labs and fields, destroying months of work. Those guys we saw are just pawns trying to make enough to afford old T-shirts, food for their families, cigarettes, and cheap beer. I hope we don't have to go back. I don't want to be there if the shooting starts. I couldn't handle that."

"You talk about it like we don't have a choice, and that

maybe we'll have to go back."

"No. Well, yes. Maybe. I don't know. I didn't have a choice with you," he said with a sigh.

Mindi looked pained.

"No, no, no," Jeff said, "I'm glad it worked out. I'm so glad I met you. But it's still weird that we don't have a choice. Something else is in control."

Neither said anything; they just looked at each other, considering the situation.

Mindi broke the silence, quoting a famous movie line. "Life is like a box of chocolates."

He stood up and pulled her to her feet and embraced her. "It'll be fine. And for me, I had a mission: to get you to go to school and to break up Rick and Carolyn. The best part is it got us together, which made it all worth it. No. We'll have to wait and see."

Jeff smoothed her hair. "What d'ya say we call it a night?"

"Yeah. Who woulda thought?" she said.

"Maybe I'll see you tomorrow, here or in Cartagena."

"Where's that?"

"Cartagena is on the coast of Colombia, a major drug shipping hub. It was mentioned in a video on YouTube."

Mindi shook her head. "Oh. When I woke up, I thought it was kind of cool that I did what you've been doing, but now I'm not so sure."

"It *is* cool you did it too," Jeff said. "Right now, let's not take it too seriously."

"Sure. I get it. Ciao for now?"

"Yeah. Ciao."

They stood so close that their images dissolved in a fluttering of commingled glitter.

15

CHAPTER 2

Jeff awoke before his alarm and went to the living room to meditate while listening to a guided meditation recording that helped him focus his breathing. Twenty minutes later, with a deep sigh, his eyes fluttered open. Gentle rain pattered against the window. He'd make a copy of the meditation DVD to send to Mindi.

Jeff had a bounce in his step. Nothing could keep him from having a good day. The feeling of success permeated everything he did. After work, he went to the gym and had an intense workout, a positive counterpoint to the meditation. To avoid conflict, he'd take the path of least resistance. But if conflict was on the menu, he was ready.

~

He turned out the light next to his bed and hoped he'd see Mindi again in his dream. He felt like a schoolboy with his first love.

When the floating stopped and grayness cleared, he

discovered that wherever he was, it wasn't with Mindi. It was twilight and his host sat alone in an outdoor restaurant. Cloth napkins, matching dinnerware, a view of a marina, a beach below, and blue ocean water beyond. He felt a gentle, warm breeze as the sun began to disappear beyond the horizon. His host reached for an iced cocktail glass and took a drink. Jeff enjoyed the cool taste of the expensive gin and tonic. Compared to the discomfort of the jungle cocaine laboratory, this was a good leap.

The golden color of the skin on his host's hands ended at manicured fingernails. He wore two rings, one on his right pinkie with a huge clear stone, a diamond perhaps, and on the ring finger of his left hand, what appeared to be a bejeweled wedding band. Jeff felt his host's impatience when he checked the time on his gold Rolex Cosmograph—7:45. The watch had no day or date window to give Jeff information that could be valuable in fixing the date of this dream. He did not know what the watch cost, but the familiar cliché came to mind: "If you have to ask the price, you can't afford it." Financial excess and conspicuous consumption rarely impressed Jeff, but tonight he might make an exception for the watch.

All his leaps earlier this year had been directly related to each other, so he assumed the same applied to this one. Since this leap followed the making-cocaine-in-the-jungle leap, this man could be near the top of the food chain of illegal drugs. Whatever the man did for a living, Jeff was certain he never got his hands dirty.

Jeff couldn't tap into the guy's thoughts, and he tried to keep his own thinking to a minimum. Whatever mission this might become, to make someone of this level paranoid was surely not in the best interests of whatever had brought him here.

With that thought, which he worked hard not to dwell on, he remembered Mindi. Was she around here somewhere, and if so, how would he know?

His host turned around in his chair—first to the left, then slowly to the right—and surveyed the dining area, as if he was expecting someone.

The answers will come, Jeff. Be patient, he told himself.

A few minutes passed. The man finished his drink, and without being summoned—as if cued—the server arrived with a fresh drink.

This guy's a big-shot. What am I doing here? Could Mindi be here too?

The man spun around again, quickly this time, and Jeff felt his host's impatience. Was that a touch of paranoia? The feeling tempered, then another burst of impatience flashed through his mind.

The wait didn't bore Jeff. Many people dream about being able to sit in a luxury outdoor restaurant in the tropics, enjoying a cocktail, looking out over an azure-blue bay, and watching people on the beach and marina below. So he enjoyed the moment.

But he did start to feel the effects of the cocktail. Why were his host's thoughts not available to him, just his feelings? *I can't wait to tell Mindi about this luxury.*

As Jeff thought of Mindi again, the man looked around nervously, then rubbed his temples and eyes and looked at his watch. Now Jeff heard his thought. *She's an hour late.*

He was waiting for someone. Had he already eaten? No. The table bore no evidence of a completed meal. The utensils were still wrapped in their napkins. The server brought another drink.

The man had been there for over an hour. This was his

third drink since Jeff had arrived, and he'd hadn't even had an appetizer. Several couples and small groups arrived, and others finished their meals or drinks and left, but the man continued to sit and watch the water and the rising moon, looking around whenever Jeff thought of Mindi.

They heard a woman's voice above the gentle conversation in the dining courtyard. The man turned around to look and recognized the statuesque, raven-haired woman with a black lace shawl over her shoulders, a short red evening dress, and lovely legs ending in gold high heels with a matching clutch bag.

He rose and took a few steps toward her. She reached out, and he kissed the back of her hand. With a heavy Latin accent, he said, "Miranda, my dear, I am so glad you could join me this evening."

She answered graciously in cultured English with a Latin accent equaling the man's. "Carlos, my apologies. I had business that could not wait. I trust you were not waiting long. And why so formal? I have asked you to call me Mindy, as all my friends do."

Now Jeff understood why every time he'd thought of *his* Mindi, this man, Carlos, had become agitated. *What is she to him? A lover? A prospective lover?*

Carlos held the chair for her. "I have been enjoying the evening. It is quite comfortable, and now that you have joined me, it has become most charming." He signaled the server and said to the woman, "What would you like to drink, my dear?"

"Strawberry daiquiri, *por favor.*"

The server nodded, then looked at Carlos. "*Señor?*"

Jeff watched her large dark eyes as Carlos gazed into them. Finally, Carlos looked at him and said, "*Sí, otro gin-tonic, por favor.*"

He retrieved the empty from in front of Carlos, bowed gently from the waist, and retreated.

Their behavior and posture indicated to Jeff that they'd not shared intimacy, but he knew Carlos wanted to. Their social status was equal.

Miranda started the conversation. "So, Carlos, how is Sofia? Have you heard from her?"

Carlos smiled. "My daughter is fine. She called me from Boston just yesterday. Her studies, she claims, are going well. She says she is interested in a young man from a good family who will graduate this spring and who has plans to join a law firm there."

"Will she be staying in the States?"

"Well, she still has a little over a year until she gets her degree. I was hoping she would return to Colombia. It has been lonely since her mother passed, with my only child being away where I cannot protect her." He paused a moment, then added, "And Roberto, have you heard from him?" He smiled.

Miranda returned the smile, then watched as the frosted stemmed glass was placed on the lace paper coaster and Carlos's long drink glass set in front of him. The server straightened and looked at Carlos, who politely dismissed him with a nod.

They shared a silent toast toward each other, then Miranda set down her drink, looked at Carlos, and said, "Where were we? Oh, yes, you asked about 'Berto." She said the name with the gentle trill of the *r* consistent with native Spanish speakers. "He is in San Francisco, on the yacht. I am missing him. He will be there until the end of the week, then sailing south. He calls me regularly." She took another sip from her glass and waited for Carlos to continue the conversation.

Carlos took the cue. "Well, my dear, do you have

good news? I appreciate you did not wish to tell me over the telephone."

"Quite." She retrieved a slip of pastel-blue paper from her clutch bag and handed it to Carlos.

"'Berto asked me to give it to you and expects you will share it with Alejo."

Carlos took the offered note, opened it and read the delicate feminine handwriting: *26 de junio en el puerto.* He nodded, then looked up. *"Gracias."* He placed the paper in the pocket of his linen guayabera shirt.

"Thank you. Now, shall we have dinner, my dear?" Carlos raised his hand to signal the attentive server who placed leather-bound menus in front of them. They perused their options. Jeff noted the name of the restaurant, looked it up later, and confirmed they were in Cartagena.

Jeff quietly observed the scene, becoming certain of the significance of his being there. The caution they'd taken in relaying the message on the note suggested that drugs were involved. He made a mental note of the names: Miranda, Carlos, Roberto/'Berto and Alejo. And June 26 at *el puerto. Interesting that Mindi and she share the same name.*

At that thought, Carlos's head jerked up to look at Miranda. He put his hand to his forehead and pressed his temples.

Miranda's eyebrows rose. "Carlos, are you alright?"

At that point, without the use of his escape word, Jeff awoke in his bed in Seattle.

He watched the shadows on the ceiling, disappointed it had ended so abruptly. He'd enjoyed the pleasant, warm evening in a luxury restaurant with the cocktails and a view.

But then, he rationalized, he'd had little control for the past six months, anyway. His dreams had taken him to the

21

where and when of something else's choosing. He'd called it "the universe," his generic label for an unknown authority. In centuries past people would've called it God's will, but Jeff didn't believe in the monotheistic concept of an omnipotent being making the sun come up and moving the stars across the sky. Yet he and Mindi were again being subjected to something unseen, outside of their control.

His acceptance of the powerlessness didn't prevent him from being curious as to what made these dreams happen. In his experience, things happened for a reason—there was always a cause and effect. He wanted to understand the cause, the science, of these dreams and leaps. But he could be patient. So long as they didn't get hurt, they'd treat it like a mystery story where the ending would eventually be revealed.

Jeff recorded the dream in the journal and ended the night's entry with the comment, *Can't wait to see if Mindi had a dream tonight too.*

He looked at the clock and felt that he'd be able to go back to sleep, especially after sharing, albeit virtually, three gin and tonic cocktails.

He fell back to sleep and immediately returned to his gray cocoon, floating and hearing Mindi's voice.

"Jeff? Jeff, you there?"

"Yes, Mindi." He answered right away and walked through the silently opening gray doorway toward Mindi.

"Jeff, I had another falling dream tonight," she said, eyes wide and shining with excitement. "I fell, relaxed, and floated for just a moment, then was in a woman's mind." She waited for a moment for Jeff to track.

Before she could get started again, Jeff held up his hand and said, "Just a minute. Let me guess."

Mindi nodded but fidgeted, showing how keen she was

to talk.

"Her name was Miranda, and she was drinking a strawberry daiquiri."

"Oh my gosh, Jeff, you were with Carlos!"

"Yes. When did you get there?"

"While she was riding in a limo pulling up to the restaurant. She tipped the driver 20,000 pesos. Is that a lot? They had accents. Where were they?"

"Colombia."

Clearly Mindi had had a good time with the game, and Jeff didn't want to deflate her ego with the seriousness of the subject of their leaps just yet.

So he asked, "How long did you stay there? I wanted to stay but left without saying ciao. I was having a good time, felt the alcohol glow from his gin and tonics, and it was a beautiful evening. Did you have dinner?"

"Yes. She had a seafood salad; he had lobster. She seemed to enjoy it, although I couldn't taste it."

"You can't taste . . . yet. It'll happen soon enough. I wish I could've stayed for the lobster. What did they talk about?"

"Small talk. He talked about his daughter, how she'd met a guy, that she wanted a new car, and he was going to arrange for her to pick up a new BMW Series 6." She thought for a moment. "He had some fabulous rings—and that watch! My father always wanted a Rolex."

"Yeah, I noticed. A Series 6 is expensive, even for a Beemer. What else did they talk about?"

"She was having her kitchen redone. They were going to have the latest appliances. That was one of the things that"—she paused so she could enunciate Miranda's husband's name—"'Berto was checking into in San Francisco. This is so exciting, Jeff. I may have grown up in a suburb of Los

Angeles, but I'm a hometown girl. I've never seen this kind of stuff before."

"Me neither, just in the movies. It is kinda grand, but remember, maybe they dined on the backs of those peons we saw in the jungle."

Mindi frowned. "Peon. That's such an ugly term."

"I know that's the way we use it here, but I looked it up. If that was Mexico, they'd be called 'braceros.' But in Central and South America, they're 'peons.'"

"Okay. Well, I guess the leaps might get old. Is it getting old for you?"

"No, not really. This is a whole new twist than before."

"Okay, I get it. I'll try to keep it low key. Why do you think we're doing this? And we still don't know who, or what, is behind it."

"I'm sure this time it is cocaine."

"Is that what that note was about?"

"That's a good guess. Miranda must know what it's about. June 26 at some port. Some type of rendezvous, maybe a drug shipment. Other than that, we don't know the when, except it's June, but what year? Last June? Next June?" Jeff paused. "One more thing. I influenced Carlos while he was waiting for her to arrive. Every time I thought about you, thought your name, he got all agitated—I could even feel his nervousness. He'd look around, looking for her, probably because you share the same name."

She shrugged. "It's a common Latin name."

"Yeah, I get it." Jeff nodded. "If these leaps continue, and you end up in someone's head again, see if you can persuade them to look at a calendar or their phone so we can date-stamp the trip."

"Okay."

"By the way, I've got my days off and my flight. ETA is noon on Wednesday. I'll text you the details. I can't wait. I'm more excited about seeing you than drinking gin in Colombia."

They looked at each other with a smile and, as if on cue, stood up and gave each other a hug, and then at the same time said, "Ciao for now," smiling as they sparkled away.

~

Jeff went to work with a renewed sense of purpose. Craig stopped by Jeff's office to talk details about a client and remained in the chair after they'd finished talking about the project.

"Anything else?" Jeff asked,

"Well. Yes. I'm still a little shocked about you and Charlene," Craig said. "You two seemed so close, like you might have even gotten married soon. Was it because of Mindi that you broke up?"

Jeff owed Craig an explanation, but of course, he couldn't tell the whole story. "No, Craig, absolutely not. Remember when we went over to the peninsula a couple of weeks ago? I did propose. I thought she was interested, but I misread her signals. She's not ready for marriage. We didn't fight; we handled it like adults. That all happened before I met Mindi at the Halloween gala." Jeff hoped Craig wouldn't press any further.

Craig said nothing but leaned forward in the chair, eyebrows raised, expecting more, so Jeff continued. "Charlene broke it off. I was willing for it to be the way it had been, but I guess she couldn't do that. I thought I'd handled it well." Jeff and Craig looked at each other and, hoping to close the conversation, Jeff added, "I'm glad we had the time together we did."

That seemed to satisfy Craig. "Okay. Good. To be honest, I was a little worried how you were taking the breakup."

Jeff smiled and nodded. "Thanks."

Craig continued, "You know, I'm still a little concerned that you spent so much time with my cousin now that you're in rebound. You just met her that night, and you spent every day with her while she was here. I had offered to take her to the airport, but she was emphatic that you would drive her. She's really taken with you. I hope you know what you are doing."

Craig's tone sounded protective of both his cousin and his friend. Jeff couldn't tell him he'd known Mindi for six months, and that, in fact, she'd known *him* for two years in her time, rather than one week, as it appeared.

"Yeah, it does seem that things got moving rather fast, but Craig, I assure you, right now things are platonic . . ."

Craig shifted in his chair, apparently uncomfortable. "Why did you feel you needed to tell me that?" he said. "Yes, she's my cousin, although I do kinda think of her as the sister I never had . . ." Craig waited for Jeff's reply.

"Yeah, that's why I felt I needed to tell you."

"Hey, I'm not my cousin's keeper. I just don't want anybody to get hurt. I trust you to run your own life—you've done well so far." He chuckled and looked around the office as if the status of the office indicated how well Jeff could handle things.

"Thanks, Craig. By the way, to show you there were no hard feelings between Charlene and me. She has me in mind to be a model in ads for the men's LaDormeur makeup line in a few weeks. She's not mad at me for trying to rush things along, and I'm okay with how things are turning out. Imagine me, a model, huh?"

To which Craig replied with an air of joviality, "Oh, *puleese*, mister jock sir, gimme a break. I can see you're already picturing yourself trading in your Toyota Camry for a Porsche Carrera and being a Southern California stud. Do I get bragging rights that I once collaborated with you at such a pedestrian job as software management?" Craig stood and finished with, "I'll just leave you with your daydreams. Next time you talk with Mindi, tell her I said hi and tell her not to break my friend's heart."

Jeff smiled.

"Jeff, you're okay. That's all I wanted to know. Golf this weekend?"

"Sure," Jeff replied, then with mock disappointment added, "I got nothing else going on."

~

That night, Jeff went to bed thinking about his conversation with Craig and his now not-so-secret interest in Mindi. As with every other time Jeff was lucid dreaming, his dream started with the familiar sensation of falling, but this time it felt different in a way Jeff couldn't describe. He'd learned to be patient with this strange hobby of his, so he relaxed and the floating began.

Suddenly, the grayness parted, providing him with a view through a windshield on a freeway at night. The driver looked down at the speedometer, and Jeff glimpsed an Audi logo on the steering wheel.

Nice ride, Jeff thought.

Car taillights marked the road ahead with red punctuations.

The headlights, like a string of glowing pearls in the oncoming traffic, struck his eyes as the cars moved past while the driver negotiated a stretch of Interstate 5 North, just past the downtown Seattle exits. They approached the bridge that would lead them toward the University of Washington, visible off to the right. Below them was the bridge across the ship canal. Jeff drove this road daily. Lake Union spread out to the left of the freeway, and the Space Needle sat beyond at the foot of Queen Anne Hill.

This is strange. Who is this guy?

The driver moved deftly through the traffic, smoothly changing lanes, and eventually signaled to take an exit that Jeff had taken for the last year and a half when driving to his ex-girlfriend's house.

As Jeff realized this, the man took his right hand off the wheel and rubbed his hand over his eyes, massaging first his right temple then switching hands and rubbing his left temple.

Jeff knew the route this car was negotiating well. When they turned left onto Charlene's street and stopped in front of her apartment building, Jeff gasped, his mental control slipping. The driver looked around, trying to find the source of the sound in his mind, shook his head, got out, and walked around behind the car. When the man glanced at the temporary paper license plate in the back window of the Audi, Jeff saw the expiration date: June 30, 2018. The driver caressed the badge of the Audi A8L and focused on the front door of the building.

Charlene appeared, smiling. He opened the passenger door as she walked toward him. She kissed him gently on the lips and, with the grace of a dancer, turned and sat down. He paused and admired her thighs before slipping back into the driver's seat. With a quick glance over his left shoulder, he pulled away from the curb.

"I was really looking forward to seeing you tonight," Charlene said. "Where are we going?"

"You look fabulous tonight, my dear," he replied, his Latin accent unmistakable. "Would you allow me to surprise you?"

"Alejandro, you are such a tease. How could I deny you that?"

Alejandro? If Alejo was a nickname for Alejandro, this could be the Alejo that Miranda mentioned in her conversation with Carlos. Why else would he be in this guy's head? In the last six months of leaps, a pattern had revealed itself—the dreams had all been connected.

Jeff noted his own lack of jealousy, regret, or disappointment. He felt no anger toward Charlene, nor any feeling of happiness for her. What he did feel was extreme curiosity. What did Charlene have to do with this scenario? Whatever Charlene's involvement, Jeff felt concerned that this man may be related to the cocaine trade.

Alejandro looked in the rearview mirror and Jeff saw the corner of the temporary plate again and thought, *New car tags are only good for sixty days! So I've traveled to the future?* Alejandro felt that thought as pressure in his temples, which caused him to blink and rub his head again.

They joined traffic on the southbound freeway entrance without a word spoken and no more affection displayed after that first quick kiss. Gentle jazz emanated from the sound system.

Familiar landmarks passed by until suddenly Jeff awoke in his bed, his curiosity in full activation. He knew from his past experiences the answers would come, but this time he might not like the answers. Both he and Mindi had possibly seen two sides of a cocaine operation: first the jungle, then a posh, presumably Colombian restaurant. That Charlene was dating someone with a Latin accent called Alejandro—nickname possibly Alejo—who drove a new, top-of-the-line Audi that cost eighty thousand or more, could certainly point to a relationship with the drug traders of the previous dreams.

As he wrote in his notebook, Jeff identified in himself some insecurity regarding the lack of extravagance in his life. The feeling was quickly discarded as he took inventory of what he did have: a good paying job he enjoyed and his health; and would have, he was certain: a wife, a home, and a family. Conspicuous consumption truly wasn't his thing.

If Jeff's hunch was correct that these people were engaged in smuggling cocaine, the wealth certainly wouldn't be worth the cost of one's peace of mind. But how was Charlene involved in this? He didn't want her to get hurt from being involved in something illegal. He stopped himself . . . *Don't jump to conclusions.* This guy, Alejandro, might just be a rich guy associated with a client, his name a coincidence. They might be a good match. After all, she was truly in the big leagues now, working for a major ad agency with a worldwide cosmetics company as a client.

Jeff's mind, in analysis mode, noted his concern for Charlene, not because he loved her, though. They had a history, of course, and mutual respect. He hoped he wouldn't have to interfere in her life to keep her safe.

To the room, Jeff said, "There you go again, Jeffy. Let it go for now." But it wouldn't let go. While waiting for sleep to come, he replayed Carlos and Miranda's conversation. And in doing so, the name Alejo resurfaced. He'd look that up tomorrow, see if it was a nickname for Alejandro. Then he slept.

CHAPTER 3

When he awoke the next morning, he texted Mindi: *Wait till I tell you about my dream last night.*

A few moments later, his phone chirped with her reply: *Me too.*

The famous line from Sherlock Holmes popped into his head—*Watson, the game is afoot.* Feeling excited, Jeff returned: *Call me.*

His phone rang. "Hey," he answered. "That was quick."

"Yeah," she said. "Wild night dreaming."

"That was a statement, not a question. Did you dream too?"

"Yes, but you go first."

Jeff told her about the new Audi and being in Alejandro's head when he picked Charlene up for a date. "My dream ended before they got where they were going, so I don't know where they went or what they were doing. I was glad—I didn't want a repeat of the Carolyn and Rick thing. And . . . I leaped into the future."

Mindi just said, "I know."

"You know what? That I went to the future?"

"No, I don't know about that, but I know where Charlene and Alejandro were going. I was in Charlene's head—"

"Why am I not surprised?"

"—and it all wasn't that much fun. So how did you find out we went to the future?"

He told her he saw the temporary license. "The expiration date is June next year. That's seven months from now. Temp tags are only good for two months, so we were there sometime between April and June. Okay, now why wasn't it fun? They didn't, uh, do anything, did they?"

"Not while I was there. They might've later on." She paused a moment, then said, "I'm sorry, Jeff. I didn't mean to sound flip about that."

"No worries. I'm really not jealous. I thought I might be, but it doesn't bother me."

"Good. I'm glad," she said, her tone compassionate.

He smiled and nodded. "I'm more concerned why we were shown that at all. Where did they go?"

"He flew a small jet plane. I sensed he was showing off. They drove to Boeing Field and left for Friday Harbor for dinner. Pretty extravagant. But I was cold and a little scared. I wished myself out before they touched down."

"Okay. Do you want to know what my theory is on this?"

"What?"

"You noticed he has an accent, right?"

"You mean he might be from Mexico . . .'"

"Or Colombia."

"Yeah."

"Yeah, that's what I'm talking about. Carolyn and Rick's leaps followed a pattern. This might be the same."

Mindi's voice rose. "Charlene's involved in drugs?"

"Well, Charlene *never* did drugs, not even cannabis, let alone cocaine or worse. She likes wine. It's obvious the guys in the jungle were involved, and we suspect the couple in the restaurant. Why not Alejandro? He could be the Alejo that Miranda mentioned."

"Hmm. People change, Jeff. Look at what her dad did, and no one knew until later."

"You may be right," Jeff said with a sigh.

"I hope not. Say, I'd better go. This isn't like the gray room where we can talk and still sleep too. I've got to get ready for work."

"Sure. But hey, I just remembered something you said."

"What?"

"You said you felt cold in the airplane, right?"

"Yeah, what about it?"

"Your sense of feelings is advancing. That didn't happen for a while with me."

"Oh," Mindi said. "Is that important?"

"Heck, I don't know. Maybe. But keep track and write it down."

"Okay. And Jeff . . ."

"Yes?"

"Seriously, it was kind of fun at first, being in Miranda and Charlene's heads. But I've been thinking about Charlene. Not just because you and she have a history. It's because, well, Alejandro is so much like the guys that I dated before I quit going out."

"What do you mean?"

"He only wants one thing: to feed his ego and have sex, not a serious relationship."

"I see," Jeff said. "I'm sorry it affects you that way. I wish there was some way I could ease that for you, but someone or something else is in control of these dreams."

"I know. I'll deal with it. Oh, and if drugs *are* involved with Charlene and that guy, be careful and please don't let it distract you. We need clear heads if we have to intervene somehow."

"I hear you. Thank you. I do appreciate you being Al Calavicci to my Sam Beckett." He was referring to the characters in the 1990s TV show, *Quantum Leap.* "Ciao."

"Sure thing, always. Ciao." She clicked off.

Jeff half expected the phone to turn into glitter.

~

A few days later, Jeff called a business meeting for him and Mindi to meet in their dream's gray room. The leaps seemed to be becoming more streamlined. They often bypassed the familiar falling and floating in the all-enveloping grayness, and sometimes their lucid dreams started with them in their chairs facing each other, wearing whatever they'd worn in their real-time to bed.

In mock board-meeting style, Jeff said, "I suppose you are wondering why I've called us all together tonight."

Mindi flashed him a big smile. "Jeff, you are so silly. You don't need a reason to call. I'm happy to be here."

"Me too." Jeff returned her smile and watched her until the expectant look on her face told him to say something. "Oh yeah. We've got stuff to talk about. First, did you get the meditation video DVD I sent?"

"Yes, I did."

"Does it work for you?"

"I've only used it twice. First time, I nodded off. Then the next time, my brain was busy. My father called it the 'committee,' my self-talk, who's active in my head."

"I understand. That'll pass. Keep trying, because I think meditating makes coming to the gray room easier and faster for me. No falling and floating. I just come right here."

Mindi nodded. "That's the way it's been for me, you know."

"Yeah, you're a natural. I resisted it for a while. You're catching on to the senses quickly too. I'd like to see if you can visit in my mind like I used to do with you. There're other things we might be able to do too, but I don't think it's up to us yet. They just seem to happen."

"Like what?"

"My imagination has a list, but no point in going into them now. They'll happen if *they* want it."

"Who're *they*?"

"Purple dragons or little green men in flying saucers," he said with a smile.

"You're a silly tease. Well, Prince Charming, I think you've done very well in rescuing this Snow White from the dragons. How much better can it get?" Mindi gave an impish smile and her body language told Jeff she had something else on her mind besides riding around in drug dealers' minds. Jeff didn't run with the cue.

Mindi let it go. "I heard what you were thinking a moment ago about different leaps."

"Damnit, Mindi," Jeff said with a smile. "It's one thing to read *their* minds when we're riding around in them, but it's an invasion of privacy to be reading my mind."

"You're one to talk. Invading someone's privacy is your MO. I'm not the one who was in a bathroom stall with someone uninvited." Mindi tried to maintain a straight face while staring him down.

Jeff's jaw dropped. He stared at her, shaking his head. "How . . . do you . . . know that?"

"Jeff? Really? How *would* I know?" Her smile told him everything was okay. "That was one of the first times I felt you in my head, though I thought it was Shirley then. There was one time here you thought you'd hidden your thoughts. I only caught part of it. Mostly that you didn't want to embarrass me. I was pretty sure then, but your reaction now confirms it. Right?"

Jeff had anticipated the need to use basic "thought modes" during a leap or visit to the gray room, but might forget to be "quiet" and either blurt out his thoughts, or at least, not keep them especially private, which could then be heard by the host, or Mindi here in the gray room. During a leap, he could use Quiet Mode #1 when he could ask the subject subliminally to show him something like the time or date or where to find something. Quiet Mode #2 was totally private thoughts, not to be shared with the host. It all sounded well planned and efficient, but it took great concentration, and sometimes the dividing line blurred, and a host couldn't even be counted on not to respond to Quiet Mode #2 thoughts, meant to be hidden. He needed to coach Mindi for when she leaped into someone. Quiet Modes #1 and #2 were beside the well-established way he'd learned to intentionally communicate with the host telepathically.

Jeff nodded, continuing to stare at Mindi, surprised she had known this secret of his. He had tried to keep it to himself.

"I'm not busting you for not telling me," Mindi said. "I know you were there by accident." She tapped her temple. "You didn't mean to be here, right?"

"You are incredible. You put all of that together, and . . . you don't resent me for not telling you. Wow."

"I hope me telling you relieves you of the burden of carrying that around. I know you well enough to know that's one of your, uh, things—not wanting to share shame or doubt. Now, is there anything else I should know? If you don't want to say, I can tell you."

Jeff frowned. "What are you talking about? I don't have any other secrets. Except I locked my brother Mark in a trunk when he was five and didn't let him out for a while."

"That's cute. No, not that. You are so sweet, Jeff. So very sweet. I know you're afraid to, well, approach me about, well . . . Umm." She was trying to circle back to talk about the feelings she'd hinted at a couple of minutes ago. She lowered her eyes.

It took a moment for Jeff to realize what she was getting at, and he took the opportunity to now tease her in return. She looked up, her eyes pleading for him to help her out.

He said, "Where's that confidence you had a minute ago?" He tipped his head sideways and raised his eyebrows.

They communicated wordlessly for a moment, then Jeff said, "Yes." He gave her a little smile. "I am reluctant to make a serious pass at you. Yeah, we sorta talked about the sleeping arrangements when I come down for Thanksgiving . . ." They searched each other's eyes for another moment. "I feel like a schoolboy with his first crush, afraid of rejection." He paused a moment. "That's not the most important thing, though. I'm afraid that I'll scare you . . . and that'll mess things up . . . I don't want you to be . . . afraid." He paused, feeling helpless. "Do you blame me?"

"Oh, Jeff." Mindi stood and reached out her arms for a hug. He put his arms around her and held her. Though he felt her close to him, he knew she was physically a thousand miles away in Gardena. The border between reality and a lucid dream remained.

They eventually let go of each other but stood close, each

a little embarrassed but relieved that the subject, and their feelings, were now out in the open.

Mindi broke the silence. "Well, what do we say now?"

His look was contemplative and serious, which prompted a concerned look on her face.

"What?"

He blurted out, "What kind of vegetable side do you want at Thanksgiving? Green bean casserole or Brussel sprouts?"

She looked at him for a moment, then burst out laughing, a refreshing tension release that Jeff matched. They laughed until tears streamed down their faces, real tears that now blurred the line between dreams and reality.

When their laughter waned, they gasped for breath, then looked at each other as if seeing the other for the first time and started laughing again.

As they wiped their tears, Jeff said, "Good thing you weren't wearing mascara. It would be running down your face."

Mindi's eyes widened in amazement, and she burst out laughing again. When she'd composed herself, she said, "Jeff, you've got to work on your pickup lines. Both of those were terrible."

"Well, I obviously need help. Are you available?"

Mindi replied in a calm voice, making sure she wouldn't embarrass her friend, "Jeff, of course. I'm here for you as you've been for me."

Jeff sighed. "Thank you. Well, this was a good company meeting. Everyone has action items. I move to adjourn. Do I hear a second?"

Mindi grinned. "Meeting adjourned."

With huge smiles on their faces, they said "Ciao" and awakened, each in their own beds, twelve hundred miles apart but feeling closer than ever.

Jeff answered his cell phone without glancing at the caller ID. "Hello, Jeff Marlen."

"Hi, Jeff." A pause. "Charlene."

This was the first they'd spoken since she told him they should no longer be a couple. Jeff was grateful to her for the way she'd approached the breakup after having read his dream journal and learning about his dreams, her father, and Mindi. He knew the information in the journal had affected her on many levels.

Jeff checked his own emotional temperature. He had no regrets and no resentment toward her. She'd been right in saying he wasn't in love with her, that he'd fallen in love with Mindi. He resolved to be as smooth as possible in this conversation.

"Charlene, thank you again for those tickets to see the play. It was a good show. Mindi loved it too."

"You're welcome, Jeff. Mindi texted her thanks. I'm glad you both had a good time. Now, what I called about. When we were in Santa Monica, I mentioned I thought you'd make a good model for the men's product line for LaDormeur. Do you remember?"

"Of course. Charlene, I trust your judgment, but it's not something I would ever have thought of. What do you have in mind?"

"Okay. Good. We've started working on the campaign for the release of men's products, so if you're interested, I'd like to send you some paperwork to look over. If you want to go ahead, you'll need to get an agent. I'd recommend that you check with Mindi's agent to see who she might recommend." She took a long breath. "I've given it a lot of thought, and I'd like to have the two of you together in the ads."

Jeff smiled, imagining the photos. "Sure, send it over. I'll be down in LA over Thanksgiving. I'll call her agent."

"Sounds good, Jeff. The sooner the better. I'm finalizing the schedules."

"Okay. One more thing, if I may?" He sensed tension on the other end of the line.

"Yes?" She hesitated in a way that confirmed it.

"How is your mom? Did you share any of what you learned from the doctor with her and your sister?"

"Oh, Jeff. Thanks for asking." The tension released. "Originally, I wasn't going to because Dad's life was so full of secrets. But after I talked it over with Gail, it didn't seem right to hide anything more. We felt it was better that Mom knows everything. Dad was probably going to tell all of us about his cancer when he got back from Egypt. We're sure he wouldn't have wanted us to worry while he was gone. And considering his diagnosis, we believe he'd have torn up his confession letter about the affair. I'm sure he was thinking about that at the end. That makes me even sadder. But fate had different plans. And I didn't tell them how I found out about the cancer. Your secret, uh, is still a secret. Don't worry about me having shared it, okay?"

"Thank you, Charlie, for everything."

"You're welcome. Thank you. Call me after you've gone over the paperwork."

Jeff couldn't wait to tell Craig that the modeling gig was going to happen.

～

Mindi awoke after another night of no dreams in the gray room, but she and Jeff had talked on the phone and texted every day. She didn't have to be downtown until one o'clock, so she'd have time to meditate. Sitting cross-legged on her big pillow, she pressed *play* on the DVD player and took deep breaths as the sitar music from the recording set the mood for her meditation. The spoken instructions told her to visualize sitting beside a quiet stream, the water flowing gently past her. She was to let her thoughts float past like leaves passing by, floating on the water.

Mindi descended into the desired alpha state. Ten minutes into her session, at peace with herself, she felt she wasn't alone but resisted opening her eyes. Instead, she treated it as another thought to acknowledge and then let float by. She heard someone say her name softly in her mind. *Mindi?* She tried to dismiss it as just another leaf on the stream and took two deep breaths to press the thought back, but she heard her name again, soft and low. *Mindi?*

Taking that as a signal that her meditation was over, she opened her eyes, stretched and got ready for the day.

Jeff called her on the phone while she was having breakfast.

"I was just getting ready to call you. Nice surprise," Mindi said.

"Yeah, how're you doing today? You've got a meeting with your agent later, right?"

"Yes, I'll mention that you're looking for an agent and see what she says. You don't have any headshots yet, but I've got a couple of pics on my cell phone I can use to get you started."

"Great. Thanks. If you get any names, I'll see if I can set up an appointment for right after Thanksgiving."

"That sounds good. Oh, hey, I've got a question for you."

"Sure, what?"

"I was meditating to that recording you sent. I think I was doing it right."

"Yeah," Jeff said. "The best thing to get out of it is nothing at all. You turn off everything, and realize, well, nothing at all." He gave a short laugh. "That's the tough part of selling meditation; there's nothing to get. You give up everything for a short time but realize so much."

"I guess I was close. But here's my question. After I was, oh, in the zone, I heard my name. It was said softly, as a question. I tried to let it float by. When it happened again, I ended the session. What was that about? Did it ever happen to you?"

"M, I'm sorry."

"For what?"

"That was me. I was meditating right then too. Without trying, my inner vision opened up, and I saw you by the stream. I didn't plan it, and didn't mean to spoil your session, but I called out to you. You were nice and peaceful. Sorry I messed up your time."

"That is so cool. No, don't apologize. This is what you were talking about, right? Being able to be telepathically connected at a distance. Did you intend to do it?

"No, it was another accident. We might be onto something. I'm glad you said something. I wasn't sure you heard me."

"Yeah, I'm glad it was you."

"Call me later, or better, let's meet in the gray room."

"You just called me 'M.' Is that your new nickname for me?"

"I guess so. It just slipped out. Craig's the one that nicknames everybody. I guess he's got me doing it now. Is that okay? Some people don't like things like that."

"No, its fine. I think it's kinda cute. Makes me think of James Bond's boss's name, M."

"I'd rather think of you as Moneypenny," he said with a smile in his voice. "Ciao."

~

Mindi climbed into bed after reading Jeff's text with his ETA at LAX for his flight at Thanksgiving. She started to dream and fell, but after first feeling off-balance, she took a deep meditative breath and immediately transitioned to floating. Then she found herself in someone's head, looking at a laptop screen on a kitchen counter. The sound of oldies on the radio hovered in the background. She watched the screen as the man's hands worked the keyboard and mouse. Her host moved with quiet efficiency, searching the internet for information on telepathy and out-of-body, OOB, experiences.

What the—? That's the same stuff Jeff and I are working with, she thought.

The hands froze above the keyboard, and the hands' owner looked up and said, "What . . . ?"

Mindi recognized the voice. *Jeff! Is that you?*

Jeff's hands covered his eyes, turning her view dark. He rubbed his eyes, then the view returned, and Mindi felt the touch of his fingers rubbing his temples.

Jeff, it's you?

"Yeah! Yeah, give me a second."

He went into the bathroom and looked in the mirror. She saw his smile.

"Mindi, you did it! Wow, it feels sorta like a mosquito in my head buzzing around."

Interesting way to put it. I never thought of it that way, but yes.

"What day is it for you? Are we doing this real-time, or did you leap from the future?"

I just reread your text and went to bed. What? It's, uh, Wednesday the fifteenth.

"Yeah! We're doing this real-time. I was wondering if you might have gotten here from the future. If so, I'd have to take my 'curiosity anti-itch medicine' to keep from asking you what we'd been doing in the meantime. No need."

So how does it feel, being on the receiving end?

"Strange. So this is what it's like."

Mindi gave a little chuckle. *This is fun.*

"So . . . you were thinking about me when you went to sleep?"

Yes.

"This is so cool. You're asleep right now, and I'm awake. I can't believe we're in real-time, no time travel."

You were looking up stuff on telepathy, right? Are you finished? May I hang around and watch? And we can talk.

"Sure, I'd like that." He went back to the computer. "There's been a lot of research done on telepathy," he told her. "Particularly by governments who want to use it for spying. There's nothing specific on government sites. A lot on conspiracy sites. I didn't expect to find any reports on duplicable results because they wouldn't publish anything that had actually worked. They'd keep it secret, so the enemy doesn't find out. They'd want to weaponize it in private. But I'd hoped to pick up a nugget or two."

If not government, what about private or university research?

"University research is often financed by government grants—sometimes private money from corporations or individuals. They'd keep that quiet too. Don't tell the competition you could spy on them. And if I did find results, I wouldn't trust them. They could be phony results to throw others off the trail."

So we can't trust what you find?

"Yes, and we can't trust what we *can't* find either. Make sense?"

I guess so.

"Here's what I think. You and I've had some success. Like right now, but it's hit-and-miss. And even if we perfected it, we'd never make it public."

You're taking this pretty seriously.

"Yes, it's the way I am, and I won't apologize. If I hadn't taken it seriously, I wouldn't have anyone to cook me a turkey next week, right?"

Is that the only reason? Mindi said with a laugh in her tone.

"What if it were?"

Oh, Jeff, you're not that shallow. A turkey isn't the only reason.

"I do know what I want. Anyway, when you're learning to swim, don't you start out in the *shallow* end?"

Funny pun. Okay, okay. You made your point. So we start with turkey and green bean casserole, and then . . . ?

"I *like* what's on the menu."

Mindi laughed, which made Jeff laugh. They both felt the connection.

"Well, make sure you document this dream. We might see patterns and opportunities."

You're always the computer documentarian.

"Again, if I hadn't written it all down, you wouldn't be in my life right now."

I know, Jeff. I wish I was as disciplined as you are. I admire that.

He smiled. "Hey, young lady. You have strengths, like

your ability to memorize. I don't do that well. You've got other stuff . . . that's quite admirable too." She heard the smile in his voice.

Well, thank you . . . Okay, mutual admiration society meeting is over. What's next?

"I'd like to do something we've never done before: try to target a leap to a specific person, place, and in real-time."

Okay, who?

"First, you. When you're awake and I'm asleep. Do you have any early days in the next week before I come down there?"

I'm working for Jeri at Denny's on Tuesday. Shift starts in the morning at six. I'll be up at 4:30.

"Okay, what if I try to catch you before you get to work?"

If you're too early, you'll catch me in the shower. Don't do that.

"If that happened, I'd escape right away. And I'd text you so you'd know I didn't stay. Okay?"

Okay.

"Great, we've got a plan. You're already asleep. Do you want to stick around while I change into my pajamas?"

She laughed. *No. Thanks anyway.*

"Good night. Sweet dreams—that pun intended too. Ciao."

Ciao. Thank you for being there.

⁓

Monday night, Jeff stayed up late planning his targeted leap in real-time. He'd dozed off, did not know how long he'd been asleep, and was falling in the gray cloud. He hoped to target Mindi on the bus, so he relaxed and began to float.

Mindi, Mindi, Mindi, he called. Nothing happened. He

remained suspended.

A doorway opened, the entry to the gray room. *Darn, I missed.*

Mindi was there, dressed in her pink sweats, hoodie, and bunny slippers. They stepped toward each other, gave each other a hug, and sat in their chairs.

Jeff smiled. "Well, I'm glad to see you, but it looks like I missed. You're still asleep."

"Yeah, what time is it?"

Before Mindi could reply, a doorway opened in the gray space about twenty feet away. A man appeared and watched them for a moment. When Jeff noticed him, he sucked in a breath of alarm and glanced at Mindi.

Eyes wide, she leaned toward Jeff and said, "That's Alejandro!"

The man took a step forward. Jeff stood and started toward him.

The man hesitated and broke eye contact with Jeff, glanced at Mindi and said, "Do I know you? How do you know my name? Where am I?"

Jeff waited, looked back at Mindi and mouthed, *Escape!*

Mindi nodded and they both said, "Ciao."

~

Jeff awoke in his bedroom with the television still on. He texted Mindi:

You awake?

The phone rang. It was Mindi.

"Mindi!"

"What the hell?"

"You did good. You didn't hesitate," Jeff said.

"How did he get into our dream?" Mindi asked, her voice a combination of anger and fear.

"Don't know. I don't like this—a stranger in my dream."

Mindi let out a laugh. "Strangers in my dream? How many times were you—"

"I know, I know. But this is different. That was Alejandro. He dated Charlene."

"He *will* date her, next year. Remember?"

"Okay." Jeff dropped into analysis mode, thinking out loud. "The temporary license on his new car means we were in his and Charlene's head about six months from now. Let's call them Alejandro and Charlene version 2018. Our dream tonight is real-time, version 2017. You and I know I time traveled backward, both by me leaping into your mind and then visiting the gray room version of you in 2015. And we have at least one data point that we can time travel to the future. Now we have a hitchhiker who was dreaming when he visited us. Was he lucid dreaming? Did he know and will he remember? And was that Alejandro version 2017 or version 2018?" A long pause passed. "We have no way to know."

The phone line remained quiet for long enough that Mindi said, "Jeff, you still there? Did we get disconnected?"

"No, I'm still here. Sorry. I was thinking. This could be dangerous. I'd rather use our talents for fun than with potential drug dealers. This changes things. How can we avoid it?"

"Do you remember when I told you about my first conversation with Ingrid?"

"About it being dangerous."

"Yes. She said it might be more dangerous to *not* get involved than to get involved. But dangerous for who? And she said we should trust ourselves to manage whatever comes our way."

"Do you think this is what she was talking about?"

"She knew things about us I didn't tell her. Who knows what she knows? So what's next?"

"Well, you go back to sleep. You've got to get up early and go to work. We need to talk more when I get down there. We'll avoid the gray room for a while. Sleep well."

"Ciao, Jeff. I'll call you when I get off work today."

"Good."

They disconnected.

CHAPTER 4

Charlene Thomsen was in the conference room at the advertising company's office, packing things into her briefcase. She'd been in Santa Monica for the last four months coordinating the launch of her client's campaign, LaDormeur Cosmetics. Tonight she would fly back to Seattle for Thanksgiving dinner the next day with her sister and mother. This would be her last visit to Southern California until after the first of the next year.

Margarite Laughlin, Charlene's lead assistant, entered and stood a short distance from her, waiting until recognized.

Charlene looked up and smiled. "Hi Margarite, I'm going home tonight. The airport is going to be swamped, but I'd rather wake up in my bed at home than fly early tomorrow. Where are you having Turkey Day? You've been as busy as me, I can't imagine you hosting a dinner."

"No. Roger and I are going to his parents' ranch in the valley. His whole family will be there. My folks are back in Texas. Say, the reason I came in—if you have a moment—there's someone with LaDormeur that's been meeting with

Mr. Casswell today. The guy's in his office now and said he wants to meet you. He's pleased with the success of the campaign."

"Who is it, Margarite? Haven't I met everybody by now?" Charlene said with a touch of irritation in her tone. She woke up her phone that sat on the table next to her and checked the time. "And why now?" She would rather not meet with him, but if the top brass wanted it, she would accommodate.

"His name is Alejandro Sarís," Margarite replied. "He's a big investor in LaDormeur."

Charlene shook her head. "I haven't heard of him. Where's he from? Why does he want to meet with me?"

"As I understand it, he's silent money—not on the board but owns a huge block of stock. Apparently, he's loaned a substantial amount of money to the company at nominal interest. I've heard that money was used to get our program started. Boss says it's because of him we could keep things on the fast track. He's a high roller." Margarite smiled and shifted her weight.

Charlene sighed. Margarite's explanation appeared to be an attempt to convince her to make a little time to honor the boss's request. "Why now? Where's he from?"

"He got here earlier this afternoon and has been with Casswell since. I overheard that he's flying back to Bogotá tonight."

"Bogotá? Colombia?"

"Yes. He's Colombian, and . . . he's real good-looking, Charlene." Margarite lowered her chin and looked over the top of her glasses with a smile. "Please, may I tell him you'll talk with him for a few minutes? I'll tell him you have a flight to catch."

"Alright, Margarite. Give me about ten minutes to get all

this packed up. Have him come down here, or did they want me to come up to the tenth floor?"

They heard a man's voice with a sophisticated Latin accent, "Pardon me, where might I find Señorita Thomsen?"

Margarite and Charlene turned toward the door. A man stood there dressed in a charcoal-gray bespoke suit, properly buttoned, his tie knot and collar perfect, his cufflinks on display the proper distance beyond his suit's sleeves, his suit pants creased as if they'd just come from the cleaners, and his Italian-style wing-tip shoes brightly polished. He looked as if he'd just stepped out of the pages of *Gentleman's Quarterly*.

Charlene paused a moment, realizing she was in the presence of one of the individuals responsible for her being able to easily afford her new Mercedes.

With confidence, she stepped forward and said, "Good afternoon, I'm Charlene Thomsen. May I help you?"

Margarite stepped back and exited the conference room with an apologetic backward glance at Charlene.

Alejandro bowed slightly at the waist without breaking eye contact.

Charlene offered her hand, and he took it in proper business fashion with a firm grasp that Charlene returned. "My name is Alejandro Sarís. I'm very pleased to meet you, Ms. Thomsen."

They faced each other for a second. Charlene, somehow succeeding in not being intimidated by his style and handsomeness, replied, "Glad to meet you . . . Mr. Sarís." She gestured to a chair opposite her.

As he sat, he admired the photographs on the walls of the models in the current advertising campaign. Charlene sat at the head of the table, looked directly at him, and said, "I understand you wanted to talk with me. How may I help you?"

Alejandro glanced at the airline tickets sitting next to her briefcase across the table, then back at her. "I don't want to keep you, Ms. Thomsen, but I have heard so much about you concerning your success here. I wanted to thank you personally."

"I have a marvelously talented team, both here and in my offices in Seattle," Charlene said. "The credit truly belongs to them." She nodded to indicate that nothing more needed to be said about the subject. "And I understand that much of our ability to get action by the media was because of your influence. Is that correct?" She found this man very much to her liking, and the absence of a wedding ring indicated his approachability, but she kept the conversation professional.

"Ms. Thomsen, your reputation about your willingness to share credit for your success has preceded you. And I must reply in kind that any influence I have been able to exercise toward your success is due to my financial advisers."

He paused a moment, then continued. "I see you are about to depart. I was prepared to invite you to join me at the cocktail lounge across the street, but I shall not intrude on your schedule."

"Mr. Sarís, thank you for the invitation, but yes, I do have a reservation, and in order to make my flight, I will have to be efficient with my time. Perhaps when I return after the first of the year, we could meet for lunch?"

"Well, I also have a flight to return to my home. My plans are to remain in Colombia until after the new year has begun. I will have to check with my assistant to see what my schedule will be. Perhaps I can have him call you?" He reached into his pocket, took out a gold engraved business card holder, and they exchanged cards.

53

"Ms. Thomsen, it has been a pleasure to meet you. I find you as charming and lovely as described by those who introduced your name to me upstairs. I look forward to meeting with you again."

He stood and offered his hand, which she took. Instead of shaking it, however, he held it in a gallant manner, as if to raise it to his lips, but then merely moved her arm to show that would've been his intention if this hadn't been their first meeting. He let go of her hand, bowed slightly, and with a nod left the room without looking back.

Charlene watched until he turned the corner into the hallway, looked down at her hand and sighed. She cast him from her mind and got ready to leave the building.

~

Mindi sat in her Honda Civic in the cell phone lot at Los Angeles International Airport, waiting for Jeff's flight to arrive. She felt like a schoolchild, excited and shy. He would text her when the plane touched down and again when he knew at which entrance to meet. She'd already rehearsed the drive to make sure she could do it easily—the holiday surge in travel had made the busy terminal even more crowded. She felt she was being silly, but this was an important visit for her. After all the dream visits, and that wonderful week with him in Seattle a couple of weeks ago, she was excited. She checked her makeup in the mirror for the umpteenth time. Soon he'd be here!

Her phone chirped. She looked at the text: *On the ground, see you soon [heart emoji]*

It was a short drive. She didn't want to get there too early, because security might not let her idle at the curb, but she didn't want to keep him waiting. In just a few minutes she'd arrived, crowded on all sides by other drivers also intent on picking up their travelers.

There he was!

She left the car running, jumped out and threw her arms around him. He held her close, and they kissed. He folded himself into the compact car's passenger seat and she merged into traffic, confident as a taxi driver. She put her right hand on his arm, then reached for his hand. Their fingers interlocked. She gave a squeeze of love and negotiated their way toward the supermarket near her apartment in Gardena.

Mindi felt him staring at her while she drove. "Jeff!" She tried to sound like she was scolding him, but it came out betraying that she liked the attention. "You're distracting me. I've gotta drive."

He smiled. "Well, where should I be looking? You're doing a fine job. What I'm seeing is better than that." He motioned at the traffic.

"Oh, Jeff. Stop. If you want to help, please get my purse and open the side zipper. There's a shopping list of stuff we need to pick up."

"Well, you know, Mindi, that's a little outside my comfort zone."

"What are you talking about?"

"Mom told me never to go into a woman's purse."

"Nice sentiment, and I appreciate it, but first, I asked you to. Second, it's the zippered pocket, and third, there's nothing in my purse that you shouldn't see, unless you count the pepper spray that I keep close to the top and easy to reach."

"Now I'm on alert." Jeff grinned. "A weaponized woman is my driver. My respect level just went up. Should I go to code red?" He got the list and set the purse on the back seat.

Mindi shook her head. "Now *I'm* on alert. You never know how safe you are when you pick up someone at the airport and they put your safety equipment out of reach in the back seat." She enjoyed the sparring. Jeff's imagination and sense of humor complemented hers. This holiday was going to be fun.

"I bought a fresh twelve-pound turkey. Does that sound okay?"

"I'm sure it is. I've never cooked a turkey except to help Mom baste it. You're in the lead. I'll help."

~

As they carried the shopping bags from the car into her apartment, Jeff said, "Looks familiar."

"Yeah, Sherlock Holmes," Mindi said with a grin. "Did you ever wonder how things would've gone if you could've found the apartment and rung the bell when I was home?"

"Yes. I imagined you would've called the police and had me arrested. Things were still improbable back then. You and I wouldn't be here right now. I'm glad I had the self-control not to go any further. I could've contacted your manager."

"My doctor calls this 'delayed gratification.'"

He turned around in a circle, taking in familiar sights that he'd only seen in his dreams when he'd visited during his leaps.

She assembled ingredients and got out the mixing bowls for meal prep.

Jeff washed his hands, and as he dried them, she handed him the box of stuffing mix and said, "Directions are on the side."

After they completed their preparations for the next day's

meal, they walked hand in hand through the neighborhood. Their conversation centered around what Jeff had learned about the cocaine trade and Pablo Escobar in Colombia in the 1980s and early '90s. He told her that the violence that had surrounded Escobar's cartel concerned him, but only now because Alejandro had appeared in their gray room, and he seemed to have recognized her.

They agreed that if Alejandro appeared in their dreams again, they'd escape immediately, like before, with no discussion. Though Jeff said nothing to Mindi about it, he had considered the possibility that this Alejo could track her down in real life through Charlene. He would have to come up with a plan for that.

They walked in happy silence, each reflecting on their comfortable evening together. Once back at the apartment, Mindi said, "Beer or wine?"

"What are you having?"

"I was going to have a glass of white wine, but knowing you like IPAs, I did a little homework last weekend and bought you some Washington craft beer. You saw it in the fridge, didn't you?"

"Yes, indeed. That was thoughtful. Thank you. I'll have one of those. Where are the glasses? I'll pour."

"In the cupboard to the right of the sink."

He started toward it and Mindi dashed in front of him, turned and faced him with her back to the counter as he was about to reach for the handle. He stopped short to avoid a collision. She leaned into him. He held her shoulders to keep from crushing her. She stood on her toes, put her arms around his neck, and gave him a long, slow, passionate kiss.

Powerless to resist, without thinking or protesting, Jeff returned the kiss as she leaned back against the counter, him pressing into her—their first kiss of true passion.

When they came up for air, Jeff said, "Wow. That could've been a disaster. Did you mean to do that?"

Mindi smiled. "Are you pleased?"

"Well, yes, of course."

"When I saw I could ambush you, I figured I'd take the chance to let you know how I felt. You've been too shy to make an approach toward me, so I figured I needed to take command. I hope you don't mind." The look in her eyes pleaded with him to agree.

Jeff answered her by lifting her toward him and giving her another long kiss. He then stepped back a half step and said, "No, I don't mind at all."

She laughed. "I don't think the etiquette books say anything about who should make the first move, but I'm not keeping score. I just didn't want to miss the opportunity . . . Does any more need to be said?"

"Well . . ." he said, his tone sounding as if he would disagree.

"What?" she demanded.

"Well, where *is* that wine glass and the corkscrew?" He smiled at having teased her.

Mindi relaxed. "Okay, wise guy." She handed them to him.

He poured and they touched their drinks in a toast and said together, without pre-planning, "To the future."

~

Mindi and Jeff fell asleep wrapped in each other's arms. His dream started as he leaped into a host driving a car at night. It wasn't the Audi. A cell phone rang, and Jeff watched as the driver pressed a button on the steering wheel that answered in hands-free mode. The ring on the driver's little finger told him who it was. The caller asked in Spanish, "Do you have the information?"

Jeff recognized the voice, although he understood little of what was said. Carlos replied in Spanish, "Yes, delivery is expected as planned."

Based on their professional yet polite, businesslike tone, Jeff was sure it was about business. He noted Carlos wasn't at all deferential to Alejandro.

In English, Alejandro said, "Carlos, would you please speak English?"

"Of course. But why do you ask?"

"I prefer to do my business in English. I am trying to teach my children to speak it. Much of my business is in the United States. It keeps my mind sharp and makes my English better."

"*Sí*, no problem. My *inglés* is not as good as yours, but as you wish."

"*Bueno*, Carlos. Please let me know if there are any changes. Otherwise, I will make arrangements precisely as we did the last time."

"Very well."

"Good. Goodbye."

As soon as the call ended, Jeff awoke. The clock said 12:35 a.m. Mindi lay next to him, sleeping the sleep of the innocent. He got up, grabbed his journal and sat at the dining-room table to document the dream, disappointed he hadn't gotten the date for the leap. He felt certain the leaps were related. Alejandro *was* involved in a business deal with Carlos, Miranda, and Roberto. He cautioned himself not to assume it was about cocaine. But his gut told him it was. What else could it be? He'd learned there were no coincidences with these dreams.

He finished his dream journal notes, got back into bed, and cuddled up next to Mindi and fell asleep.

~

The next morning, while Mindi made coffee, Jeff sat at the table with his dream journal open.

She set a cup of coffee in front of him. "That's your dream journal? May I read it?"

"Do you want the old one? The one Charlene read?"

"Yes—that's not it?"

"No, this one is new. The other's in the safe at my apartment."

"Why do you have that one out? Anything interesting?"

Jeff slid it across the table to her. She looked at it and back at Jeff. Jeff tipped up his chin telling her to read it. She started, then glanced at him with a question in her eyes.

He nodded, then looked back down as a signal to read further.

When she'd finished reading the three short paragraphs, she said, "Really? Last night while I was asleep?"

"Yes. Did you dream?"

"No, not that I remember. You were in Carlos's head while he was driving and talking to Alejandro about a delivery?"

"Yeah, I think so."

"What does it mean?"

"I'm feeling it's what we assume."

Mindi frowned. "Are you sure?"

"Pretty sure we're in for some more dreams."

They looked at each other for a long moment, and then both shrugged.

Mindi closed the notebook and said with a resigned tone, "Let the games begin."

Jeff shrugged again. "Let's enjoy the holiday. My appetite is already growing. We haven't even had breakfast yet. I cook a mean fried egg and toast. You game?"

Thanksgiving passed in true fashion. Dinner was fantastic, and they resisted the temptation to fall asleep watching the football game afterward. Jeff suggested they go for another walk around the neighborhood.

"Why don't we drive over to Manhattan Beach?" Mindi suggested. "It's only fifteen minutes from here. We can walk out to the water, go out on the pier. I don't know if the aquarium will be open, though. What do you think?"

"Sounds great! I love the ocean."

At the beach, they joined many other like-minded people enjoying the temperate Southern California climate—a pleasure as always.

They held hands. Mindi shared with him that this was one of her favorite places, that she and her parents had come here to enjoy the waves and people watch.

"I hope you have lots of memories like that," Jeff said.

Mindi nodded. "Yes, it was good for a while, until Dad started drinking."

They walked on a few more steps, then Jeff said, "If you don't mind, may I make a comment about what you just said? I trust I'm not out of line."

"Sure. What?"

"Over the last few months, when you talked about your father, I noticed you never called him 'Dad,' you always referred to him as 'my father.' You just called him Dad. Did you notice?"

"No, I didn't. Hmm." She studied the sand as they walked

on. "Thank you for noticing."

They walked in silence until Jeff said, "Say, I've been thinking that when we dream together, we've no way of knowing the other is nearby."

"Yeah."

"We need to be able to tell each other we're there. We know our hosts can hear us when we're in their heads, so could we have a code?"

"Like a spy's password?"

"It can't be complicated. Just one word that's strange enough they'd be likely to repeat it out loud in surprise if we say it loud enough in their mind."

"One syllable?"

"Yes."

Nearby, a guy threw a Frisbee for his dog. A breeze caught it and sent it toward the couple. Jeff caught it adroitly and tossed it back.

The guy shouted, "Sorry! Thanks."

Jeff waved.

"Frisbee," Mindi said.

"What?"

"It's two syllables. But nothing a drug dealer would ever say in conversation. We'd recognize it, no?"

"Frisbee. I like it."

CHAPTER 5

In the 1980s, Pablo Escobar first set up the trade routes for his product into Miami in balloons in the stomachs of commercial airline passengers called "mules." When traffic increased, the Medellín Cartel smuggled kilos of the drug inside legitimate cargo shipments of appliances, food, and coffee beans. The cartel then bought a Bahamian island, Norman's Cay, and established an air route using their own airplanes, thence into Florida.

Eventually, the cartel set up overland routes into the United States through border crossings from Mexico. The North American Free Trade Agreement, NAFTA, made it fairly easy to get their trucks through. Authorities intercepted many shipments using drug dogs and spot checks, but not all. Once the wholesale shipments of powdered cocaine reached the burgeoning market in America, organized crime, as well as small-time drug distributors whose earlier distributed drug of choice had been marijuana, took advantage of their existing distribution system to move tons of cocaine into the noses of affluent Americans.

It was estimated that back then, it cost one thousand dollars to refine a kilogram of cocaine, and another four thousand to smuggle it into the United States, where it could sell for a street value averaging one hundred dollars per gram. At one thousand grams per kilo, it was a very profitable business. Crack cocaine, crack for short, typically cost the same per gram as powdered cocaine, however the high, the rush, was faster and more intense. Both forms were highly addictive.

Alejandro Sarís lived in this world. Not as a user, although he wasn't averse to it when either the social or a sexual opportunity called for it, but his wealth, originally from his family in Bogotá, had skyrocketed when he found that his money could be multiplied several times over by financing shipments from Colombia to the United States. In the beginning, he had carried five hundred kilos himself in his private airplane into southern Florida. Although he wasn't risk-adverse, he felt it was better for business to pay others to take chances. Busts were now seldom. However, he preferred to be the silent partner in nearly all transactions, isolating and insulating himself from the gamble of spending time in court, embarrassment to his family, financial penalties that might ensue and, of course, risk of imprisonment.

He'd made so much money in just a few years that he'd looked for ways to invest in legitimate businesses, all the while maintaining a relatively low profile. When the business decision was a good one, and the profits rolled in, he let it ride and compounded the profits.

There were other more high-profile investors who shared his investment in LaDormeur, which kept the main spotlight off him. The emerging cosmetics company was a personal choice, not only because it could quietly advance his standing in the business world but also because it could put him in close contact with lovely young women.

After this latest visit to Southern California, he'd flown back to Panama City for a brief visit with business contacts there. From there, he would fly to Medellín for the same reason, then he'd drive home to the capital of Colombia, Bogotá. When he'd traveled north for his trip to Los Angeles, he'd left his vehicle in Medellín.

He used these stops to show the elites and minor capos in the cocaine trade that he was interested in their success and to reinforce his influence. He also enhanced the standing of his drug partner's high quality luggage manufacturing business. Popular in the American market, the luggage had become one more method of getting the illegal product past customs inspectors.

He checked into the Medellín Marriott, dined alone at Restaurante Elcielo there, and turned in early to be fresh for the almost nine-hour drive back to his home in Bogotá. He could have chosen to fly, but lately he enjoyed driving his newest toy, a fully equipped Land Rover Discovery First Edition, on highways through the lush green jungles of central Colombia where he'd grown up. The time alone with the expensive sound system gave him a welcome break, allowed him to wear more comfortable clothing, to leave the suit and tie for those he wished to impress.

At the hotel, he turned out the light but left the curtains open and allowed the city lights to cast their soft glow on the ceiling of the well-appointed hotel room. He fell asleep immediately.

He began to dream, and in time was in REM sleep that morphed into a feeling of falling within a cocoon of grayness. He didn't know from where he'd fallen or to where he might be falling. His initial reaction was panic, but when he controlled that, a floating sensation took over. He was aware that he was dreaming, the hallmark of a lucid dream. Within moments of the realization, the gray parted, and he saw a gray horizon that extended in all directions with no end point.

A doorway appeared, phantom-like, opening silently. Although disoriented, he approached it and saw a man and a woman talking while sitting in matching gray overstuffed chairs. They looked at him as he stepped through the doorway.

Alejandro froze as the man stood up as if to advance toward him.

The woman leaned forward and said to the man, an edge to her voice, "That's Alejandro!"

Alejandro tensed and looked at the woman. "Do I know you? How do you know me? Where am I?"

"Escape," the man said, then they both said "Ciao" and disintegrated into glitter.

Alejandro jerked awake in his hotel room bed with a clearly etched memory of the dream. He lay there for a few moments, threw the covers back, and, with an unsteady motion, pushed off the bed. He stood for a moment as he rubbed his face with both hands, then moved toward the bathroom.

He'd seen the woman somewhere, but where? The dream troubled him because of its clarity and persistence. He'd never had a dream like that before.

He lay back on the bed and watched the landing lights of the airliners on final approach while he replayed the dream. He soon drifted back into a restful sleep.

Alejandro awoke feeling fully rested with the memory of the dream intruding on his thoughts. After breakfast, he claimed his SUV from the valet and began the four-hundred-kilometer drive home.

He scoured his mind for the woman in the dream who

knew his name but found no answer. If he saw the man again, he felt sure he'd recognize him.

Alejandro parked his car in the expansive driveway of his villa near the base of Monserrate Mountain that overlooked the city of Bogotá to the northwest. The view was a welcome sight after the crush of humanity in Los Angeles. As he carried his suitcases into the hallway, he heard his children playing upstairs. His attractive wife of ten years came through the doorway, wiping her hands on her apron.

Karina spoke in Spanish. "Alejo, I am so glad you are home. Why do you insist on driving all that way? I would have picked you up at the airport."

Alejandro put his arms around her. She wrapped her arms around his neck, and they gave each other a long, slow kiss.

"I've missed you so much. I don't like it when you leave, but it's so special when you return. Your trip was a success, was it not?" Karina said with a smile, then she called upstairs, again in Spanish, "Mateo, Maria, your father has returned."

The boy and girl, aged seven and six, bounded down the stairs and hugged him tightly.

"Please, Kara," Alejandro said. "We agreed to speak English so you can practice and the children will be fluent for business as they grow. *¿Por favor?*"

"I am sorry, Alejo. I am so glad to see you. Are you hungry?"

In unison the two children said, "*Papá, ¿me trajiste algo?*"

"Kara, my dear, please . . ." He gave her a look of loving frustration.

Karina returned his look.

"Children, please let us practice our *inglés*, okay?"

"*Sí*, Mama," Mateo said.

"*Yes*, Mother." Maria looked at Mateo and stuck her tongue out.

"Papa, what did you bring us?" they said together.

Alejandro kneeled, put his arms around his children, and said, "Of course I brought you something. But let us have Mama finish her preparation of dinner, and after our meal, we will see what I have in my suitcase for you. You have been good for Mama while I have been gone, no? If so, can you wait?"

The two children pouted and swung their heads in disappointment, but each said, one after the other, "*Sí, papá, podemos esperar.*"

He gave a stern look at each of them, to which they repeated in English, in unison, "Yes, Papa, we can wait."

"Go back upstairs and put your toys away, wash up, and come back for supper."

⁓

The last two days since Thanksgiving had been satisfying for Jeff. He thought he'd been happy before, but these days with Mindi had been fantastic. Even though they'd been together for only three weeks in real-time, they'd known each other for over six months in their dreams. Their friendship had developed backward to most, having learned significant personal details of each other's past very early upon meeting. The intimate part of their relationship, because of the virtual nature of their early months, had developed in a nontraditional way as well.

The telepathy and astral projection abilities came without an instruction manual, but the couple's experience with Alejandro made them aware that they could be in danger in both the physical world and the metaphysical.

While they were on holiday, though, they put all

concerns away for the time being. It had been years since Jeff had visited Universal Studios, and when he mentioned he'd like to see the new Harry Potter ride, Mindi was enthusiastic. They spent the day in Hollywood completely immersed in the world of make-believe, even though they lived with an equally amazing world of their own in their dreams.

That night, he once again found himself in the gray room standing a few feet from their overstuffed chairs. His first thought was whether Alejandro would join him there. And if so, how would he handle it?

A doorway opened, and he tensed, but it was Mindi, her expression as concerned as he felt.

"What's this?" she said. "We just kissed good night. What are we doing here?"

"I don't know. This is strange."

Mindi looked around. "I thought Alejandro might be here."

"Me too. What should we do?"

"Well, someone or something is setting our agenda, so we wait and see?"

They moved toward their chairs, intending to sit, but before they got there, they both dissolved into glitter.

Instead of waking up in bed, Jeff was falling again. Abruptly his view changed to seeing through the windscreen of a small airplane flying at night. The digital avionics of this aircraft looked like something from Star Wars. Was this Alejandro?

With that thought, his host looked to his right and saw Charlene, who was looking out the window to her right. Alejandro scanned the gauges and glanced out the window to his left. Lights pooled at the houses on the shoreline of the islands below, punctuating the darkness.

Jeff remembered their code word, and in his mind, blurted out, *Frisbee!*

Alejandro's head snapped to his right just as Charlene turned toward him. One after the other they said, "Frisbee?" Then shook their heads and laughed.

"What was that about?" Charlene said.

"I don't know. Why did you . . . ?"

She shook her head. "I don't know."

Alejandro looked puzzled for a moment, then returned his attention to being a pilot as he keyed the comm button. "Boeing Tower, Pilatus 9889HK, ten southwest at 2,000, inbound for landing."

The radio replied, "Pilatus 89HK, cleared runway 13L."

With his Latin accent, "Roger. Cleared to land 13L, Pilatus 89HK."

"Alejo, this has been so much fun," Charlene said. "Such a surprise. You really know how to impress a lady. My first airplane flight to go for dinner."

That comment by Charlene made Jeff consider that he and Mindi may have actually leaped back into this couple's date where he had missed the flight and when Mindi left it early. If this *was* the same night as before, it raised the question on the linearity and the continuity of leaps into the future. What crossroads had they returned to and made to take another future path? Apparently, travel to events in the future was not as fixed as time travel was into the past. He mentally shrugged and easily accepted he might never know the answer. Surely they needed to learn something for this mission—otherwise they wouldn't have been put here tonight.

He watched as the competent pilot brought the airplane in for a smooth landing. At the hangar, after post-flight procedures, Alejandro reached for the logbook. Jeff expected the flight log to be on an electronic tablet or laptop, but no, it was an old-school logbook for the Pilatus PC-24 in which Alejandro wrote April 21, 2018, and the details of the flight.

They *had* leaped forward in time. Jeff had what he needed, but he wanted to see what might happen next.

Charlene, in a hasty movement, unfastened the seatbelt and started to stand.

"*Un momentito, por favor,*" Alejandro said as he put his hand on her arm. "Remember, I must let down the stairway."

She waited while he stepped through the narrow doorway into the cabin, pressed the button on a panel and watched the stairs descend. When she stepped up to him, he reached out and slipped his arm around her waist, and pulled her to him.

She leaned away from him briefly, then leaned forward giving him a kiss that had no invitation in it at all. "Alejo, I'm not feeling well."

"My dear, I trust it was not the meal. It seems they serve the best there."

"No, no, it's not my stomach. It's a headache." She rubbed her temples, pressed her palms into her eyes and took a deep breath. "Alejo, would you mind if you just took me home? But please, call me tomorrow."

They made their way down the steps. Alejandro spoke with a young man to confirm what services for the airplane were expected.

Jeff felt satisfied. It had been a successful leap.

He awoke and turned toward Mindi, who was up on one arm, looking concerned.

"Oh, Jeff, I've got a horrible feeling about this."

"What do you mean?" He sat up and held her close.

She held onto him as if he might leave her.

"Mindi?"

71

They made eye contact.

"What is it?" Jeff said, gentleness in his voice.

"It's the airplane and the money. And Charlene. I know you don't love her—we've been all over that—but it must feel strange to be there anyway, so close, when you're there in the mind of someone else kissing her."

Jeff stroked her hair and said nothing for a few moments.

"It's okay. Thank you, but she was right. I don't love her. Sure, we had a connection, but tonight didn't bother me. It's over. I'm in love with you." He touched her chin and turned her face to look at him. Her expression was full of wonder.

"Jeff, you haven't said that before, but—you really mean it. I've been hesitant to tell you. I love you too."

They kissed, and when they pulled away, she said, "You're a much better kisser than Alejandro."

Jeff looked at her with surprise. "Well, thank you." He smiled, gave her a quick peck on the lips and said, "Could you tell why Charlene was feeling bad?"

"It was probably me that gave her the headache. I was bold and wandered around in her head, opening doors in her mind."

"That's interesting. You looked around? How did you do that? Did you find anything?" He motioned for them to go into the kitchen.

"Well, no. I didn't know what to do. I think I stirred things up, though."

"Hey, how about the Frisbee thing?" he said as he made the coffee. "That made me laugh."

"Yeah, that worked well. I think with some practice we can do other stuff. The whole drug thing puts a damper on this being fun, though. Makes it scary."

Jeff nodded. "List time. One, we only have one data point

on it, but it looks like we can let the other know we're there. Two, we know we went forward in time. That was April 21, next year. Three, you can snoop around."

"Maybe we can do that some more and find something useful. Do you think we can make someone happy, angry, curious, or scared, rather than just give them a headache?"

Jeff tilted his head thoughtfully. "Or suspicious, cautious, or tired. I don't know. You know, I suspect this is all happening to us because we're supposed to keep Charlene out of trouble."

Mindi's head snapped around. "But not get into trouble ourselves."

"Well sure. Did you have anything particular in mind about what kind of trouble?"

"Alejandro might have seen a LaDormeur ad and put me and Charlene together. He might ask her about me."

"Wouldn't she respect your privacy, not give out private information?"

They looked at each other as if the answer hung in the air between them, shrugged, drank their coffee, and wrote in their dream journals. They exchanged them and read what the other had written.

"Well, we got up a little early. Shouldn't we go back to bed?" Mindi said in a coquettish tone.

"After this coffee, I'm not sure I could sleep."

Mindi grinned. "Who said anything about sleep?"

~

Jeff and Mindi stood on the sidewalk outside departures at the airport saying their goodbyes, both reluctant to accept that Jeff had to return to Seattle. Being together at Thanksgiving had been a wonderful visit—as the duration and intensity of their goodbye kiss indicated.

They made a date to meet in the gray room that night, so their parting wasn't nearly as disruptive as it would've been without their paranormal abilities.

Jeff sighed as he watched her drive away. While he sat at the gate waiting for boarding, he looked up Pilatus PC-24 on the web and saw a base price of nine million dollars. Of course, it could be leased, but that would still be a hefty monthly budget item. Its range, with no passengers or cargo, was twenty-four hundred miles, so it could easily make it from Colombia to Seattle with just one stop. And according to the manufacturer's website, it could land on unimproved airstrips.

Like a law enforcement agent, Jeff thought, *Great smuggling plane.*

~

Back home and asleep, he went to visit Mindi in the gray room as they'd planned. She sat in her chair already, smiling.

"I found a website that says time in lucid dreaming follows the same time structure as real-time," Jeff said. "Fifteen minutes here is fifteen minutes on the clock in the bedroom. I should wear a watch to bed, see if I can bring it with me here."

"Interesting. When we first started coming here, we wore what we wore to work. Then it changed to what we wore to bed. I don't wear my bunny slippers to bed, though, but when I come here, I've got them on. And the time you wanted your robe, presto, you were wearing it."

He laughed. "What if we went to bed naked? Would we show up here that way?"

"Leave it to you to think about that." She chuckled. "And

I already did."

"Okay, maybe we can try that sometime, but not if Alejandro might show up. That would be too much for me to take."

"Spoilsport. Okay, I'll be good. Why don't you 'think' your watch right now?"

Jeff then felt the watch on his wrist. Their dream world had just given up another secret.

"There you go. What time is it?" she asked.

"Twelve thirty-seven."

"Okay. Now, do you own a gun?"

Jeff looked up at her. "Why do you ask?"

She shrugged. "Just wondering."

"No, I don't. I never felt I needed one. The police and the military get paid to protect us. Dad took us to the shooting range to teach us how to use one a few times, though, so we could learn about firearms safety and all that. If I felt I needed one, I'd get one." He gave her a chance to reply.

She said nothing.

"I don't think a gun would be much use here in dreamland," Jeff said, "except to scare someone. We can't get hurt here, can we? We'd just wake up."

Mindi frowned. "Or would we?"

"What? Not wake up? I don't know. I don't want to find out. But I understand why you asked. I told you, the history of the drug trade is violence. I'd hate to think that in real-time we'd need to protect ourselves. You've got your pepper spray and alarm, don't you?"

"Yeah, but that wouldn't be any good against someone with a gun."

"I'll have to give that some thought."

She stood and put her arms around his neck, leaned back

and said with a twinkle in her eye, "Are you thinking what I'm thinking?"

"What? I wasn't, but now I am," he said with a smile. "Here? Do you think we can here? In our dreams?" He looked at her and smiled. "Oh, yeah! But . . ."

She finished his sentence for him. "Alejandro?"

"Yeah. We can lock the door and close the shades in the apartment, but how do we lock the door to our gray room?"

Ten-foot-tall gray walls suddenly surrounded them and their chairs. Jeff stepped toward the nearest wall and pushed it. It didn't move.

"Solid." He turned toward her. "That was you?"

"Yep. You did the watch; I do walls." She waited a moment, looked at the solid, featureless walls and said, "But I don't do windows." She chuckled.

"Cute." Jeff smiled and rapped on the wall with his knuckles. "Good job. There's no style though, but good construction. And we don't need a door, huh? We'd glitter outta here, right?"

Jeff had just finished his sentence when they heard a a man's muffled voice coming from the other side of the wall. They looked at each other, and then around their new confined room.

"Hola? Hello," the voice said.

Jeff dropped into a crouch, looked at Mindi and mouthed silently, *Alejandro!*

She turned around in a circle, eyeing the walls, and when she looked back at Jeff—as she told him later—she was startled to find that Jeff's head had turned into a massive dinosaur.

He put his human hand with a raised finger up to the dinosaur mouth to signal silence and nodded sideways, motioning with his hand and eyes for her to leave.

She whispered, "Ciao," and her glitter settled toward the floor.

Jeff walked up to the wall, touched it, and it too, dissolved into glitter. By the time the wall was gone, Jeff had fully transformed into the image of the aggressive velociraptor from Jurassic Park.

Alejandro stood in silk pajamas, not ten feet away, his eyes widened in terror. Jeff stalked menacingly toward him, then lunged, roaring like a lion—he didn't know what kind of sound a dinosaur might actually make. The frightened man retreated, back-stepping as Jeff advanced and roared again. Alejandro turned and sprinted toward the indistinct horizon. Jeff gave chase, still roaring. After a few dozen yards, Alejandro's image turned into glitter and disappeared.

Jeff laughed and looked down at his dinosaur hands as they changed back into his human form.

He left with a ciao, woke up in his own bed in Seattle, and telephoned Mindi.

"Jeff!" she said.

Jeff was laughing so hard he could hardly catch his breath.

"That was brilliant," Mindi said. "By the way you're laughing, it worked. Tell me."

Jeff controlled his laughter, took a deep breath and said, "I went full velociraptor on him and chased him until he became glitter. I wished I'd been able to catch up with him. I bet he almost peed his fancy silk pajamas." He started laughing again.

"That was quick thinking, Jeff. Do you think it will stop him from coming back?"

"I have no idea. I hope so. I also hope he doesn't figure out he could turn into a T-Rex. I'd be outmatched."

"Do you think he would do that?"

"I'm glad you didn't get scared when you looked at me."

"Just for a second, but I figured it out. I wonder if we can control our hosts like that when we leap into them."

"I like that, you're always thinking. Sure, but only if they're not friendly. I wouldn't want to do that to Charlene. But it could be a useful tool."

Mindi frowned. "Why did he show up again?"

After a long silence on the line, Jeff said, "I don't have an answer for that. Like us, he probably can't control it. Let's say good night, and talk tomorrow, 'k?"

"Right. I love you," Mindi said.

"I love you too. Ciao for now."

"Ciao." They disconnected.

Before turning off the light, Jeff wrote the whole episode in his journal, and then fell asleep, considering all the things they could do with their developing talents. His last consideration before a dreamless sleep engulfed him was how he could get into someone else's gray room and create images in their minds that way—even nightmares.

CHAPTER 6

Carlos Cordoba was part of the supply chain of cocaine for the wealthy addicts in the United States, and he was a strong link. His role, in cooperation with Alejandro, was to arrange transport from the jungle manufacturing facilities to laboratories and storage throughout Colombia, where the cocaine awaited shipment abroad. They'd decentralized their warehousing so that if one location became compromised, they wouldn't lose an entire shipment of up to twenty tons.

Carlos was paid handsomely for his efforts, and his income from cocaine was several layers deep, highly laundered, sheltered, and primarily offshore. He routed a small amount through his leather luggage and bag factory in Medellín, with the corporate books reflecting what appeared to be legitimate sales. His company paid him handsomely. He had few vices besides his daughter going to college in the United States, luxury cars, and the fine dining he enjoyed. He was careful to operate under the radar of the authorities, had no criminal record, and his name appeared nowhere in newspapers within Colombia, not even in the social pages. He gave generously, and anonymously, to the church and local charities. He hadn't even a traffic ticket in his name.

Through his efforts, chemicals moved quietly into the jungle, and the raw product moved equally quietly through to the labs, where it was processed and then stored until it was put in transit. A small array of street kids and lieutenants informed on the position of the army and local police patrols if they got close to a site. With such intel, the business operated with virtual impunity, having few losses or arrests.

If any of the cartel's people proved disloyal or happened to get arrested, they were sacrificed to the legal system along with a small amount of drugs. Individuals had only limited knowledge of those further up the hierarchy, so authorities would only find a short trail to a dead end. If those arrested tried to negotiate leniency and decided to flip, the organization isolated them completely—hopefully without them being liquidated, as had routinely happened three decades ago. The threat of a serious reprisal was always present, however, and that, plus the generous pay, kept the workforce loyal to the system.

Because of this relatively benign system, they had a minimal need for soldiers, the *sicarios*, who shed blood that risked bad press and had in the past eventually turned public opinion against the cartels. Experience from the 1980s and 1990s in their country, Colombia, and in Mexico taught that the quieter and more concealed their operation, the greater the amount of profit that was distributed upward.

~

Jeff landed in Carlos's head in his Mercedes just as he pressed the button to disconnect a hands-free phone call. Was this a continuation of the same dream as before or a new one? No matter, he was here to learn something.

With Jeff watching through Carlos's eyes, the drive was on the city's highway and residential streets until arrival at a nice house in a nice neighborhood. Carlos pressed the button on the remote for the garage door. His Rolex said 8:07 p.m.

When the door opened, Carlos parked the car in the two-car garage beside his Range Rover. He waited for the automatic door to close, latched it, and entered the house. A dog shuffled and whined around the corner in the laundry area, and Carlos opened the door on a very pleased German Shepherd in a large wire kennel.

"Max, good boy," Carlos said in Spanish as he scratched his dog's ears. "Did you miss me?"

Elated to see his master, the dog pranced, head-butted Carlos's thighs, and gave a happy whine.

Carlos wandered into the living room, took off his jacket, and then unclipped a concealed semiautomatic pistol from his waistband.

Jeff mentally gasped at the sight of the gun. Carlos poured himself a drink from an unmarked crystal decanter, sat down in a leather recliner, and turned on the television news without sound.

Jeff decided he needed to try what Mindi had done by looking around to find what day Carlos was in now. Intuition guided him into a passageway in the man's mind, and he stopped in front of a closed portal. With a virtual hand, he touched the doorway and witnessed Carlos's memory of a restaurant breakfast of huevos rancheros while reading Spanish-language newspapers, *El Universal de Cartagena*, and then the *Medellín Herald*, both dated *20 de mayo, 2018*.

He had traveled forward in time again. *But what was that*

date of this *day?*

Carlos rubbed his forehead and the back of his neck as he felt the strain of Jeff's concentration.

Return to the optic nerve, Jeff thought, and immediately he again saw through his host's eyes.

The pressure now off, Carlos responded to the recently stimulated memory of the newspapers and looked at a newspaper on the side table. It was one those from the memory. Jeff had his answer, May 20.

Carlos lit a cigarette and stared at the ceiling, deep in contemplation.

Jeff tried but couldn't read the man's thoughts. He found the odor and taste of the cigarette repulsive and felt intolerant of it, but he needed to stay to learn what he could.

June 26, he thought, hoping to stimulate a helpful response, but the only answer he got to his inquiry was the memory of the Cartagena dinner with Miranda and explicit thoughts of how he wanted to sleep with her. The memory dissolved when an image of 'Berto formed, validating that his desires would never be satisfied. Jeff watched the memory of Carlos reading the note and putting it in his pocket, but he got no more information about June 26.

Why not? There has to be more.

Not wanting this to be a wasted leap, Jeff planned to go back into Carlos's memories for more information, but he suddenly awoke in Seattle feeling nauseated. He dropped two seltzer tablets into a glass and wrote the entire event in his dream journal, including feeling sickened by the smoking. He knew from previous experience that the host's alcohol affected his mind too, and speculated that the same applied if the host used other drugs. Clearly, not all leaps would be fruitful.

~

While Jeff slept in Seattle and visited with Carlos in Medellín, Mindi—in Gardena—had a lucid dream of a visit with a woman she, at first, didn't identify.

She was preparing a meal in a relatively modern kitchen, though one somewhat different from what Mindi was used to. The sound of Spanish spoken on a television came from the other room. *Am I in Colombia?*

She carried two plates, each with half a tamale and a serving of rice and beans, and placed them on a table next to a bowl of cut fruit. Two tall glasses of milk also sat on the table.

In Spanish, Karina said, "Maria, Mateo, come eat your breakfast."

The sound of running feet preceded the entrance of two well-groomed children. They sat at the table and, before eating, placed their cloth napkins in their laps, crossed themselves, and mouthed a quiet prayer of thanks.

"When you're finished, wash up and get your sweaters. Your father wants to take you to the market to do some Christmas shopping. Okay?"

Mindi felt her smile at them before she turned and went back into the kitchen where Alejandro was leaning against the counter, drinking a cup of coffee. He smiled at her, set his cup down as she approached him, and put his arms around her. She shook the hair out of her eyes and closed them as he leaned in and gave her a warm kiss. Mindi did not enjoy it, although she felt that the woman did.

Oh my God, he's married and has children! And in a few months, he'll be with Charlene! Mindi's anger bubbled up from within her mind and into Karina's.

Karina's enjoyment ended as she backed away from the embrace and looked suspiciously at her husband. She closed her eyes and rubbed her temples.

Alejandro's hands held her gently at the waist.

"Karina, are you feeling alright?"

Karina shook her head, and a flash of denial dismissed the negative feelings Mindi had just shared with her. "No, Alejo, I'm fine. You have a good time with the children. They are looking forward to spending time with you. They missed you when you were gone."

He slid his arms around her, pulled her to him and gave her a tender hug. Now with his hands lightly resting on her shoulders, he smiled at her, kissed her forehead, and then walked through the swinging door to talk with his children.

It bothered Mindi that she was being shown this scene. He loved his wife and kids, so why would he want to cheat on them?

As soon as Mindi completed that thought, Karina spun and looked at the door through which Alejandro had just passed. The feelings of distrust returned to Karina's mind.

Shit. Mindi immediately tried to quit telegraphing her feelings to Karina, but it was too late. The women's minds were linked. Mindi had good reason to distrust Karina's husband, and Karina now intuitively felt that distrust. Jeff had cautioned her to think in the quiet part of her mind. She needed more practice.

Karina cleaned up the kitchen while Mindi considered what Jeff had said about them not creating the situations in which they were involved, but to only act as a catalyst for what seemed destined to happen. Maybe the man had cheated before. Was their marriage destined for failure anyway, and her presence would just finish the job? She shut off her thoughts again, but not before Karina closed her eyes and held her face in her hands as a wave of despair shuddered through her.

Time to go before I do any more damage. Ciao!

Mindi awoke, looked up at her ceiling, and felt guilty for the seeds she'd planted in Karina's mind.

While she wrote the dream in her notebook, her phone chimed. Jeff's text asked her to call him.

~

Jeff heard Mindi's concern on the other end of the line. "Jeff! This is just too much. How were you able to handle everything you saw and heard with Charlene's father and his girlfriend?"

"What is it?" Jeff asked. "What happened?"

Mindi told him the whole dream, what she'd thought and felt, the feelings she'd planted in Karina's mind, and the guilt she felt.

"I know. It's hard to watch other people getting hurt," Jeff said, trying to comfort her. "I tried to keep it all in perspective, but it was hard. We didn't ask to be witnesses to a train wreck, and I know you don't want to be the cause. But you didn't give her any evidence, right? You just planted some women's intuition. And is the information wrong?"

"Sure. Okay. I see what you mean, but I still feel like crap about it. Now, you wanted me to call you?"

"Yes, I did. But first, I understand how you feel and that it will all work out the way it's supposed to, whatever that is. Remember, we're not completely in control. There's nothing in particular I wanted to talk about. I just wanted to hear your voice. Maybe I somehow knew you needed to talk."

He told her about looking for information in Carlos's

head and coming up empty. "You came out better than I did, I think. I did share some good scotch, but I also got sick of his cigarette. I think the drink may have dulled my ability to find anything useful."

"Thanks for listening," Mindi said. "I feel better now. I was feeling sorry for myself and feeling sorry for Karina. I'd better get going to work."

Jeff looked at the clock in his kitchen. "Yeah, I've got to get going too. Love you. See you in the gray room tonight?"

"You got it. Ciao."

"Ciao." They clicked off.

~

Alejandro kissed his wife good night, turned over, and watched out the window as the moon seemed to be brushed by the branches of the trees in the breeze. For some unknown reason, he felt afraid to fall asleep tonight, but sleep eventually overtook him. After falling and floating, he found himself in front of the gray door again. It opened, and he stepped through but saw none of the landmarks from before—no chairs or wall. Nothing but a vast view of gray. He listened for sounds, afraid the monster would chase him again, but all he heard was his own breathing.

Then from every direction, all around him, a coarse woman's voice shouted in Spanish, "You don't belong here! You must leave!"

Sweat beaded on Alejandro's brow and it stung his eyes. He wiped it away with his sleeve and spun in a circle looking for but not finding the source of the voice.

"I know this is a dream," he said, trying to control his fear. "So let me wake up." He continued to turn, this time looking for the doorway, but it had disappeared.

A shuffling sound came from behind him. He turned and gasped in horror. Snakes covered the ground all the way to the infinite horizon, slithering toward him slowly but relentlessly. He spun, intending to run away, but the snakes were advancing from there too. They were a mass of writhing snakes, piling up and trapping him in the center of a circle.

"Be warned. You are *never* to return!" the woman's voice said.

The snakes were upon him, covering him, wrapping themselves around his limbs, circling his chest, smothering his face. He screamed, until they filled his mouth, covered his nose and ears.

He awoke on his bedroom floor with a scream, consumed by panic and enmeshed in bedclothes that covered his face and entangled his legs and arms, holding him prisoner.

The light was on and his wife was trying to free him.

"Alejandro!" she cried in Spanish. "It's a nightmare. Wake up!"

Thrashing and groaning, he shoved Karina away, and she fell backward against the wall, crying out in surprise and pain. Alejandro finally freed his head and broke free of the bedclothes. Realizing what he'd done, he reached to protect her, but she recoiled. He collapsed, helpless. After a period of calm, she tentatively approached him and helped him to his feet, put her arms around him, and hugged him to her. He shook uncontrollably, quiet for a moment, and then he began to sob.

They sat on the edge of the bed, and he looked around the room, his eyes wide with terror and confusion. She placed his hand on her cheek to reassure him she was real. His eyes closed, and his breathing and heart slowed.

Karina lifted his feet onto the bed, gathered up the covers and spread them over him, and then she climbed onto the bed and held him as he mumbled repeatedly, "Snakes. Snakes everywhere. So many snakes."

Eventually, he fell asleep.

~

Mindi and Jeff laughed so hard that they could barely catch their breath. Tears streamed down their faces, and they gasped, then laughed again until they had to hold their sides. When the laughter had finally run its course, they sat in their gray overstuffed chairs alternately looking at each other and then at the place where Alejandro had dissolved into glitter covered with their imagined snakes, which had also dispersed into a ground-fog of evaporating glitter.

"Brilliant," Jeff said. "You imitated Shirley's voice perfectly. Where did you learn Spanish?"

"That's pidgin Spanish. It was pretty bad, I'm sure. I had a little in high school, and you pick up bits living in LA. I've been studying a little lately."

"I wonder if he woke up sweating. Or maybe we made him wet the bed."

"Jeff, that's cruel."

"Well, yeah. But no worse than being complicit in selling stuff that will ruin people's lives. No worse than cheating on your wife. D'ya think?"

With a sigh, she said, "I guess. Do you think he'll come back?"

"I hope not. We're ready for him, though. Next time, we'll meet him with a million velociraptors. But . . ." Jeff thought for a moment. "But he's going to think about this because he knows it's a dream. Maybe he'll do some of the same research I did and realize he can fight back. So I'm not counting on anything. I'd like to try some more leaps into him and get into his head. Remind him of the dream while he's awake and reinforce the terror. What do you think?"

"I'm concerned that in the real world, he'll try to find out who I am. He might put two and two together and figure us out. This place is ours. I don't want to share."

Jeff nodded in agreement as he looked around.

"What's next?" Mindi asked.

"I don't know. I guess we just wait until our next leaps. See where they take us."

~

In early December in Jeff and Mindi's real-time, Jeff again found himself in a dream, looking through Alejandro's eyes, waiting in line for communion during a Christmas Mass in Latin. His wife and children were with him.

The target's right. It's before Christmas, but what's the date? Alejandro rubbed his forehead.

Jeff shut off his thoughts and formed a picture of what he wanted to find. He left the optic nerve and headed for the hippocampus, the brain's memory center, to cruise down the path into Alejandro's memories.

Jeff visualized a corridor for short-term memory and found himself transported into a space similar to that of Carlos's newspaper memory. He wandered around, touching on entryways and getting visions of Christmas shopping with his children, brushing his teeth, and reading the internet news on his laptop for *el 24 de diciembre*. He opened one passage and watched Alejandro's memory of him being intimate, hopefully with his wife. He quickly backed away, but not before he sensed that the reactivated memory had aroused real-time Alejandro. Jeff felt it briefly and thought, *Must have been good.*

The next passageway took him to the memory of Alejandro waking up from the bad dream tangled in blankets on the floor. His wife comforted him. Jeff saw the memory of the snakes, felt the man's panic. Jeff backed away with haste. He felt no regret. *It serves him right.*

The memories, although somewhat pertinent to the mission, weren't ones that would help him interfere with drug imports. He shut off his mind and meditated, looking for direction on where he should go and what he should look for. A whispered question came to him uninvited: *Where are his childhood memories?*

He wondered, *Why those?*

Suddenly, he found himself in a different part of the brain, inside another portal. He'd activated a vivid memory of the young Alejandro looking up at a man in a white suit and dark tie with skin as dark as Alejandro's. He was slapping the boy hard, back and forth, first with the back of his hand, and then with his hand open on the return swing. All the while he said, in Spanish, "I told you never to go into my office." Slap!

"I thought I made myself clear." Slap!

"You'll never do that again. Do you understand?" Slap!

Jeff understood the boy had broken a rule, and the man continued to slap him full force each time.

The boy cried out with each strike, and whimpered, "*¡Lo siento, papá! ¡Lo siento!*" I'm sorry, Papa. I'm sorry.

Jeff tried to back away from that memory but was frozen there. He felt the slaps himself and was stunned as the beating continued. He felt the boy's pain, sorrow, and shame. Jeff could finally leave, returning to see Mass through Alejandro's eyes. Tears streamed down the man's face from the memory Jeff had activated. He wiped the tears while he kneeled.

Alejandro felt his wife's hand on his arm as he wiped the tears from his hand onto his trouser leg. He looked over at her, saw compassion in her eyes, and turned away in shame. Jeff, too, felt the man's shame. Alejandro crossed himself as he sat back on the pew.

His son tapped his father's arm and stretched up to whisper, "Are you okay, Papa?"

Alejandro smiled at the boy. "*Sí, no hay problema.*" He looked back toward the front of the cathedral and crossed himself again, whispering, too low to be heard, "I *am* sorry, Papa!"

Jeff knew it was time for him to go, and mentally said, as quietly as he could, *Ciao.*

~

Mindi sat in one of their overstuffed chairs in the gray room, waiting for Jeff. He walked in with downcast eyes and a slumped posture.

"It's a little late," she said with a smile, "but Frisbee!"

He looked directly into Mindi's eyes.

She peered at his pained expression. "Jeff, what's wrong?"

"You were there, with Karina, during Mass?"

"Yes. And I saw him crying. The compassion, the love she felt toward him was immense. She really loves him, and he was going through something. She thought he was having some sort of spiritual experience. Then I felt her speculate he might be crying because he was remorseful because he had cheated, but she quickly dismissed that. And then her thoughts went back to when he'd awakened during a nightmare. She didn't know what was wrong, but she wanted to comfort him."

"Wow. Yeah, it was intense for me. I felt what he felt. We really have some power here. We've got to be careful." Jeff told her about Alejandro's memory of being beaten by his father—that he had complete recall, that Jeff had felt the punishment too, and how it'd left him exhausted.

Mindi continued to study Jeff's face and watched it soften, become less intense as he relaxed.

Jeff continued, "That's interesting what Karina was thinking, seeing him crying like that. And Alejandro's son, uh . . ." Jeff paused, trying to remember his name.

"Mateo," Mindi said.

"That's his boy's name?"

"Yes."

"Mateo saw his father crying and asked if he was okay. That beating was a profound event in Alejandro's life, and I made him relive it."

Mindi frowned. "It affected you deeply, didn't it?"

"Yes. I felt the pain and his shame. I felt it all while being slapped by his father. He knew he'd done wrong, but the boy felt betrayed at the harshness of the punishment."

"Did you feel punished?"

Jeff looked at his folded hands in his lap. "No. Well, yes, in a way. I felt the pain and his shame, something I've never felt before, and it makes me understand a little about how you must've felt when your father . . ." He stopped when he realized where he was taking the conversation. "Oh, Mindi, I didn't mean anything by that. I'm sorry."

"No, Jeff. That's okay. I'm glad you're sharing. I never want to feel that way again. I hope you never have to feel that way again."

Jeff shook his head. "It feels terrible. I don't understand why I was shown that. I think he'd buried that memory deep, and I uncovered it. I've got to be careful . . . No, *we've* got to be careful when, and if, we go crawling around in others' heads again. But if he sins now—and I don't mean that in a biblical or carnal way—but if he does wrong, he should pay. Is that what this mission is supposed to be about, punishing him?" He paused, then added, "I hope it's not. I just want to keep Charlene safe."

"I'm glad you said that. I feel the same way. If we ever find anything like that again, we've got to back away. And that goes for good memories too. While I was poking around in Karina's head, I found her memory where she and Alejandro were making love. I left right away."

"That's odd. I think I found the same memory."

Mindi and Jeff looked at each other with the same look of astonishment, trying to understand what that might mean to their abilities when visiting other's minds.

"That's got to be more than a coincidence," Jeff said. "Why?"

Mindi stood, urged Jeff to his feet, and gave him a long, comforting hug. He returned the hug and found solace in their closeness, as if it were their real bodies, rather than being out-of-body in their gray room. The border between these lucid dreams and their real world had faded a little more.

After they left the dream and returned to their own cities, Jeff wrote in his dream journal he felt sure all this was leading somewhere, maybe something huge. Bigger than what they'd done before.

~

Christmas had passed for the Saríses in Colombia. Alejandro sat at his desk in his office, typing into his laptop. The calendar on his desk reminded him it was the January 13, 2018. His children had returned to school, and the sound of Karina in the other room was comforting. Except for the return of the memory of his father beating him when he was ten, and the dinosaur and snake dreams in that huge, gray space, Alejandro's life, as he reflected on it, was perfect. He would be returning to the US to discuss the continued financial needs of the cosmetics company. Perhaps he might meet again with that lovely blond woman, Charlene.

He felt ultimately responsible to ensure the shipment in June would be successful. This would be the third shipment in a forty-foot container in the past year, and everything had gone very well before. His organization had a new truck and a trustworthy driver to move the container to a warehouse in the San Fernando Valley. The driver and the warehouse operator could be depended on implicitly. Locals in the US would, using their own networks, distribute over twenty-five thousand kilos of product throughout the West Coast. It would be a very good year.

Jeff landed in Alejandro's head just as he finished a carefully crafted, heavily encrypted email, just before it was sent to an unknown recipient. He could only discern the name of a ship—the *HMM Aisling*—and confirm the date of June 26 and the Port of Cartagena in the all-Spanish message. He wished he had Mindi's knowledge of the language and eidetic memory so he could understand more of what he'd seen.

Alejandro sat back, and Jeff felt the man's satisfaction. After a few moments, he sat forward again and typed "types of dreams" in English into a Google search. The result told him that there were normal dreams, daydreams, lucid dreams, false waking dreams, and nightmares.

He clicked a link that led to an article on lucid dreams,

and as he read the page, Karina set a steaming cup of black coffee on the desk. He looked up. She met his look, smiled, and then looked at the computer screen to see what had occupied her husband's interest.

She started speaking in Spanish, then, remembering his wishes, switched to English. "Are you still troubled by your dreams? You haven't had them again, have you? It's been some time, no?"

He nodded. "They were strange. So real. I had never had them before, and the last one was troubling." He reached around her and held her for a moment. "*Gracias, mi querida, por tu apoyo* . . . Forgive me, I forget to speak in English too. Thank you, my dear, for your support."

"You're welcome, my love," Karina said as she massaged his shoulders. "What have you learned there?"

"This says that when you know you are dreaming, it is called a *sueño lúcido*, a lucid dream. They are rare, but because one knows they are dreaming, they can be controlled. If it happens again, I wish to be in control so I will not be frightened."

"Maybe you will no longer be . . . *¿cómo se dice 'afectado'?*"

He looked up at her and smiled as he translated. "Affected. Affected by them? Thank you, I trust you are right."

She kissed the top of his head, then turned to leave.

"*Y gracias por el café*," he called after her, forgetting once again his own request to speak in English.

Witnessing Alejandro learning this about dreams made it obvious to Jeff that this man could be a worthy adversary. Alejandro had figured out the dreams, yet Jeff's knowing what the man now knew should help them in the future. Needing nothing more, Jeff left the man's mind.

CHAPTER 7

Jeff wanted to know what could be done to manipulate the future they'd seen, to change what they didn't wish to happen. What they'd been shown regarding the drug shipment and Alejandro and Charlene's upcoming relationship overwhelmed him. He felt better, however, when he remembered what Ingrid had said to Mindi: "We seem to never be given more than we can carry. However, the burden sometimes may feel unwieldy. But confidence in our own ability will help us carry the load."

Jeff closed his notebook and put the budding adventure aside. In real-time, he needed to get to work, though their dream-world activities were never far from his mind.

That night in the gray room with Mindi, he shared what he'd learned the previous night with Alejandro. "I've been thinking that with everything we're starting to control, maybe we could telepathically contact each other to let each of us know we're there."

"We've got the Frisbee thing we can do, right? But you want to 'mind text'?"

He laughed. "You're so good at getting what I mean and putting it into concise terms. I love that about you."

"I hope that's not all you love about me," she said with a smile in her voice, followed by a laugh.

He looked back at her with a what-do-you-think look on his face that made her laugh again.

"It's so good to laugh with you," she said. "I went so many years without feeling this kind of joy."

He nodded his acknowledgment and smiled. "Okay, back on topic; let's not get distracted. How much control do we have to work with?" He paused. "Let's see if we can leap into Alejandro and Karina when they're together and try to talk to each other telepathically while we're there. What do you think?"

"That sounds like a pretty tall order. Are we good enough to be that directed?"

"We'll see. I've been able to leap into Alejandro when I wanted to. I haven't been able to target a specific time, but each event seems to have given us what we need to know."

Mindi nodded. "Okay, what's next?"

"Let's ciao out of here. I'll see you in Bogotá."

"This could be fun. See you there. Ciao."

He watched her turn into glitter and then found himself awake in his own bed. His phone beeped, announcing a text from Mindi: *Going back to sleep now. Hope to see you soon.*

He texted back a thumbs-up emoji, put his head on the pillow, and thought of Alejandro as he fell back to sleep.

Suddenly he was back in the gray room, looking at Mindi, whose surprised look matched how he felt. Immediately, before they had time to more than have eye contact, he again fell and floated in his gray cocoon. When his view reopened, Jeff was on board, watching Alejandro shave. The shower behind Alejandro was running, with the sound of someone washing themselves. A check in Alejandro's mind confirmed it was Karina.

With that thought, he heard Mindi's voice in his mind say quietly, *Jeff?*

Alejandro looked over his shoulder. "Karina, what did you say?"

From the shower, she replied in Spanish, "Nothing. Why?"

Alejandro turned back toward the mirror as the shower stopped. The curtain drew back and Alejandro and Jeff watched Karina reflected in the mirror as she reached for her bath towel.

Unprepared for the view of the man's naked wife, Jeff thought loudly, *Mindi, oh my!* Then slapped a virtual hand over his mouth.

Alejandro turned around at the voice, razor still to his face, nicking himself as he looked at Karina. He said, "What? Ow!" He dropped the razor into the sink and put his hand to the cut on his face.

Mindi thought, *Jeff, you okay?*

Karina, who'd just finished wrapping the towel around her, put her hands to her temples. "What? What's happening?"

Jeff and Mindi simultaneously mentally shouted *Ciao!* and found themselves back in the gray room with a look of wonder on their faces.

"That was . . . uh, interesting," Mindi said, because she could see that Jeff was thinking of the attractive image of naked Karina.

"It sure was," answered Jeff.

Mindi snorted. "I can see what you are thinking right now. Should I be jealous?" Then she laughed, breaking the spell of wonder and surprise they'd both felt.

"I'm so sorry. It wasn't my fault." Jeff said, stepping forward to embrace Mindi and hold her close. "But hey, can't you control when you are reading my mind?"

"I guess not. It just happens sometimes. But as far as she is concerned, Jeff, it's okay. I got a pretty good view of Alejandro. He was naked too, or did you not know?"

"Oh?" Jeff said. "Really?"

"Yeah. We've got to learn how to control this stuff, otherwise we'll end up in more risqué situations than we want." Mindi stood up on her toes and gave Jeff a quick kiss.

"Yeah, I guess so. How do we do that?"

Mindi shook her head. "I don't know, but we've got to be careful. I, well, *we* messed up and used our names. I'm sure they heard us. That's something we can do something about. Do you think they'll remember? I was so disoriented, I didn't remember to say 'Frisbee.'"

"Me neither. And the escape word thing . . . Alejandro's a sharp guy. He's already starting to put some of this together with the internet search on dreams, and if it comes together completely, he'll be *really* dangerous, instead of just dangerous. How about we try to visualize leaving without saying ciao? What do you think?"

"We can try."

They stepped back and looked at each other. Mindi folded her arms together at shoulder height, lifted her chin, dropped it in a determined move, and dissolved into glitter. He'd seen this on TV. Barbara Eden as her character Jeannie did it in *I Dream of Jeannie* when she wanted to go back into her bottle.

Jeff repeated Mindi's move and woke up in bed. His phone rang. The caller ID announced Mindi.

"Hi," he said. "That was cute. How did you think of that?"

"I don't know. From watching reruns, I guess. Did I bring

you back when I phoned?"

"No. I did it too, and it worked."

"I love you," Mindi said.

"I love you too. Talk with you tomorrow."

"That *was* fun. Good night."

~

Alejandro looked in the mirror as he put a piece of tissue on the cut to stop the bleeding. His mind raced. *Voices in my head. I've heard them before. Their names. Jeff? Mindi?*

He caught sight of Karina behind him. She looked shaken and confused.

"Are the children safe?" he asked as he turned around.

Her eyes widened. "I'll go see." She left to check.

~

When researching the paranormal—witches, séances, mediums, tarot cards, and the like—Jeff came across an article about Sarah Winchester's Mystery House in San Jose, California.

Oliver Finch Winchester had been the owner of the successful Winchester Repeating Arms Company, in Connecticut, until he died in 1880. The country continued to expand after the Civil War, and the Winchester rifle became known as "the gun that won the west." When Oliver died, his son, William Wirt Winchester, inherited the company, but soon after taking control of the company, died of tuberculosis, which left his wife, Sarah Winchester, with ownership of fifty percent of the company. William and Sarah's only child, Annie, an infant daughter, died at six weeks of age, also of tuberculosis. After suffering that string of bad luck, Sarah, now a fabulously wealthy, childless widow, moved west to San Jose in 1888 to grieve. She purchased an eight-room farmhouse west of downtown and began to expand it by turning it into a fabulous Gothic Victorian mansion, albeit labyrinthine in design.

Legend had it that a psychic medium named Adam Coons told Sarah that her family, of which she was now the only survivor, had been cursed and haunted by the ghosts of the men killed by the firearms manufactured by her company. Her father-in-law, husband, and daughter, the medium was reported to have told her, were victims of vengeful spirits. The psychic advised her that the only way she could protect herself was to keep building onto her home, making rooms, it was not clear, either for the spirits to "live" in, or to confuse them. After thirty-eight years of continuous construction, the building had expanded to 160 rooms and covered twenty-four thousand square feet. Sarah died in 1922, at the age of eighty-two.

Jeff considered the role of the medium in Sarah's life and wondered if he could manipulate Alejandro's vulnerabilities in a similar way. He'd already primed Alejandro's mind with nightmares, the resurrected memory of his abusive father, and voices in his head. Perhaps they might be able to cultivate superstition to create guilt, remorse, and fear that would change his behavior enough to protect Charlene and stop his role in the manufacture and shipment of drugs.

~

After doing his homework to prepare for making a pitch to Mindi about "haunting" Alejandro, Jeff closed the notebook, went to bed, and began to dream. The doorway opened into the gray room to reveal Karina and Mindi sitting in the chairs, in conversation.

Jeff surveyed the scene. As he approached, Mindi smiled and, taking charge, motioned to a space beside her chair. Another chair appeared.

Jeff nodded at Mindi, then looked at Alejandro's wife and sat in his chair. "Hello, Karina."

Karina gave a tentative smile, and with a heavy accent said, "*Buenas noches.* How do you know my name?"

Jeff looked at Mindi.

Mindi gave Jeff a reassuring look. "Karina and I've just begun our conversation. When I arrived, she was walking around looking confused, and I told her"—Mindi glanced at Karina, then looked back at Jeff—"that this was a private space, but she was welcome here tonight. I asked her what she was doing here, how she'd found her way here, and she said she didn't know. The last thing she remembered before arriving here was that she'd turned off the bedside lamp and laid her head on her pillow."

Jeff nodded at Mindi in acknowledgment, then turned to Karina. "Karina, what do you think this space is?"

She looked around and, after a moment's hesitation, said, "I do not know."

"I'll tell you. This is a dream. Do you dream often?" Jeff waited for Karina's answer.

"Not usually, not I. *Mi esposo* recently had nightmares, though."

"Why do you mention your husband's dreams?"

"I am worried about him. He has not been acting normally. I do not know what to do."

"Have you ever had nightmares? Ever been afraid in

a dream?"

"No." She looked at her hands in her lap.

"Are you afraid now?"

"No." Voice timid, head still lowered, she added, "Well, maybe. Yes."

"Okay." Jeff paused, then said, "Karina"—he waited until she raised her head, and her eyes met his—"you don't need to be afraid now. I'll explain. This is only a dream. We are here because your mind has created us to help you cope with whatever problems your husband may be dealing with. The nightmares he had, his tears after communion, are of great concern to you . . ."

Karina interrupted. "How do you know about those things?"

Keeping his tone patient, Jeff replied, "Because we're part of your mind. We know because you know. We also know you are concerned when Alejo goes out of town, and you wonder what he does. He doesn't call you every day like you would like. You know your husband is a handsome man, and you worry that other women may show an interest in him, and that's not to your liking. Is that true?"

She nodded assent slowly, looking from Jeff to Mindi.

Mindi gave a friendly smile and nodded. Karina looked back at Jeff.

"All we can tell you is what you already believe and feel. We're not magic; we don't know the future as you don't know the future. You must rely on yourself for Mateo and Maria's sake. You are responsible for keeping them safe and secure— and well provided for. Look after yourself, because the future is uncertain. Do you understand?"

Karina nodded, and again glanced from Jeff to Mindi and back again.

Maintaining eye contact, Jeff said gently, "It's normal for you to feel concern for those you love. You have come here so that you can be assured that if you remain vigilant—"

"What is 'vigilant'? My English is . . ."

Jeff smiled. "You do know, because my words come from your mind. Vigilant means being aware, observant, on guard." He waited for a moment, then continued, "If you remain vigilant, you and your children will remain safe and cared for."

She nodded she understood.

"Karina, our time together is over," Jeff continued. "It's time for you to awaken. If you find yourself here again, it's because you're looking for answers. The answers, however, are not here, but in your own heart. Now say a Hail Mary. It's time for you to go. After you cross yourself, you will be awake in your bed, fully refreshed and ready for the day. Do you understand?"

Karina looked at Mindi, who smiled and nodded again. The woman whispered the prayer, made the sign of the cross. Her image sparkled away.

Mindi touched Jeff's arm and gave him a warm smile. "That was brilliant, and kind. How did you think of that? I was planning on stalling her. Maybe talk about her children, hoping you would join us and figure out what to do. You did, thank goodness. I didn't want to scare her with a disembodied voice, or a dinosaur, and you handled it perfectly. That was great."

Jeff smiled. "Well, we'll see. I came here prepared to talk with you about doing something subtle to frighten Alejandro—to play on his fears and build on the classic guilt that my Catholic friends have talked about that comes with their faith. Maybe get him to believe that God, or the Devil, will punish him if he keeps doing what he's doing. You did well in setting the stage for me—we make a good improv team. I was a surprised to find her here. How have they both keyed on landing here in your mind? Why are you the focus?"

Mindi shrugged. "Yeah, I don't know. It's a little scary."

"I hope she obeys me and never shows up again and, particularly, doesn't share this dream with her husband," Jeff continued. "Karina knows she's responsible for herself and her kids. I didn't have to tell her that. With her being suspicious of his activities, I don't think this will get back to him. I don't want to break them up, but I think if we play to that, she may put pressure on him to straighten up. What do you think?"

Mindi tilted her head thoughtfully. "What did you have in mind tonight that you wanted to share?"

Jeff told her the story of the Winchester Mystery House and Mrs. Winchester's superstitious beliefs. "We might be able to rely on superstition to scare them. We may have to improvise again."

"You're not *just* thinking of interrupting the cocaine business, are you?"

Jeff looked deep into Mindi's eyes and gave a little shake of his head. "No. No, I'm not. Our first concern is to protect Charlene. I think she's in danger, and that's why this, uh, mission is revealing itself—just like I was supposed to help you when the whole leap thing started, and put us together. I hope you agree that you and I both owe her, and maybe this is how we can repay the debt. I know Charlene. She's not the type to be involved with a married man. Of that, I'm sure. And especially after what she learned about her father. And I really don't think she'd knowingly be involved with a drug dealer; one with such a vast influence like Alejandro seems to have. I don't care how handsome or rich he is."

Mindi shook her head and added with a smile, "And one that's such a lousy kisser."

Jeff laughed and leaned over and gave her a kiss. "Not like this?" He kissed her again.

"No. And that's not enough." Mindi laughed, pulled him closer, and they kissed with so much passion, they tumbled to the floor with a laugh. She wrapped her arms around him and the light dimmed, but it brightened when she said, "This floor isn't cold, but it's sure not comfortable. We've got to do something about that."

~

The next morning, as Jeff and Mindi talked on the phone, Jeff said, "We got a little distracted last night. I'd like to talk more about our mission."

Jeff listed the dateline of their leaps and visits and the rationale behind his calculations. He pointed out that when Alejandro visited Charlene in Seattle, he'd probably set up a residence for access to her and to have an address to register the Audi.

"And here's the problem if we try to interfere: With us having been with them in the airplane flying back from Friday Harbor, I'm sure it made that path certain. If we try to intervene and keep him from going to Seattle in the first place, we'll likely fail, just like I failed to keep Rick from shredding the letter admitting he had an affair—it had already been found in his future. These two getting together in Seattle is immutable."

"Okay, I get that," Mindi said. "So what can we do, and how do we do it?"

"Good question. I don't know, but remember my dad

said that the answers will come if we ask the right questions. Those are the first questions."

"Sure. Next question: Do you think we can interfere with the shipment?"

"Good question. The date, June 26, is important, and so is Cartagena. But we don't know if the twenty-sixth is the day the HMM Aisling sails, the day a container gets delivered, or something else. I'll see if I can find a website with the sailing schedule."

Mindi chuckled. "Well, Sherlock, you found me, so you'll find the answers."

"Wise guy. You could grab a giant detective's magnifying glass and help me with that."

"Well, how about this? Karina's mind is easy to get into, so why don't I see if I can get her to snoop in Alejandro's desk while he's gone. Maybe he left a clue there. With seeds of suspicion we've planted, maybe I can find evidence of infidelity, find shipping information and who knows what else?"

"Sounds like a plan."

~

Mindi, operating on her and Jeff's recent conversation, went to sleep thinking about Karina's family's well-being. But Karina wasn't at home when Mindi arrived in Karina's mind. Alejandro's wife stood alone, studying the directory at the Centro Mayor Mall in Bogotá.

As Mindi rode along in Karina's mind, she noticed the lack of Christmas decorations. Although it was still before Christmas in Mindi's real-time, she was sure she'd traveled to a time after the holidays in Bogotá.

Karina tried on shoes, felt the softness of the fabrics in the nearby dress shop, and held dresses up in front of a mirror, with Mindi enjoying every moment.

Karina exited the store and glanced across the mall to a large advertising display in the department-store window. A large, floor-to-ceiling ad showed the head and shoulders of a model that both women recognized. Seeing her own face in the ad there for LaDormeur Cosmetics startled Mindi, and Karina's feet froze in place while she stared at the image of the woman from her dream.

Mindi's fear of exposure transferred to Karina, but Mindi regained her composure and sent her host a message of comfort, which tempered the rush of adrenaline. Karina walked slowly toward the window, nearly colliding with a couple. After apologizing profusely, she stood in front of the huge portrait and tried to process what she was seeing.

Mindi wanted to escape away from Karina, but her intuition told her to wait, observe, and intervene if necessary. She plugged into Karina's thoughts and, although in Spanish, she understood enough: *Very pretty, so friendly. She was in my dream.*

Mindi was relieved that Karina felt at peace with her discovery, but she dropped her guard when she thought, *Wait until I tell Jeff about this.*

Karina looked around and said under her breath, "Who said that?"

Mindi immediately, and silently, did her "Jeannie thing" and her mind was transported back to Gardena. A glance at the clock showed it was too early to call Jeff, so she wrote in her journal and went back to sleep.

~

Jeff had fallen asleep with thoughts of Mindi trying to visit Karina, and he connected to Mindi for just enough time to recognize the gigantic picture of Mindi's face in the store window in Bogotá. He had no time to say anything to Mindi and immediately bounced to a view of a newsstand, the sports magazine section. His host—Jeff suspected Alejandro—focused on one magazine, *Fútbol*. Jeff watched as he picked it up and began to thumb through it, then walked on, his gaze scanning the other magazines. Suddenly, he stopped and focused on an issue of *Vogue Mexico*. What drew his attention was Mindi's photo and the words *Miranda Madisen, modelo sensacional de LaDormeur* splashed across the cover.

Jeff heard Alejandro's thoughts. *La mujer que soñé. Vi su foto en la agencia de publicidad.* The dream woman. I saw her photo at the advertising agency.

Notwithstanding Jeff's lack of Spanish vocabulary, he understood the phrase "*agencia de publicidad.*" Forgetting to control his thoughts, he mentally exclaimed, *He saw her picture at Charlene's agency!*

Alejandro's head snapped around.

Shit, Jeff thought. *Alejandro must've heard me say her name.* Jeff tried to duplicate the *I Dream of Jeannie* exit move in his mind but failed. He was still there. *Shit!* What he should do? *Ciao!* And he was back in his bedroom, staring up at the shadows on the ceiling formed by the passing car headlights below.

⁓

Alejandro, who'd heard every word, muttered, "Charlene? Shit? Ciao?" Perplexed, he looked around the shop, shook his head, then made his purchase.

CHAPTER 8

The next evening, after their respective shopping visits to Bogotá, Jeff and Mindi arrived in the gray room at the same time.

"Your text said we needed to meet," Mindi said. "Do you want to start?"

"You first, love. Please. You look like you're bursting with information. I hope yours is good."

"Well . . ." She drew out the word.

"What? Tell me."

"It's not really that good. I leaped into Karina while she was at the mall, and she saw my advertising poster for LaDormeur." Mindi paused as the expression on Jeff's face telegraphed something to her. "What?" she said.

"I saw the poster. It was in a window, right?"

"Yes. Why didn't you say something then?"

"I couldn't. It was only for a second, then I shot right into Alejandro's head. He was buying a magazine at a newsstand. My guess, he was in Bogotá too."

"And . . . ?"

"He saw a *Vogue Mexico* with you on the cover. The tagline under your face said 'LaDormeur's Fabulous Model,' or something like that, in Spanish."

"Did you get anything of what he was thinking?"

"Oh, yeah. He recognized you from the dream, and that he remembered having seen your picture at Charlene's agency."

"Shit."

"Yeah, that's exactly what I said. And he may have heard me say that."

Mindi frowned. "That would have been late this next January or February because I'll be on the cover of the February edition. The next month's issues always come out the end of the month before."

Jeff smiled. "I'm impressed that you made the cover of *Vogue*. You knew about it? Will there be an article about you?"

"I never gave them an interview. I think the article is about LaDormeur hitting the markets. We were told, if journalists approached us, to refer them to corporate PR. Nobody contacted me, so it all came from headquarters, but yes, I did know I'd be on the cover. It's great for my career. I'm the face of LaDormeur, at least for now."

"I still think it's great. We've leaped into their future, so we have some time to do something before they know where they've seen us. We can't change that they recognized you, but it's not in our real-time. There's no way to be sure, but I don't think we've real-timed with them yet."

"Why do you say that?"

"Until you and I got together in real-time on Halloween, every time I saw you, it was always in the past. Now, when we leap, it's been into our future, *and* their future. But . . ."

"What, Jeff? What are you thinking?"

"Just a minute," he said as he thought something through

and stared off into the gray distance. "Were they in the gray room in their real-time, or were their lucid dreams putting them into their past? But when we leap into them, we are going into our future. Let's see. Does it really matter? There's really no way to tell unless we can date-stamp our leaps, but we can't date their visits." He looked at Mindi and asked, "Did you get anything from Karina that she'd seen you before?"

"Yes. When she saw the ad, she recognized me from her dream with us—which was before our visit to the mall. So she visited us in our real-time here but had traveled backward. Right? Wow. This is confusing."

Jeff said, "Okay. Now I wonder if our leap into their bathroom was into our future, or did that happen in our combined real-times?" He thought for a moment. "If things hold true, it must have been their future. So we've been with them between December this year and April of next. I wonder . . ." He got lost in thought again. "But I don't think we are leaping forward into them in any chronological order; we seem to be jumping around."

"What do you mean? Mindi asked.

"We visited them in April for dinner at Friday Harbor, then back in their time at Christmas Mass, then forward again to late January, early February, for their shopping trips to the mall and his magazines. Every time I visited with you, it was sequential, moving forward, toward my real-time into your future. Now, with us going forward in time, there are different choices to be made at each crossroad that haven't yet been anchored with the experiences, like our two leaps into their airplane trip to Friday Harbor. So let's keep documenting our time-stamped leaps and visits, to maybe see a pattern. But for now . . ." He trailed off, lost in thought, then said, "Regardless, us knowing the precise sequence is not important to keeping Charlene safe, but I would like to know for science's sake. Okay, back to business. We still need to get more info on the drug shipment. Can you give it another try?"

Mindi nodded. "Sure, no problem. I'll try to get Karina to snoop. But why can't you just leap into Alejandro and find it? Just don't trigger any more bad memories. Do you think he's tied our voices in his head to our faces?"

Jeff considered for a moment. "He's had plenty of chances to make the connection. One other thing—would he know 'Mindi' is a nickname for Miranda?"

Mindi shrugged. "Yeah, he knows Roberto's wife, Miranda, so he has to know the nickname. He'll definitely recognize us when he sees billboard and magazine ads with us as a couple, right?"

"Yep, that's stuff we can't control."

"Speaking of the ads, when did you last talk with Charlene about your contract?"

"I need to give my agent a call. I know they want to get things moving. Thanks for the nudge."

"Sure thing. We're a team."

"That we are. Next, I'd still like to get info on who provides Alejandro's crypto program. But let's call it a night."

Mindi nodded, then smiled and said, "Ciao."

"Ciao."

Glitter.

~

Charlene met Jeff's call with professional enthusiasm. "I'm glad you called," she said. "Have you signed your contract yet?"

"Not yet. I've a couple of questions for you before I get it back to my agent."

"Good," Charlene replied. "I've got some things I'd like to cover before you sign too. First, before we go any further, it's important to me, professionally, that nothing spoils our relationship with Mindi. She's a rising star, and we don't want anything to come between our client and her. So how are things between you and Mindi?"

Jeff hadn't expected this to ever come up, but because Charlene had couched the question based on their professional relationship, he felt she had a good reason to ask.

"I see what you mean, Charlie." But he also knew, because of his and Charlene's backstory, that she'd also like to know the answer from a personal point of view, to validate her decision to end their relationship. "We're doing well and looking forward to working together."

"Good, thank you for sharing. It's important to the agency, and, well . . ." The way she left the rest of the sentence unsaid confirmed Jeff's assumption about her personal interest.

"I understand," he said with a note of compassion. "It's all good; thank you for asking. What's next?"

"Before we get to your questions, let me say that normally I'd be out of the loop at this point. But because we're friends, and you're so new to the business, I'd like to point out some of the finer points of the contract. I don't want you to have any surprises later. It's easier in person, though. When could we have lunch?"

"My calendar's open today. Would that work for you?"

"Yes, how about the sub shop, eleven-thirty or twelve?

"Let's do eleven-thirty."

"Okay. See you then. Bye."

Jeff arrived early, claimed a booth, and ordered what he knew she would like. He hadn't seen her since November, and when she entered, they exchanged a Hollywood double-cheek air kiss.

"Thanks for ordering. Did you get . . . ?"

Jeff smiled as he slid her half-sub sandwich over to her.

"You haven't forgotten." She returned the smile and said, "Let's eat and small-talk, then when we're done . . ." She patted her briefcase and put her cell phone on the table.

Jeff nodded and began to eat.

Her phone signaled an incoming call. They both looked down at it, and before she picked it up, Jeff saw the caller ID—Bogotá, Colombia—along with a long telephone number starting with +57, Colombia's country code.

She hesitated, looked at Jeff, then after the second ring, said, "I should take this," but she didn't leave the table. "Hello, this is Charlene."

She listened for a moment.

Jeff watched her face and saw a slight smile cross her lips and register in her eyes.

Quietly, she said, "Alejo, I'm in a meeting right now. When's a good time for me to call you back?" She listened again for the reply, then said, "I'm glad you called. Until later."

Jeff realized that this meeting would be a double success. First, he'd got information he couldn't have gotten any other way, and second, he would lock in a great moonlighting job so he could work with Mindi. What could be better?

Charlene turned the ringer off, they finished their sandwiches, and then talked business. "This isn't a standard contract; it's more of a short-term employment agreement."

He gave her a puzzled look.

"Look at this paragraph." She rested her index finger on the relevant section and slid the paper over for him to read. "It's a six-month contract with an option for another six."

Jeff read it over twice and looked up at Charlene, a question in his eyes.

"You missed it before, didn't you? Yes, Jeff, you read it right. To put it bluntly, they, well, we *really* want you. This is one of the best contracts for a model we've ever put together."

Jeff read it over again. "Okay . . . So . . . ?" He looked up at her with wide eyes.

"So . . . can you get a leave of absence from work for six months? After that, there's a non-binding option for another six."

Jeff looked at her, then back at the contract. He'd thought it would be a part-time gig, but the contract was for a full-time job for half, maybe a whole year.

"Mindi hasn't talked about this. Does she even know about this sort of thing?"

Charlene shook her head. "It's new, but now standard for most of LaDormeur's top models. We need you to be available when we want, and we want you exclusively, but it's for a finite period, not forever. We've talked to Mindi's agent. Her contract is coming up for review and . . . Well, I'm not supposed to talk about other's contracts, but you, well, you understand." She nodded. The implication was that Mindi's contract would match his.

"I've shown your photo around, and the consensus is that you're perfect for this, and with the chemistry between you and Mindi, everyone thinks it'll be perfect. The photographers we have are great at capturing that. You've seen the layout in *Vogue*, haven't you?"

"Yes. But I'm prejudiced."

"I'd expect so. So are we. Here's the guilt trip. I've talked you up, a lot. Everyone agrees, and I'd hate to be let down. Will you talk to your boss?" That was the sale-close question.

Charlene had worn down what little sales resistance Jeff may have had. Not by guilt, but by his faith in Charlene doing her job—and especially the chance to work with Mindi for at least six months. She knew not to say anything after the question was asked, but she tipped her head sideways, indicating an answer was in order.

"Okay. You sold me. Yes, I'll talk to them."

~

When Jeff got back to the office, he checked out the company procedure for leaves of absence and found it straightforward. After he'd completed the intranet-based form, he printed out a copy, called his supervisor and human resources and asked if they had time that afternoon for a meeting.

After the meeting, Jeff called his team to the conference room, and by the end of two hours, he and his team had all the projects laid out, and the plan for handing off his accounts to others submitted to his boss for approval. And it would be approved. He and Mindi would walk on tropical beaches during a full moon *and* get paid for it.

He texted Mindi that he had great news and could they talk?

She called back immediately. "I've got a few minutes. What's your great news?"

"Two things." He told her about the call from Alejandro in Bogotá.

"Okay, that's good, but what did you talk about, about being a model?" She was eager for more good news.

Jeff told her about the terms of his contract, and the need for a leave of absence because of the way the contract was written.

"Yeah, my agent called me about mine. It sounds like they really want you, and it sounds like our contracts are similar for six months and then an option for another six. When will the contract start?"

He told her, and they agreed to meet in the gray room that night.

~

In the gray room, they discussed Christmas and planned for Jeff to be a "snowbird" and head to California for the holiday. After that decision, talk proceeded to the Alejandro/Karina situation and what they should do next. They agreed there wasn't much they could do until they got another clue to follow. June 26 was still six months away; a lot could happen in that time.

~

A new development came in their dreaming skills when, without planning to, Jeff and Mindi were falling in the gray cloud together. They later called it their "tandem leap." They could see each other at arm's length in the grayness.

"Hey!" Jeff shouted. Mindi answered back, proving they could hear each other too. They reached out and clasped hands and moved into a mock skydiving pose, pretending a wind of descent was pulling their feet and arms upward, but there was no rush of air.

After a few moments, Jeff said, "Relax."

They hung in the air, then, without warning, they were each alone in the gray. An instant later, like a switch had been turned on, Jeff was watching through Alejandro's eyes as he kicked a soccer ball to his son on the expanse of lawn at a park. Trees ringed the field and Jeff could see cars on a road beyond a tall wrought-iron fence. A few other families played in the park. Mateo deftly stopped the ball with his foot, dribbled it forward, then feinted toward his dad but sent it toward his sister, who missed it, turned, and ran after it.

Alejandro walked over to his boy, tousled his hair, and said in English, "Good move. You fooled me."

"Gracias, Papá. Tú me enseñaste."

"Okay. *Sí.* Now, in *inglés.*"

"Oh. Thank you, Papa. You taught me."

"Good, Mateo. Very good."

Again the boy said, "Thank you, Papa."

Jeff appreciated the tenderness and patience with which Alejandro treated the boy. Jeff mentally turned and started to wander in the man's mind, looking for information while being careful not to trigger any bad memories—if it could be avoided. *I want information on the shipment*, Jeff thought inwardly. Jeff felt Alejandro rub his temples, then he returned to soccer with his kids.

Good. He'll be distracted while I look around.

Jeff floated into the first passageway that appeared and focused on what might be guiding his destination. *Meditate. Watch the water flow by. Be without intent.*

A portal appeared, and Jeff reached out and touched it. Immediately, the subdued lighting in his host's office appeared, and Jeff watched a memory of Alejandro typing on his laptop. It was in Spanish, and Jeff could only make out a few words from the document. Alejandro saved his work, exited the program, opened a Google search window and after typing into the search window, pressed *Return*, and a web page for the Port of Cartagena appeared. After a few more keystrokes, he came to a table of information, then scrolled down to the *HMM Aisling*. Alejandro read it would depart June 11, and was scheduled to arrive at Long Beach on June 26.

Excitement rushed through Jeff at the discovery.

Alejandro clicked on a drop-down menu and a map of the ship's proposed route, including the Panama Canal. Another window opened showing another series of columns. The cursor moved down the column marked "Clients" and stopped on *AR&C*. His eyes moved right to the column labeled "*Cont.#*". Alejandro read the alphanumeric entry, *LADO900192*. Jeff memorized the container's number, and Alejandro, too, noted it in a small notebook. The memory ended.

Jeff wondered about the significance of the company name. AR&C? It took a moment—Alejandro, Roberto, and Carlos. Incriminating evidence—right there on the internet.

Jeff backed out of that portal and heard the children shouting, and his view returned to Alejandro's eyes. Karina was walking from the parking lot with a large wicker picnic basket. Alejandro jogged toward her, and when he reached her, relieved her of her burden, gave her a kiss, and walked with her as the children joined them at a picnic table.

In English, Karina said, "Have you had fun playing Frisbee . . ." She stopped short and looked directly at Alejandro, a confused look on her face.

His head turned toward her. "What did you say? No, we were playing . . ."

Jeff commanded Alejandro's mind for just a moment.

"Frisbee. No, uh, ha-ha, I-I mean *fútbol*."

Karina laughed. "I'm sorry, I confused you. *Sí, fútbol*."

Jeff smiled to himself, guessing that Alejo hadn't yet heard it said in the airplane over Puget Sound with Charlene. This gave him an approximate time stamp.

Alejandro passed sodas to each of the children while Karina set out paper plates. Jeff watched the bucolic scene unfold as they enjoyed their lunch on a carefree, lazy day at the park.

Alejandro drank an iced bottle of Costeña beer. Both men were feeling relaxed.

Jeff wanted to find out if he and Mindi could telepathically communicate without their hosts consciously hearing them. He quietly whispered in his mind, *Miss Model Traveler?*

She whispered back. *Yes, Mister Programmer?*

He paused. Did Alejandro or Karina hear them? Neither reacted.

I love you, Jeff thought.

I love you too, Mindi replied.

Karina looked over to Alejandro, who met her eye and smiled. Karina returned his smile, then returned to reading her magazine.

Mindi thought softly, *What's next?*

"What did you say, Karina?" Alejandro said.

He'd heard something that time.

Karina looked up at him and shook her head. "I said nothing."

It's time to go, Jeff whispered to Mindi. *I got what I needed.*

⁓

When Jeff awoke, his intuition told him his phone would ring.

But he received a text instead: *Picnic was fun. U learn anything? I got nothing.*

Jeff called Mindi back and gave her the information he'd found on the ship's movements and container number.

"You didn't find that before. How did you get it this time?" she asked.

"This time, I just relaxed, and the first door I opened had what we needed. There are literally millions of neurons in the brain, so how did I find just the one we needed this time but not before? If we're not getting help from somewhere, then we're just lucky. And if so, I should look for a winning lotto number, buy us an island and have someone bring us margaritas."

Mindi laughed. "I already won the lottery when I met you; I need nothing more."

"That's sweet. Yeah, me too. Speaking of that, when I told you I love you at the picnic, did she think it was from him? That's another clue on the kind of manipulation we might be able to do. We can do it with love, and you've done it with suspicion, a lack of trust and confidence. So how about fear, anger, joy? What do you think?"

"I liked the way it felt being with her when she felt that the sentiment came from him."

"I think he does love her, but not enough to stay faithful. I just hope she doesn't get hurt later."

"Well," Mindi said, "I won't be the one that gives her the bad news. She can find that out by herself. I don't want to hurt anyone. Look at what it did to Charlene's mother, even though you tried to stop it."

"Today was peaceful. I hope that gave her a reason not to tell that bastard about her dream with us."

"Oh, Jeff. Is that necessary? To call him names?"

"No, I guess not. But I can't like the guy because of what he does with drugs and might do to our friend, no matter how much he cares for his family."

"I understand how you feel. I don't like him either. But

I love you."

"I love you too." He paused. "Lights out? Ciao."

"Ciao."

He missed Mindi already, even though they'd just had their adventure and a phone call.

~

After their conversation, Mindi turned out the light. She pulled the covers over herself and felt a familiar movement in her mind.

Jeff? Is that you? Are you here?

Warmth enveloped her, and Jeff replied in her mind, *Yes. I know I said before I wouldn't be here without telling you first, but after I hung up, I was lying there wanting to hold you so much, and I thought of calling you to the gray room, but I ended up here instead. I'll leave if you want me to.*

No. Stay, please. It's not the same as you really being here. But it's good.

She felt his smile.

I'll stay until you want me to leave. I just wanted to hold you. Oh, Jeff. Mmmm.

~

When Mindi awoke the next morning, Jeff was no longer in her mind. She checked her phone—no text or email. While she drank her tea, she added another short paragraph to her dream journal about Jeff's visit.

She checked the time, thinking she might send him a text. The caller ID flashed and the phone rang.

She hit *Accept* with joy. "Good morning! That was nice

last night. I just wrote about it in my journal."

"Good morning." Jeff said. "Thank you for not throwing me out. I was, uh, well, feeling kind of vulnerable after our talk, and I wanted to be close."

"You're fine, love. It was just fine. We have another tool in our toolkit to make up for the distance. Besides, you'll be back down here in a couple of weeks. You were already asleep in real-time when you showed up—when did you leave?"

"I don't know—I woke up here thinking of you. So what are you doing today?"

"Another session. They want all six of us, again, in groups and individuals. There'll be some product placement with the new SPF line. They've got some cosmetics that are SPF 50 too."

"Sunblock meets the world of beauty, huh?"

"Yeah."

"Hey, I'm getting a call from Frank on my team. I think they're a little freaked out that I'll be gone for a while, so they want to make the most of me while I'm still here. Love you, talk soon. Ciao."

"Ciao."

CHAPTER 9

Jeff and Mindi spent the Christmas and New Year's holidays together in California with Jeff being the tourist, visiting the local who wanted to show him the special places that only the locals know. The couple discussed their plans for their immediate, real-world future.

They'd only visited with Alejandro and Karina through leaps a few times, and learned nothing new. Jeff had tried repeatedly but failed to find out where the encryption codes were in Alejandro's mind, or who the tech person was that either sold it to him or set it up. When Mindi leaped into Karina, she found nothing about the shipment, or Alejandro's predilection for other women. She left that subject alone.

Except for a couple of casual visits with the smuggling team in Colombia to see if there was anything new, their "hobby" took a back seat to being a normal couple enjoying each other's company in real-time—just like the billions of others in the world who stayed in the present, 24/7.

After New Year's Day, Jeff returned to Seattle to complete the transfer of his responsibilities to his team at SiLD2, his employer. He needed to contact his clients to prepare for his leave of absence, which would begin in a little over a month.

He'd been working out faithfully seven days a week, making sure that his physique was top-notch for the photographers. The last time they'd been together in the gray room, Mindi had told him, "You looked good before, but now"—she'd playfully taken the form of Tony the Tiger—"you look gr-r-reat."

When she regained her human form, Jeff said, "I'm impressed how quickly you could do that. That might come in handy."

To which she replied, "I had a good teacher," and snuggled up to him.

~

When the time came for him to go to California to begin his new career, Jeff contacted Charlene. She referred him to the team that coordinated the scheduling and logistics and in two days, Jeff was on an airplane to LAX with a driver to pick him up when he landed.

Once off the plane, Jeff waited at the curb outside arrivals, scanning traffic for a company car. He was enjoying the slightly cooler day than he'd had while visiting at Christmas, when a familiar voice with a professional air said, "Mr. Jeffrey Marlen? Your car is here."

His head snapped around in disbelief. Mindi stood there, wearing a too-large chauffeur's cap tilted jauntily to the side. She took off the hat and from a full two steps away seemed to jump into his arms. It took his breath away.

"Wow. This is some kind of service that the company provides," he said with a smile when they finally came up for air. "You didn't tell me you'd be here."

"At your service, sir!" She smiled. "I wanted to surprise you. Looks like I did."

"Well, I hope this isn't the kind of service you provide for all arriving models."

"That is true, it is *not* the kind of service I provide, but just wait until later to see the kind of service I do provide for"—she punched a forefinger into his chest—"this model." She gave a wide grin, and her perfect teeth seemed to shine with a sunburst, like in the cartoons—without, however, the accompanying *ding* sound effect.

They turned toward the car just as an airport policewoman approached. She looked like she was about to tell them they had to move their vehicle. But on seeing their joy, she merely smiled and gestured for them to proceed with a wave of her hand, before turning toward the next offending vehicle in line.

Mindi put the car in drive and looked over at Jeff. As their eyes met, she said, "Oh. About the flowers that arrived yesterday, I know I thanked you when you called, but they are *so* beautiful. Thank you, again. So thoughtful. What a wonderful Valentine's Day gift. Your gift is at home waiting for you." She winked.

~

Jeff had been in Los Angeles for a week, and what a week it had been. He hadn't realized the scope of the modeling business. He'd met so many people: stylists—makeup, hair, and wardrobe—photographers of all types—videographers, large format, wide-angle—lighting specialists, food service, grips. The list went on and on. He caught on quickly, his mind filled up with his new career.

He loved it. And Mindi loved it too. Mindi had warned him about long periods of standing around, but that gave him time to both study his new craft and reflect on the recent lack of dreams about drug dealers.

He hadn't yet come up with a plan for their mission to protect Charlene and maybe stop a drug import until one night, while he and Mindi were relaxing, watching a movie about drug smuggling. Jeff sat up straight, pressed *pause* on the remote, and turned to Mindi with purpose.

Mindi looked at him. "What's wrong?"

"Nothing. I've been trying to work out how we could interfere with the shipment."

"Okay?"

He pointed to the screen. "The DEA agents there."

She looked at the screen, then back to him. "Okay?"

"We don't have to do it alone. We just figure out how to get the DEA involved."

Mindi frowned. "How? In a leap?"

"I guess. I dunno."

"We don't know anyone. How do we know who to tell?"

"Well, I guess we just shop around for agents. Second, we'll figure out how to make them a host and get the information to them. Ask the right questions, and the answers will come. So yeah, the first question is how do we find an agent?"

"Okay, but we don't want them in the gray room."

"Like our friends from Bogotá? Absolutely not. I guess we can do a basic leap into their heads. The trick will be how to get them to believe us."

Mindi shrugged. "Where do we start?"

"I'll look up where the DEA is here in LA. We've got the container number, a ship name, a departure, and probable arrival date . . ."

"And we've got their names," Mindi said.

"Yeah, our folks we know, but we don't have details on the truck driver who picks up the container, and . . ." He trailed off, considering the list. "If Alejandro doesn't know that, and he may not, he knows who would. Probably Carlos, right?"

Mindi nodded. "Even without that, which I'm sure we'll find out, we have enough for the DEA to get started."

"Okay, we have action items for tomorrow's research."

"You know, we haven't been to the gray room for over a month," Mindi said. "Let's go there tonight, just for fun. Practice." She looked at him with a twinkle in her eye, a sly smile, "And maybe some variety." Followed by a coquettish smirk.

Jeff didn't miss that cue.

~

They fell together holding hands. Suddenly, without a jolt, they were standing in the gray room a few feet from their chairs, exactly as they'd left them. They let go of each other's hand and approached their chairs. A folded sheet of paper lay on Mindi's seat. Written across the top it was *Miranda Madisen.* Mindi leaned over to pick it up, but Jeff stopped her.

"What?" Mindi withdrew her arm and stepped back.

"Please, just a minute." A pencil appeared in Jeff's hand. "Did you just find that?"

"No, I just made it, for a tool."

Jeff, using the pencil so he didn't have to touch the paper, lifted open the folded note to read what was written on the inside.

"Why did you do that?" Mindi asked.

"I don't know, being careful—just a hunch."

She leaned over to read it. It was in all capital letters and had an exclamation point. *I KNOW WHO YOU ARE!*

A chill passed over them, and the hairs on their dream arms and necks stood up. They looked at each other and then in all directions, out to the infinite horizon.

"Jeff." A long pause as she continued to look around. "This is creepy."

"I know." He folded the paper closed again and left it positioned exactly the way it was when they first saw it. "Let's go. We have to talk."

When they returned to real-time, they sat on the edge of the bed, alternately asking the questions that were on both their minds.

"What the . . . ?"

"Who . . . ?"

"When . . . ?"

"Why . . . ?"

"How . . . ?"

Then they both fell silent.

Jeff broke the silence with a chuckle. "The only thing we didn't ask was 'where?'"

"Was it Alejandro or Karina?" Mindi said.

Jeff shrugged. "Don't know. Block letters—could be either one. They're our only suspects. But . . . if they could find the room, someone else might have too."

"Yeah, but they're the only ones who've seen me. It had to be one of them."

"They both know you're a model because they've seen your face," Jeff said. "Did the window ad have your name on it?"

"No."

"Then it had to be Alejandro, because he used your full stage name from the magazine, not your nickname. I told you I saw him doing some research on dreams, so he understands lucid dreams and wants to take control, starting with the note. We couldn't scare him now if we caught him again."

"Then we're sure it's not Karina."

Jeff shook his head. "She's a sweet person. No, it wasn't her. Here's the thing—if it comes to a choice between your well-being, Charlene's, or Karina's . . ." He left the sentence unfinished, then said, "Minn, I think you should leap into her and plant some more seeds of his cheating. Make her more distrustful of him. We need him to be on edge, and a change in her mood would help. We know it won't stop him from taking Charlene to dinner, but it might make it a lot less fun."

"I don't like doing that to her, but you're right, it might help. So that takes care of who. What about when?"

"Alejandro saw the magazine next year, so he must've time traveled back to leave the note, although I'm sure he doesn't know it. That really doesn't matter though. We have the result."

Mindi nodded. "Okay. Next is how."

"How?"

"Yeah, how did he leave the note?"

"I conjured a robe, watch, dinosaur, snakes, pencil. You made bunny slippers and a wall, so why not a note?"

"Sure."

"And the why is to take control—now that he's figured out the process. Did he do that to test us? He doesn't know *what* we're doing, that we're working to keep Charlene safe and maybe stop the drugs. He's just shooting in the dark, hoping to hit something."

"I don't like that you used the term 'shooting.'"

"Figure of speech, but I understand. Okay. We've got that figured out. What are we going to do now?"

Mindi shrugged.

"I'll work on getting info on the DEA tomorrow. Let's call it a night, sleep on it. We can talk in the morning."

Mindi nodded. "Yeah."

They kissed good night, put their heads on the pillow, and breathed evenly, and immediately were dreaming again and were back together in the gray room, their chairs a few yards away in front of them. They were confused at being back so soon and started to say something to each other when the sound of a cough drew their attention to a door opening opposite them.

Mindi waved her right hand in a circle over her head and became invisible—a new move Jeff hadn't known they could do, and copied her. Up close, they could see each other as barely discernible air disturbances, like heat waves in the air. They stood still and watched Alejandro approach the chairs and look at the note. His frown told the couple he was disappointed that it hadn't been disturbed. He turned away. His image settled to the floor as glitter.

They both awoke in their bedroom.

Jeff said, "He came back to see if we had taken the note."

"Yeah, and we were sent back to confirm it was him. Why weren't we there when he put it there? This gets curiouser and curiouser. Is that why you didn't want to move it?"

"It was just a hunch; it might not have been important. Anyway, how do you think we could mess with him in his real-time, and make him think that something is wrong with their plans, and maybe make him paranoid? We need a Plan B."

Mindi brought their dream journals and handed him his.

"Thanks." Jeff thumbed back through the pages in his journal. "Here's something—gives me an idea. The first time I leaped into Carlos in his car, they were on the phone. Alejandro's incoming number was blocked. He keeps it a secret." Jeff paused a moment. "It was blocked on the call to Carlos. But I saw a full number when he called Charlene at lunch. So he must have two phones: one for business, one for personal. That's a drug dealer's trick. We saw that in that movie."

"What do you have in mind?"

"If I had the numbers, I could use a burner phone, maybe two or three with different phone numbers, and call him to make him think what he's doing is not so secret, that his drug phone was hacked and that *we* know who *he* is and what he's doing."

"What do you think he'd do?"

"I don't know and don't care. He's a drug dealer; there's got to be a lot of money riding on this deal, a natural amount of caution and hopefully some paranoia. I'd like to crank the paranoia up a notch or two. If I were him and thought my number was hacked, the first thing I'd do is change phones. Then we mess with that new number, and keep doing it. If it were me, the next thing I'd do is take inventory of who had my number to figure who might want to screw with me. Maybe we can divide from within. I don't know. He's wasted our time worrying about the note; let's waste a little of his time by having him worrying about his associates. I need a phone number to get started."

Mindi frowned, deep in thought. "Do you think Karina

has them?"

"It's the first place to look. If she does and you could get those numbers, I'll do something with them." Jeff grinned. "Let the games begin, Watson."

Mindi chuckled. "G'night, Sherlock." They kissed good night.

~

Their ability to leap into known subjects had become as easy as driving to the store.

Mindi watched through Karina's eyes as she finished putting on her makeup and begun on her hair. The sun illuminated the bedroom through the window next to the elegant antique dressing table with three-sided beveled mirrors. In the mirrors, Mindi could see a matching dresser on one side, a wardrobe and stand-up mirror on the other side, and a four-poster bed, complete with canopy and side curtains, behind her.

Karina brushed her hair as Mindi concentrated on getting Karina to open her phone and the contacts directory. But all Karina did was hit the home button on her smartphone as if to check to see if she had any messages or missed calls.

Darn it. Mindi tried again, but Karina merely reached toward the phone, shook her head, and went back to brushing her hair.

Mindi had read about telekinesis, the ability to control objects at a distance by mental power. What if? They'd never tried it, but now was a good time. Then there was remote viewing; could she see the phone without looking through Karina's eyes? The phone lay on the dressing table, just out of view. While Karina was looking in the mirror, Mindi only got an occasional glance of it.

Karina, subconsciously aware of Mindi's interest in the phone, looked again, paused for a moment, and then went back to brushing. Mindi backed away from the optic nerve, closed her virtual eyes, and concentrated on her meditation breathing. The phone on the polished walnut of the tabletop appeared in her mind. *Wow*, she thought. With a virtual finger, she pressed the home button on the iPhone and it awoke.

Was that really the slight click of the button Mindi felt or just her imagination?

She stole a look through Karina's eyes and saw her still at work on her hair, the phone out of her field of vision.

Mindi refocused. The phone lay there awake, but now she needed Karina's password.

Darn. She returned her attention to Karina, who was buttoning up her blouse.

Mindi concentrated. *What's the password? What's the password?*

Nothing.

Mindi had been studying her Spanish. She said three times in quick succession, *¿Cual es la contraseña?* What is the password?

A number flashed three times in her mind. *2653. 2653. 2653.*

Mindi returned her vision to the phone. It had gone back to sleep. Her psychic finger pressed the button again, and the phone awoke with the number pad in clear view. She pressed 2-6-5-3. The home screen appeared. *Success!*

She touched the phone icon, then *Favoritos*, then selected *Alejo*. She pressed the information symbol. And there were his listings. She memorized them.

Excited, Mindi went back to Karina's field of vision.

Karina was now walking back toward the dressing table to fetch her phone, the screen again black. Karina pressed the home button and saw Alejandro's contacts listing open.

"What is this?" She cleared her phone, put it in her pocket, and left the room.

Mindi visualized the Jeannie move and awoke back in her bed, alone. Jeff was in the living room in deep meditation. She documented her evening's success along with the phone numbers in her journal. She watched him for a few minutes, then returned to the bedroom to wait for him but fell asleep.

~

The next morning Mindi found Jeff sitting at the dining table writing in his journal. Her journal lay next to it, open to last night's entry. An empty coffee cup signaled that he'd been up for a while.

"Good morning," she said. "What did you do?"

He looked up, answering with a smile, "Well, I wasn't nearly as productive as you, it seems. How did you figure out how to do that?" He gestured toward her journal. "How you got those numbers was so cool. Brilliant!" He stood and gave her a hug, then held her at arm's length to get a good look at her. "You are beautiful, smart, *and* talented. You're a natural. We have no limits."

Mindi leaned toward him and gave him a kiss. "Thank you, but *you* started it. You need to do that."

"Of course. But now that you can do it in a leap in a dream, I want to see if you can do it in real-time. If so, I'll put you on stage and have you bending spoons."

The puzzled look on her face told him the reference to the stage psychic from the 1970s and 80s was lost on her.

"The illusionist, Yuri Geller, bent spoons in his performances. Many thought it was just a trick, but some claimed he worked as a spy for the US and could erase Soviet computer disks at a distance," Jeff explained. "So where do we start?" He looked around the kitchen, and his eyes settled on his coffee cup. He put a fresh mug and coffee pod in the coffee maker and said, "Here, sit here. See if you can push the *Start* button."

"Now?"

Jeff nodded and stepped behind her.

She stared at the button. Nothing happened. She closed her eyes and visualized her finger pressing the button. Nothing. She strained, clenching up her face, furrowing her brow. Nothing.

"Relax. Meditate like you said you did with Karina's phone."

She turned and looked at him. He nodded encouragement.

She sat with her feet flat on the floor, hands lying in her lap. With eyes closed, she took four long, slow breaths in through her nose and exhaled out her mouth.

Jeff looked from her to the coffee maker. The appliance seemed to quiver, but nothing more.

Mindi's shoulders slumped as she opened her eyes and said, "Almost, Jeff. Almost. Right?"

"With practice, you'll get it. Maybe we should've started with a phone."

"I'll practice later. I know I'll get it," she said with confidence.

"Right."

She pointed to his journal. "You finished?"

"Just a couple of more lines, then, yes. But it's not as interesting as what you did."

"Give me the CliffsNotes version."

"Sure. I'll be right back and tell you." He headed for the bathroom.

Mindi repositioned herself in the chair to get into the meditation pose—back straight, legs crossed on the seat, hands palms up on her knees, forefingers forming a loop with her thumbs—and tried again.

With little effort, the Keurig on the counter six feet away clicked, and the brewing cycle started. Mindi opened her eyes and looked at the coffee maker. Jeff had returned to the room and stood watching her with a smile. She grinned at him. "How about *that?*"

"I think *you* truly are *my* teacher now, my sensei. Wow."

"Your coffee is served, sire," Mindi said with a flourish.

"No, my dear, that cup is yours. You earned it."

Jeff brought the coffee and creamer back to the table, sat down, and told her what he had learned about the United States Drug Enforcement Administration during his meditation last night.

"I decided, rather than go to sleep and try to connect with Carlos or Alejandro again, I'd attempt a different type of astral projection, an actual out-of-body experience, but not into someone else's body like the leaps we've been doing. And it worked! Last night was a night of firsts for both of us!"

He put his arms out from his shoulders like wings and waved them as if flying.

"You were flying? Ingrid's book talks about that."

"Yes. When you went to sleep to visit Karina, I googled the DEA and found where their offices were. I found what I wanted and meditated. Then, while sitting right over there on my pillow"—he pointed, then raised his hand toward the ceiling. She looked over reflexively—"I gently rose through the top of my head, up through the ceiling, and looked down at the apartment. I could see the whole block and the city in the distance. There were cars moving on the street. A guy from down the block, wearing his bathrobe, walked his dog. It was a true out-of-body experience like the books talk about. At first, I thought it was my imagination, but as I continued to rise, I knew it was real." He looked at her and smiled.

Mindi's eyes widened. "Okay, okay. Go on. What did you do then?"

"I headed up toward the Federal Building on East Temple. I don't know LA that well, but somehow I flew right to it. I circled it and wondered, if someone on the sidewalk had looked up, would they see me? But of course, I was a ghost, so they wouldn't have.

"I flew, at first like Superman in the movies, with my arms stretched out in front. Then, like a fish, arms by my side." He put his hands by his side and wiggled. "Then I pretended I was sitting flying an airplane, kinda like Wonder Woman in her invisible jet. What felt more natural, though, was upright, like this. There was no wind."

He leaned forward a little, like the figurehead on a ship.

"There was a guard in the lobby reading a magazine. I drifted right through the glass in the door and floated in front of the directory—the DEA is on the seventeenth floor. I looked over the guard's shoulder at the camera monitors, but they got all fuzzy when I leaned in close. I checked out his logbook. Then I went upstairs. Well, I didn't take the stairs. I just thought about what floor I wanted, and I just sort of zipped into the DEA offices. The lights were out, but there was enough light for me to see the names on the *Who's in/Who's out* board." Jeff pointed to his journal. "I wrote the names I could remember. There's an Agent Ramsey, Agent Thompson, Agent Moreno, and a couple more. I'm going to look them up on the internet while we're waiting around at the studio and see what I can find. I'd say that was a pretty good night."

Mindi just stared at him.

"What?" Jeff said.

"What you did was fantastic! You minimized it when you got started telling me. That's every bit as good as me pushing buttons. Better, I think. I want to do that."

Jeff grinned. "I want us to go flying together for fun. Think of where we can go and what we can see. And it doesn't cost anything. All we do is meditate. And it might make our mission to get the bad guys and save Charlene a lot easier."

"Do you know what that sounded like?" Mindi said with mock seriousness.

"What do you mean?" Jeff searched for her meaning in her eyes.

With lightness in her voice, Mindi said, "It sounds like the plot from an adventure movie. We get the crooks and save a damsel in distress."

Jeff laughed. "Yeah, I guess it does. But how would you say it?"

Mindi got up and put her arms around him while he remained in the chair. She bent down and nibbled on his ear. "Well, I like the subplot better," she said, "where the two heroes spend a lot of quality time focusing on the logistics of their relationship."

CHAPTER 10

Jeff found the DEA agents listed on the government website and chose Agent Antonio Moreno, based on his Hispanic-sounding name, figuring it would be poetic justice, or just ironic, if one Latino handled the arrest of another.

On the next attempt of an out-of-body excursion, they wanted to see if they could do it together. They sat side by side, but as he rose out of his body, she remained on her pillows in her meditation pose. He waited for a moment, hoping she might join him, then tried for a telepathic connection but got none. Apparently, it was something she would need to work on.

Where should I go?

He rose above the roof and traveled toward the northwest, sailing a few hundred feet above the ground. He enjoyed the feeling of flying. The books said that flying in a dream or meditation is a symbol of freedom. No feeling of vertigo or fear of falling. His only thought of a destination was Antonio Moreno, which was a common name. How would he find him? He flew over what he learned later were the Santa

Monica mountains. The city lights off to his left stopped at the coast of the Pacific Ocean, with only darkness beyond. He continued northward, wondering where he was going. He'd studied maps of the area, but what he'd learned didn't seem of benefit tonight. Where was Beverly Hills? Bel Air? Sherman Oaks?

In a short time, he descended toward one of the dozens of identical housing areas over which he'd already flown. Many of the homes had swimming pools, solar panels on the roofs, and RVs in the driveway. He dropped through the roof of a house that looked like any other. *This must be where Agent Moreno lives.*

Inside, dark and quiet, Jeff floated feet down above the floor. But gliding along like that now felt unnatural, being inside, so he visualized himself walking and immediately had the sensation of the floor beneath his feet. He crept through the house, being careful not to make a sound, and soon realized that care was unnecessary. Being out of his body, he wouldn't make any sound.

Jeff turned the corner into the hallway that led to the bedrooms and first heard, then saw a man in a home office typing on a computer. A moment of disorientation followed, then Jeff found himself in the man's mind. *Antonio Moreno?*

His host, in response to hearing his name in his mind, looked around the room, then down at his phone to see if he had a call or a text. Agent Moreno rubbed his forehead and looked at the computer screen. Jeff briefly saw a daily report of a drug surveillance operation on the waterfront.

Another thought slipped out of Jeff's mind. *How did I do that?*

Moreno heard that too. He pushed back his chair, stood, and turned toward the door, then paused, looked back at the screen and saved his document. He cocked his head, listening. Jeff was also on alert, now aware this man was very sensitive to his thoughts. *I've got to be quiet.*

The agent heard that too. He spun around and looked toward the curtained window. Jeff heard the man's thoughts: *I know I heard something.* Moreno pulled open a desk drawer and took his Glock 17 from its plastic holster. Jeff mentally flinched at the sound when the agent chambered a round. Moreno remained still for a moment, then, hearing nothing, moved to the side of the doorway and listened again. He looked around the doorjamb into the dark hallway, then stepped through and crept toward the closed door at the end of the hall. Holding the gun behind his back, he pressed his ear to the door, then opened it. In the bed lay Moreno's wife, asleep. The agent closed the door, being careful not to let the latch make a sound, then searched the rest of the house. He checked his children's bedrooms; they were in their beds asleep. He returned to the office and replaced the gun in the desk. He sat, continuing to listen, then returned his attention to the unfinished report.

Agent Antonio Moreno was a fifteen-year veteran of the DEA, and prior to that he'd spent three years as a field operative for the FBI. His record was officially unblemished.

Jeff had learned, since these dreams started, to trust his instincts and to go with each situation as it was handed to him. His gut said this guy would be useful. What Jeff hadn't learned, however, was how to monitor his thoughts as well as he would've liked. His thought, *How can I feed him information he'll trust, not just have it come from a ghost in his head?* slipped out into his host's mind.

Agent Moreno heard the word "ghost" in his mind, turned and looked toward the door, then made the sign of the cross.

What if. . . ? I'll do it! Jeff thought silently. Then, with full intent to plant the seed in the agent's mind, he said, in a full mind voice, *Alejandro Sarís! Investigate Alejandro Sarís.*

Moreno glanced at the ceiling, reached toward the drawer with the gun, then stopped. "What?" he said out loud as he tried to focus on where the voice had come from.

Investigate Alejandro Sarís, Jeff repeated.

Moreno typed *Alejandro Sarís* into a blank document. Leads often came as a hunch; he would follow this one tomorrow.

Mission completed, Jeff visualized the "Jeannie move" and opened his eyes back in the living room. He remained still for a moment.

Mindi was still in the meditation pose. He heard her voice in his head. *Did you have a nice trip?*

Before he could answer, either in his mind or in real-time, she opened her eyes, and with a peaceful look on her face, said aloud, "Well? Nice trip?"

He grinned. "Oh, yeah. So much new we can do. What did you do?"

She stood and offered a hand to him, encouraging him to stand. "As you started to fly away, I saw you lift up through the ceiling, but I couldn't move. I waited for you to come back. You didn't seem to be gone long. Where did you go?"

Jeff described his flight, the automatic leap into the drug agent's head, and the agent's sensitivity to him. "The guy has a strong will. When I gave him Alejandro's name, he wrote it down to check out later."

Mindi's eyes sparkled with excitement. "Great. We can activate switches and control people's movements too?"

"Well, sort of. And there's probably more we can do."

"That's what I'm talking about. Suggestions are one thing, but can we actually encourage them to do things?"

"Good question. We'll have to try more things. Last night showed that it's gotten easier to get into people's minds, so that might work. Best of all, to leap, we don't have to go to sleep. We can just meditate and go."

~

The next day, at their real-time jobs, Jeff and Mindi worked a twelve-hour day. The photoshoot started at Disneyland, then, after a break, moved to the studio. Though tired, they were living the dream.

Once back home, they fell asleep immediately and found themselves in the gray room. Alejandro's note was still there.

Jeff moved the note aside and sat down, motioning for Mindi to sit.

"What if he shows up?" she asked.

"I don't know. But I have a feeling he won't. We're here for something else tonight. I can feel it."

"You're right, Jeff," a familiar, but disembodied, female voice said. "Don't be alarmed, it's just me."

Ingrid materialized in front of them, dressed like a hippie as she'd been in her bookshop.

Startled, the couple stood and started toward her.

"Please. Sit," Ingrid said with a smile. "You've had a long day." Another identical chair materialized for her, and they all sat, the couple's eyes still wide with wonder.

"I see you're surprised to see me. I hope you're pleased." She smiled again. "Truly as surprised and pleased as I was to see you when you each came into my shop."

Jeff and Mindi said nothing; they stared.

"Please don't be alarmed. You're in awe that I could find you, no?"

Mindi spoke first. "Yes, Ingrid. Yes. How did you?"

"I must answer your question with a question. How do you do what you've learned to do?"

"Uh, we just did, I guess," Jeff said with a shrug.

Ingrid nodded.

Jeff continued, "We were afraid you may have been—"

Ingrid interrupted. "Someone less friendly? Yes, I understand. I shan't stay long. I have three important things to tell you."

Jeff nodded for her to continue, and Mindi leaned forward a little.

"First, I'm sure you suspect otherwise, but I am not in control here. I'm like you; I do not know what's guiding us, if anything at all. Jeff, you have questioned the universe, wondering where these talents come from that give you a chance to act on what you know to be right. Am I correct?"

Jeff gave a quick nod.

She turned to Mindi. "When we last spoke, you asked a similar question about a higher power. The answer I gave is that I don't know." Ingrid waved her arm, indicating the gray area in which they sat. "This *is* all a wonderful mystery." She smiled. "And you asked about danger. Do you remember?"

Mindi nodded.

"Things may happen that will cause you to reconsider continuing what you call 'your mission.' But it may be more dangerous to not go forward with what you're presented. Do not waver."

"And the third thing is your concern that your privacy here has been invaded. Is that correct?" She looked from one to the other. "You have learned many talents. I want to share with you something that I discovered quite by accident. You can make this space totally private without building walls or creating monsters to scare trespassers away. If it had been in place, I wouldn't have been able to join you unless you'd given me permission."

"Okay, how does that work?" Jeff asked. "How do we hang a do-not-disturb sign?"

Ingrid smiled. "Well put. You work with computers. You have 'toggles' to turn on and off privacy settings, correct?"

"Yes."

"Just set the toggle to private."

"How?"

"How did you make these chairs appear?"

"Oh," Jeff and Mindy said together, their eyebrows arched in understanding.

"And if you wanted to, you could imprison a visitor. That takes a bit of energy, but it is possible."

"Why would we want to do that?" Mindi asked.

"Well, it could keep them from doing harm to themselves or others in their real-time. In effect, you create a sleep from which they only awake when you release them from here."

"Like a coma?" Mindi said.

"Well, yes, that could describe it. Be careful, though. It can be distressing for others in *their* real-time. Their friends or loved ones might be affected by their inability to awaken them. If you ever use it, use it wisely, because it can create anguish for the innocent. Too long of an imprisonment could drive them insane and cause permanent damage. I tell you this because you both have clear gold auras, and you wish to do no harm." She paused. "Do you know what a 'golden aura' is?"

They shook their heads and waited for her to explain.

Ingrid obliged. "Those with auras like yours are spiritually advanced souls. Few are born with one fully formed. Like many virtues, in time, an aura is polished into high quality, but only by those who are deserving. And many who have one don't know about it or understand its significance if they do. Even so, they have great compassion and are highly intelligent, with a desire to do good and assist others. They are great friends and excellent leaders. They are modest in personality and live modestly, using material possessions and wealth to extend care to others. They may, however, overextend themselves, pushing the boundaries of their abilities even to their own disadvantage. As in all things, there are benefits to moderation and meditation."

Ingrid waited as they absorbed what she'd told them, and even though she sensed they had more questions, she held up her palm in a gentle movement, letting them know she was finished. Then, with a smile and tip of her head, she waved her hand in a signal of goodbye and dissolved in a flutter of glitter.

They watched the chair in which she'd sat sparkle as it, too, dissolved.

~

After writing in her dream journal, Mindi laid her pen on the kitchen table and said, "She's one of us."

Jeff leaned back in his chair and lifted his hands palms up. "But what are we? In martial arts, high proficiency is marked by the color of your belt, with the black belts being the highest. If this were based on that, she surely has a higher degree belt than we do."

"Remember when we talked about predestination versus

free will?' Mindi asked. "You said that the situations we find ourselves in might be predestined, but the outcome might depend on what *we* choose to do. Was she telling us we must make the right choices, and when things look like we may want out, we have to stay in the game? That reminded me of my grandfather. He was a Vince Lombardi fan. You know who he was, don't you?"

"Of course. Coach of the Green Bay Packers back in the sixties, won a couple of Super Bowls. Why?"

"Gramps was always teaching us grandkids something: how to whistle, how to use a slingshot. When we got older, he showed us a motivation video that Lombardi made called *Second Effort*. The message was about mental toughness, that when you're down, get up and try again."

"Sure, good advice. Was he on your mom's or dad's side of the family?"

"He was Mom's dad. We were fond of him. We cried a lot when he died."

Jeff reached over and took her hand.

She looked up and forced a smile. "I haven't thought about him in a while." She shook off the melancholy and said, "Okay, what's next?"

"Well, I think I'll go back to Moreno and see if I can find out if the seed I planted the other night has sprouted about checking out Sarís. What do you think?"

Mindi nodded. "Good. And how about I give a little visit to Charlene and see what's going on there, maybe find what they're doing in Seattle?"

"Great." Jeff stood, then leaned over and gave Mindi a kiss. "Time to get ready to go to work. The real world calls."

That night, as they cleaned up after dinner, Mindi said, "Hey, how about a change of plans? I'd like to go with you to your new DEA friend. Okay?"

They settled onto their pillows, crossed their legs, straightened their backs, closed their eyes, and took the breaths to synchronize their breathing in an even rhythm.

Telepathically, Jeff said, *Ready?*

Yes.

And with that exchange, they both rose and looked down on their physical selves in the darkened living room. Then they looked up and rose through the ceiling.

Wait, Mindi telepathed.

Jeff paused about fifty feet above the apartment building. Mindi "stood" a few feet below him, surveying the view with wonder. She looked up at him and smiled. He put out his hand. She rose and took it, and they headed off toward the south.

"This isn't the way I went the other night," Jeff said. They traveled a short distance and then descended toward the port at Long Beach.

"I bet this is where Moreno will be tonight."

They settled, as spirits, a short distance from a black Chevrolet Suburban with heavily tinted windows and US Government license plates. They had landed not at the container shipping terminal but across the waterway, in the parking lot of a large private marina for pleasure boats. Jeff let go of her hand and put his feet, seemingly, on the ground. Mindi still floated, ghost-like, a few feet above him.

She looked down at him and said, "How did you do that? I'm stuck here."

"Yeah, feels funny, doesn't it? Just imagine you've landed, and you'll land."

She frowned.

"Relax. It'll happen."

She took a deep breath, closed her eyes and was standing next to him. "I could feel your hand," she said, "but I don't feel the air. There's a breeze—look at the flags there."

Jeff nodded. "Yeah, I don't get it. I can feel the ground and your hand, but we can walk through walls and fly through roofs." He looked around and inclined his head toward the Suburban. "Let's go over to the spy car."

"How do you know it's a spy car?"

"The license plates and tinted windows."

They stood next to the SUV, and Jeff put his finger to his lips, reminding her Moreno was sensitive and might be able to "hear" them. Jeff reached for the door handle as if to open it, but his hand passed through it. He paused for a moment, considering what to do, and then he floated through the closed door into the back seat. Mindi's eyes widened in wonder and grew wider still when Jeff's hand came out through the closed window and beckoned her inside. She took another deep breath and as she breathed out, stepped forward and slipped easily through the closed door to join Jeff in the back seat.

Wow! She couldn't help the big grin of delight that spread across her face.

The two men in the front seat were drinking coffee and watching, through the windshield, the boats on the other side of a high chain link fence.

Jeff pointed to the man in the passenger seat and, without a sound, mouthed, "Tony Moreno."

She nodded.

The agent in the driver's seat said, "It's cold in here; is the window open?"

"No, but I feel it too." Moreno zipped up his dark-blue windbreaker with the white letters *DEA* over the left breast.

Jeff leaned forward and looked at the clipboard sitting

151

on the console between the two agents, then he sat back and signaled Mindi to look. She read *Surveillance Order* and the agents' names, *A. Moreno and J. Clark. Location: Cabrillo Marina. Surveillance Target: Yacht, Miranda II, Cartagena.* After reading, she sat back against the seat, noticing that though the upholstery didn't move, it nevertheless supported them.

Jeff motioned to Mindi to follow him, then "climbed out" of the Suburban. They walked in the direction of the agents' attention, passed through the chain link fence without using the gate that divided the walkway from access to the docks, and stopped a few paces from the water. Jeff pointed at a large luxury yacht that looked like an ocean racer—long, low, sleek and modern, glossy white, and with long windows nearly the full length along the hull on both the upper and lower decks. The flying bridge and lounge area on the bow deck were sleek, and it appeared to be moving fast while still in its berth. The name across the stern, in gold, red, and blue script, said *Miranda II Cartagena.*

They followed the walkway down the dock-ramp, turned left on the dock, and approached the impressive, gleaming white vessel. Lights were on inside. Mindi, who was thoroughly enjoying the experience, walked up the few steps onto the gangway and then drifted down onto the stern deck. Jeff joined her, took her hand, and they walked forward along the starboard side of the ship. A man in a white uniform came out of the cabin. They stopped short, and he walked directly toward them, not seeing them, of course. They failed to step sideways, and he walked right through Jeff. A pace further on, he stopped, looked back the way he'd come, and then shook his head, as if he'd felt something.

Mindi pointed to the door through which the crew member had come. Jeff nodded his agreement, and they floated into a luxurious lounge area occupied by two men, both in expensive running suits, who were playing backgammon. A drink sat beside each man on a dining table large enough to easily seat eight. The two explorers stood next to the two men and watched the game.

The men remained silent as they rolled the dice and moved their game pieces with the speed of experienced players. When the game was over, the winner, in English but with a heavy Latin accent, said, "'Berto, that's three in a row. Are you now convinced I am a better player than you?"

'Berto smiled. "Jose, I refuse to admit that to you."

To which Jose, in Spanish, replied, "I admit you are a formidable opponent, but you are still not as good as I am." He laughed, put out his hand, and they shook.

Jeff smiled at Mindi, then tipped his head sideways toward where they should go next. They walked through the double doors to the rear deck, turned right, and took the stairway leading below decks. On their way toward the bow, they passed a spiral stairway that led up to the main salon, where they'd just been. Down a long hallway were the stateroom doors, all closed. They heard voices and found two crew members, one of whom they'd seen on deck, in a small crew lounge area next to a well-appointed galley.

Mindi and Jeff continued further down the passageway and found another set of stairs. These led down into the engine room, which housed two massive engines. They walked beside the pristine-looking machinery—not a tool or spot of oil could be seen.

They continued their snooping, not knowing what they might find, if anything, but enjoying their self-guided tour of this rich person's toy. Finding nothing of particular interest, they climbed up one deck and passed through the first door they found near the vessel's portside bow into a storeroom, a curtain drawn across the single porthole.

Jeff felt along the wall, then said, "Can you turn the light on?"

She felt around with her incorporeal fingers. "I can sense it, but I can't make it work."

They backed out into the passageway and investigated every stateroom along the passageway. The largest was a fabulous luxury suite.

"Have you seen enough?"

"Yeah, I think so."

They floated up through the roof and enjoyed the flight back toward Gardena.

"So that's named after Roberto's Miranda?" Jeff said as they cruised along.

Mindi laughed. "Isn't it obvious he's quite fond of her?" Then, "We need to practice our telekinesis so we can turn on lights."

Jeff nodded agreement, then said, "The Feds are watching the yacht, so there must be some reason they're there. We've been brought into this in the middle of the game. I wished we knew if we're the catalyst to get something going or . . . something. Either way, this could be fun."

Mindi replied playfully, "There's only one thing better than this. What do you think?"

He looked over at her with a small, puzzled frown. "What do you mean?"

She gave him a suggestive look, one he'd enjoyed many times before.

His face lit up with understanding. "Up here? In the air? Really? D'ya think we can?"

"Why not try? It won't be like we're really in public, right?"

He looked around as they flew leisurely northward. "At five hundred feet?"

"I know, it won't classify for the mile-high club, but"— she pointed up—"we can head up there, if you like." She flew higher, laughing, with him in pursuit.

~

Alejandro had filed his flight plan and was enjoying working through the preflight checklist. He lovingly rubbed his hands over the polished fuselage of his twin jet Pilatus PC-24 that would take him from Bogotá to Mexico City, then to Bakersfield, California, with the final leg to Seattle. He had two stops that weren't on the flight plan, however. One was to pick up cargo at a private airfield outside of Medellín. He wouldn't deplane in Mexico City when he refueled, so Mexican customs wouldn't be concerned about what he might have on board. If anyone did come around, a little "palm-grease" would surely solve any issues.

He'd take a short nap there, then be on his way in the late afternoon for another four-hour flight to a rancher's airstrip east of Bakersfield to unload the cargo under a full moon. He'd be on the ground for no more than twenty minutes. His associates could be counted on to get the packages to his friends at the marina in Long Beach. Then a short hop to Meadow's Field in Bakersfield to refuel, where he would again stay onboard for a few hours' sleep in the plane. Then the next day, a short two-and-a-half-hour flight to Seattle would be pleasant, ultimately landing at Boeing Field.

Alejo had called Charlene from Bogotá, and she'd agreed to meet him for dinner the next week. He would take delivery of his new Audi in Seattle. He wanted to impress her.

These moves had worked before; no reason to believe they wouldn't work now. He'd also planned a visit with a real estate agent, having requested three choices of condominiums that overlooked either the waters of Lake Washington or Elliott Bay. These new investments would be worthwhile when added to his portfolio, and his business agent would take care of the details. They would give him a good reason for returning to Seattle regularly to be with that beautiful woman.

While sleeping in the plane in Bakersfield, he had another of the strange dreams where he was in that large gray expanse occupied solely by the two large, gray, overstuffed chairs. He remembered the nightmare when the disembodied voice had told him to be careful and the fear when the dinosaur chased him. And the snakes! But he'd since seen the woman's face on the magazine cover, so he knew who she was. If he was attacked or threatened again, he would simply wake up and no harm would come to him; they were merely dreams.

The monochromatic area was unoccupied except for the chairs. He walked over to the chair in which he'd seen her sitting and wished there was some way to leave a message. As soon as he'd thought that, he was holding a piece of paper on which had already been written the name from the magazine cover, Miranda Madisen. He turned it over, and on the other side was written, in block letters, *I KNOW WHO YOU ARE!* How the words got here, he couldn't imagine, but it was, after all, a dream.

Alejandro looked at the paper that had appeared in his hand and then back at the chair. He folded the paper in half and set it on the chair with the name facing upward, adjusting it so the name was clearly visible. An inspection around the chairs revealed nothing of interest. With a shrug, he sat down in the other chair, waited a moment, and in the next instant, Alejandro was back in the cabin of his airplane shaking off the veil of sleep. After using the toilet and small but adequate galley services on board, Alejandro sat and watched the minimal amount of activity around the small airport in Bakersfield until he again fell asleep. He enjoyed a restful, dreamless sleep and awoke the next morning ready to continue his journey.

The dream remained in his mind, however. He was still puzzled as to the reason for having these dreams.

CHAPTER 11

Mindi had leaped into Charlene's mind while having dinner with Alejandro in the subdued light of an upscale restaurant with a view of Lake Union in Seattle. Charlene had just taken a drink of wine, dabbed at her mouth with her napkin, and returned it to her lap. Mindi tasted it.

"So you flew all the way from Colombia to Seattle in your plane—alone?"

Alejandro smiled and explained modestly that the automatic pilot system did most of the work. He told her that all he had to do was program where he wanted to go, and the airplane, with the help of GPS satellites, control towers, and beacons, did the rest. He had little to do except take off and land, and the computer guided or assisted much of that.

Mindi wanted to know what day and time it was. Charlene's iPhone sat next to her silverware, and seeing a chance to practice, Mindi reached out a virtual finger and depressed the home button, making the screen light up. Charlene glanced down and saw it, giving Mindi a clear view of the time and date superimposed on a selfie of Charlene and what might have been her sister and mother against a backdrop of large green fir trees. *8:47 p.m., March 16, 2018.*

"Apologies, Alejo," Charlene said. "It looked like I was getting a call." She drew her fingers and thumb across her eyelids, and finished by massaging the bridge of her nose. When she opened her eyes, she smiled and said, "I am so glad you called last week. I'm flattered that you came all this way to see me."

He smiled in return. "Well, it is such a pleasure to invite you to dinner. I needed to be in Seattle to investigate some investments, but I admit, it is because of you that I scheduled this trip."

Mindi heard Charlene's thoughts after Alejandro finished his sentence. *You charmer, you. You know just what to say.*

Unable to control herself, Mindi gave a sarcastic laugh, because she knew this guy was a player—with a wife and two children at home. She realized that her uncontrolled reaction had come out a little too loud, but she stilled her thoughts a little late; Charlene heard the laugh and turned her head abruptly to see where it had come from, so close by.

"Is everything alright?" Alejandro asked.

"Oh, yes. I just thought I heard someone laugh."

Mindi stayed and watched as Alejandro's entire conversation included the right balance of questions and attention to Charlene's answers. He commented at just the right moments and answered appropriately the questions asked of him. He seemed to know how to avoid seeming narcissistic yet conveyed the right amount of self-confidence to appear charming.

After three glasses of wine, both Charlene and Mindi felt the relaxing effects of the alcohol, but Alejo didn't seem affected by what he'd drunk. Alejandro wound up the dinner by announcing that he had an early appointment the next day and was grateful for the wonderful evening that Charlene had shared with him.

His comment surprised Mindi until she realized his strategy—leave them wanting more. She saw right through Alejandro's plan, but she also had to admit that if she didn't know what and who he was, she, too, could be attracted to him for the same reasons as Charlene. As soon as the thought formed in Mindi's mind, she regretted thinking it, because if Charlene felt it, she would read it as a validation of her growing desire. *She's probably going to sleep with him anyway*, Mindi rationalized, and hoped Charlene wouldn't fall for him and get hurt, in serious trouble . . . or worse.

While Alejandro drove Charlene back to her apartment, Mindi decided to wait to leave until she'd confirmed her suspicion that Alejandro wouldn't expect to be asked in for a nightcap. She was right. He gave Charlene a chaste hug, then waited until she'd entered the apartment building. Charlene turned and smiled at him as she closed the door.

Once inside her apartment, Charlene draped her sweater over the back of a chair, went into the bathroom, and looked in the mirror. This triggered a memory in Mindi of when she'd looked into the mirror, knowing now that Jeff had been in her head then. Mindi had felt someone watching her, just as she was now watching Charlene. The difference was that Mindi had thought, in error, that it had been her alter ego, Shirley, the nascent multiple personality whose job it was to protect Mindi from the world and had been gently sent away when Jeff came into Mindi's life.

Mindi waited to see if Charlene suspected she was there. After Charlene searched her eyes for a long moment, her only thought, still slowed by the wine, was, *I'd better be using more of my LaDormeur moisturizer.*

Mindi chuckled at that.

Charlene turned her head to listen, again having heard Mindi, who quickly "Jeannie-nodded" and exited.

~

Jeff settled in next to Mindi. Her even breathing and the rapid movement of her eyes under her lids told him she was dreaming and likely traveling. *Where is she tonight?* He and Mindi were both convinced that only a small portion of their leaps were under their personal control. He pictured themselves as soldiers, following orders on a mission. *No,* he told himself, *we're more like spies, following the dictates of some unseen handlers.*

Jeff fell asleep without thinking about traveling, yet found himself in Alejandro's head, flying his fancy airplane. The sun had given up its last rays off to the left as it began to circle around fields and equipment yards illuminated by the yellow glow of sodium vapor lights. The lights of a city or town sparkled in the distance.

Alejandro, with Jeff literally on board, watched out the window and continued to circle. His cell phone chimed. He answered in Spanish, "Yes, I'm searching now." He waited a moment, saw a flashing light, then added, "I have you, bye."

He checked his instruments, then landed on a dirt airfield used by the ranchers. Clearly, the plane was designed for unimproved airfields, in addition to paved runway airports. As soon as he landed, a late-model SUV drove up and cut its headlights. A large man in coveralls met Alejandro at the bottom of the airplane's stairs, and they shook hands. The entire transaction took place without a word between them.

Alejandro opened the cargo door of the airplane and helped load five boxes with a US-based grocer's logo on them into the SUV.

The SUV pulled away. Alejandro kicked the dust from his shoes, entered the plane, and sealed the automatic stairway. He wiped his hands, fastened his seatbelt, and was again airborne for the short hop to land at the Bakersfield airport. The plane taxied to the general aviation hangars as directed by the tower. Jeff saw the flight plan with the ultimate destination as Seattle. He noted the date and noticed that the flight log conveniently did not include the stop in the farmer's field.

Will anyone comment on the dust on the fuselage? Jeff wondered. Would anyone care? Who would dare to mention it to someone who could obviously afford such a high-end mode of transport?

Alejandro drifted off to sleep. Jeff awoke in Gardena and lay considering the events in the dream until he fell asleep to awake refreshed in the morning with the sound of activity in the kitchen. Mindi was at the stove and smiled at him and said, "I heard you getting up. I couldn't wait to tell you where I went last night."

"That's what I was going to say," Jeff said with a smile.

They shared a hug and a kiss. Mindi handed Jeff a plate of bacon, eggs, and toast. Another "normal" day had begun.

Jeff started the conversation. "Do you realize how far I've come—we've come—in these dreams? I can't imagine what else we might be able to do next." He told her about the boxes unloaded at night at a farmer's airport in California.

"What do you think was in them?" Mindi asked.

Jeff shrugged. "I don't know. I searched his mind but didn't find anything. I'm guessing it was some kind of illegal merchandise; illegal, at least, because they won't pay customs duty fees on it."

While Mindi cooked her eggs and toast, he asked, "What about your leap? Any success?"

Mindi looked over at him and said, "I was in Charlene's mind, having dinner with Alejandro next March." She filled in the details of the date, Alejandro's charm, and how she'd controlled Charlene's phone to get a time stamp. "We couldn't make up a story like this that anybody would believe." She sat down opposite him and started on her breakfast.

As he ate, he nodded thoughtfully at her. "This is good. You are good. Thank you."

"Is that a thank you for breakfast or a thank you for being good?"

His smile answered both her questions. They read each other's journal entries, making sure they had missed no details from each other's story.

~

A few days had gone by with no leaps. This morning, Jeff awoke with the memory of a dream he'd had. Strangely, it had not been a lucid dream. Before the lucid dreaming started months ago and became commonplace, he'd rarely awakened during a regular dream, which is usually only remembered for a short time. Jeff sat on the edge of the bed, struggling to hold on to the details as the dream began to recede. It began with Mindi and him in the gray room discussing a plan to interfere with a drug shipment when they spotted Alejandro eavesdropping nearby. The dream morphed into the couple fleeing but powerless to get traction under their feet as they clambered over a cascading mountain of boxes marked with grocery store logos. Alejandro chased them, and

Tony Moreno followed a few paces behind.

"I know who you are! You're after my drugs," Alejandro shouted. "I know who you are! You're after my drugs."

Jeff was still stumbling forward when he heard Mindi yelling from behind him, "Jeff! I'm caught!" He turned to go back, but the dream ended abruptly, leaving Jeff feeling anxious. It took him a moment to process the helplessness he still felt.

Jeff transcribed the dream and his observation that this was a "normal" dream, obviously drawn from the subjects and substance of their mission, and in a few minutes the anxious feelings abated.

~

Moreno awoke with another dream like many others that he considered an "occupational hazard." He was chasing two men and a woman, none of whom he recognized. The woman called to a man ahead of them. Otherwise, the subject of the dream, probably about drugs, was common for him, and he thought nothing more of it. The dream dissipated and, with Moreno absorbed by his waking duties, was promptly forgotten.

~

Mindi awoke alone in bed feeling anxious because of a dream in which she'd been running, being chased, then caught by Alejandro. She'd stumbled, unable to escape. It wasn't a lucid dream, just a regular dream her subconscious had stitched together. Thankfully, the dream, along with the stress and fear it created, began to fade.

She joined Jeff in the kitchen. While they enjoyed their morning coffee, she read the latest entry in his dream journal and the memory of her dream came flooding back.

Jeff stopped paging through the morning paper and glanced over as she finished reading his journal. She looked at him with her eyes wide.

"What?" He put aside the paper.

Speechless, she looked at the notebook, then up at him.

"Oh, yeah. Strange to have a normal dream after all we've done, right?"

Still stunned by what she'd read, her expression didn't change.

Jeff frowned. "It was just a normal dream. What's the problem? Shouldn't I have written it down?"

Mindi shook her head. "No, no. *I* had the same dream. Just before I woke up, I stumbled. Alejandro caught up to me, and I called out to you."

She and Jeff just looked at each other for a moment, then Jeff slid her journal in front of her, put the pen on the cover and said, "You'd better write that down."

~

Alejandro awakened with a memory of a normal dream, where he'd watched the man and woman talking with each other in that bedeviling gray room about interfering with his shipment of drugs. The dream then shifted, and he'd chased them up a hill of falling cardboard boxes, shouting at each other, using their names. A man wearing a jacket with the letters *DEA* emblazoned on it had been chasing him.

He admitted to being a little superstitious, but he could logically interpret and calculate clues. He and Karina had heard those same names before, and he'd seen the dark-haired woman's face and name on the magazine cover. He had seen them in that vast, gray room. She was a real person. Was this "Jeff" a real person too?

He smiled as he realized a spirit, a *friendly* spirit, had sent him this dream as a message to warn him of impending danger to his business. He would take seriously the warning that these two demons wanted to interfere with him and his partners. The essence of the warning did not fade like the dream's details, forming into firm resolve to protect himself and the shipment—at all costs.

~

The two agents watched the unmarked Ford Transit van park near the gate at the marina in Long Beach. The driver made a call on his cell phone.

Moreno got out of the passenger side of the Suburban, wandered over to the van, and showed his badge to the driver, who made eye contact and nodded. The driver retrieved a clipboard from the door pocket and handed it to the agent. With his back to his partner in the Suburban, Moreno removed something from under the clip and deftly slipped it into his shirt pocket and returned the clipboard.

The automatic gate snapped open. Moreno walked back to his rig, sat sideways with the door open, and lit a cigarette. The van driver stacked boxes on the hand truck—the open one on top showed plastic bags of fresh vegetables.

Both agents watched as the van driver rolled three more loads of boxes through the gate, and the two crew members loaded them aboard the *Miranda II*.

"What did you say to him, Tony?"

"I just told him there'd been some problems with break-ins, and we'd been asked to keep an eye on things. He didn't look closely at the badge." He looked back over his shoulder and smiled. "Used my thumb."

The other agent chuckled. "Yeah, works every time."

Moreno took a final drag on his cigarette, stepped down, and rubbed the tip on the asphalt, scattered what was left with his shoe, then walked to a trash can and put the butt inside. He knew where the security cameras were and didn't want an angry harbormaster calling downtown, complaining of agents littering his parking lot. Other agents had gotten memos before, and he didn't want something so trivial ending up in *his* file.

~

This would be the last photo session for another couple of weeks, and it would be a non-standard shoot. What made it different was the art director wanted it to be a whole-day session with multiple models and multiple photographers for a related series of ads, each with a different product and different models with the beach backdrop for each that would run across all media. They had been told it would be a long day.

They'd been at Venice Beach early. The sun was coming up and the sky to the west was still dark, forming a moody horizon. The rising sunlight from the east cast long shadows toward the water that the art director liked. She wanted as many shots as possible as the sun climbed overhead. Throughout the day, they shot video for TV spots and stills for magazine and billboard ads. When they weren't in the makeup tent, they were on set, waiting, or taking direction from the half-dozen photographers that kept moving around and asking the models to move and pose for the camera, and pose for each other—a complicated day.

There were over a dozen makeup models, some in swimsuits, some in street clothes, yet all barefoot in the sand and surf. The photographers shot close-ups, wide-angle groups, individuals, and couples, all having a good time. As the sun moved, at the command of each photographer, grips moved the reflectors, scrims, and lights. Further back from the water, a crowd of citizens congregated to watch the unusual photoshoot that looked as complicated as a set for a motion picture.

By midafternoon, the clouds moved in, and the models hoped shooting might be called, but the director saw great expression in the clouds and wanted to use the sun that broke through as a natural backdrop. By the time they wrapped in the late afternoon, they were exhausted from the long day but went to a local lounge for tapas and drinks.

Jeff and Mindi fell asleep as soon as their heads hit their pillows, and they immediately found themselves inside the now familiar minds of Alejandro and Charlene. When Mindi realized where she was, she immediately, in her mind, said quietly, *You there?*

Jeff telepathed back to her, *Frisbee.*

Mindi chuckled.

Alejandro and Charlene were walking toward the ocean on North Venice Blvd with the crowd. For Jeff and Mindi, it was the second time that day. The couple approached a group of people watching the action on the beach. A photo shoot was in process with models, photographers, grips, and attendants efficiently moving around. Alejandro led the way to get a closer look but remained a respectable distance away, to avoid being a nuisance to the work going on.

Trusting that Alejandro wouldn't hear his projected thoughts, Jeff telepathed to Mindi, *This is* our *photoshoot!*

Alejandro didn't notice Jeff's statement, his focus being on the beautiful women in swimsuits. One woman held his interest for a very long moment—Mindi.

Jeff, too, watched Mindi on the beach from earlier that day, while he calculated that her mind was next to him in Charlene's head while her body slept in Gardena. He gave up trying to work out the logic.

The photographer lowered her camera and motioned to someone else to move into the frame. The male model turned around—it was Jeff. Alejandro concentrated on the action.

Mindi whispered to Jeff telepathically, *Can you see that? There we are. We are here, and . . . How is that?*

Charlene looked around, then touched Alejandro's arm. "Did you hear that?"

"What, Bonita? Hear what?"

~

Mindi was concerned about Charlene's question to Alejandro and responded by being quiet. She wanted to call out to Jeff but didn't dare. She was glad she hadn't used his name, because Charlene *had* heard her and would've heard Jeff's name had she used it. What was she to do? If she "Jeannied" herself out, and she didn't answer Jeff when he reached out to her, would he call out to her louder and give himself away to Alejandro?

Mindi concentrated and focused on Jeff's mind without using words. She couldn't get his attention. Then an idea hit her. In a loud inner voice, she called out as if she were calling to Jeff but only said, *Jeannie!* Mindi awoke in her bed next to Jeff, who was sleeping, his mind still in Alejandro's head

169

sixteen miles away, and earlier that day.

A few moments later, Jeff stirred, opened his eyes, and said, "Is everything alright? I heard you escape." He sat up. "Is anything wrong?"

Mindi said, "Charlene heard me talk to you and asked Alejandro, 'Did you hear that?' He said he'd heard nothing. I was afraid if I said more, she'd get suspicious, and I felt I had to leave. I'm glad you heard me leave. How could we be there, watching ourselves in our past?"

Jeff shrugged. "I don't know. We time traveled back a few hours to see ourselves on the beach, and that's interesting, but I think the important question is, what were *they* doing there?"

"It would be easy for them to fly to LA in his plane. Charlene gets to visit a special photo shoot, gets to hang with the guy, and have a holiday. He shows off his expensive toy and his money. It's pretty obvious that Charlene's interested in him."

Jeff nodded. "Well, that answers the why and how they got there. The when was earlier today." He looked at the clock. "Well, actually yesterday. I didn't notice them standing there at the shoot. Did you?"

"No," she said.

"So the who, what, where, when, and how of them has been answered. But missing is the why *we* were there to see them watching us work. He already knows you're a model." An instant later, Jeff realized the reason. "That's it! We were there to see that he has placed my face in the real world *and* now knows we work together. That completes the loop when he saw us together in the gray room. In spy language, we've been made. Well, sort of."

"What do you mean, sort of?"

"He may not know for sure that am I the 'Jeff' guy from

our bathroom leap, though he probably suspects it. He's seen us together in the gray room and now us working together."

He waited for Mindi to interject, but she just nodded, so he went on. "Although . . . It *was* just a name in the bathroom . . ." Jeff was trying to deny that Alejandro could have put the name, face, and voice together, but relented. "He's not stupid. He'll figure it out. I just hope Charlene doesn't find out what we're doing. It could ruin your career."

"I'm not worried about the job," Mindi said. "I can get another."

"Have we given him any reason to suspect we know about the drugs?" Jeff said.

Mindi thought a moment. "No, I don't think so. But even so, he could still be dangerous. We have to stay out of their heads, stay ghosts so they won't hear us again."

"Yeah, that's safer. The downside is we can't find out what they're thinking unless we're in their heads."

"We still could leap if we stayed quiet. You know, when you'd leaped into my mind, when you said nothing, I was paranoid that someone was watching me. Or it gave me a headache. See what I mean?"

"Agreed. We still have 'frisbee' if we disguise our voices in their heads, and we can go ghost and leave their minds if we need to talk to each other."

"If we leap while they're asleep, then we can search around."

"I agree. But we can't start nightmares with bad memories . . ."

"Yeah, we've got to be careful. And quiet—like we're breaking and entering."

"Agreed."

"You sure are agreeable tonight. Is there anything else you might be agreeable to?"

CHAPTER 12

Jeff still had research to do on the illicit product's shipping schedule. Tonight, while Mindi slept, and maybe traveled, Jeff did *his* exploring on the internet. He looked up the *HMM Aisling* and saw that it had a regular route up and down the Atlantic coast, from Brazil to Argentina to Uruguay, Venezuela, then to Cartagena and Barranquilla. After that, through the Panama Canal, stops on the west coast of Mexico to San Diego, and then Long Beach, Los Angeles, and points north.

But Jeff was only interested in the Cartagena to Long Beach leg of the route. With six stops in between, allowing for no significant delay, the ship would spend twenty-four hours in each port. Add sailing time between ports and through the canal, the trip would be sixteen days. Arrival was scheduled for the Port of Long Beach container terminal on June 26, and he knew the sailing date from Cartagena was June 11. Records he found online showed there were rarely delays. The note given to Carlos Cordoba by Señora Valencia in the Cartagena restaurant had now been thoroughly decoded. But it didn't answer why the *Miranda II* was docked at the

Cabrillo Marina, with Roberto on board, just across the water from the Long Beach Container Terminal. Maybe he just wanted to be close by when the container was unloaded. Still, that seemed like an extravagant luxury if no one on the yacht was ever to handle the product.

He was happy that his research had paid off, but he still would have liked to know how to tie those on the yacht to the shipment and pass the information to the DEA.

Jeff wanted to get into Roberto's mind to validate the June 26 arrival of the drugs from Colombia, so he returned to the marina in his astral body. Lights shone in the harbormaster's tower through the windows that overlooked the marina. On a whim, Jeff went in. Did the short-term berths need reservations? Did they need, like a hotel, check-in and checkout dates? Could he find out what plans had been made for the *Miranda II* at the marina?

A few papers were on the desks. Several computer terminals lined the walls, most of which had dark screens. But one on the counter was awake, and it had a spreadsheet open on the screen to exactly the type of information that Jeff was looking for, but it didn't show the *Miranda II*. Reflexively, he tried to touch the keyboard, but his hands were useless. He closed his eyes and tried to duplicate what Mindi had done with the phone and coffee maker, but he couldn't. *Gotta get Mindi on this.* At that moment, a man wearing a short-sleeved shirt with a pocket protector full of pens walked into the room and stepped up to the computer terminal.

Pocket-protector guy scrolled through the spreadsheet and made some entries. Jeff thought, *What the hell*, and leaped into the night employee's mind. At first, the man shook his head and rubbed his eyes as if trying to fight Jeff's intrusion. But the man's cell phone rang, and the distraction allowed

Jeff to slip in past the resistance.

During a pause in the man's personal conversation with a woman, Jeff whispered in his mind, *Look up the* Miranda II*'s records.* The man continued the conversation, and the couple made a date to meet for coffee when he got off shift. After the call ended, the clerk hit a few keystrokes on the keyboard and the pages with the *Miranda II*'s information appeared on the screen. Jeff had just memorized Roberto's phone number and the departure date when he heard the clerk's thought, *what am I doing?* He closed the screen.

Jeff floated over to the *Miranda II*, satisfied that the detour had given him a couple of data points that could prove useful.

On the yacht, 'Berto sat in the lounge, alone and asleep with a book on his chest, mouth open in a silent snore.

Jeff slipped into 'Berto's mind more easily than the guy in the harbormaster's office and found him in deep sleep, perhaps between REM sleep sessions. *What can I do here?*

He passed through an unmarked portal into a bare gray room and called out, "Hello? Anybody home?" Jeff heard what sounded like scuffing feet. He realized he really didn't want to be seen and became invisible.

Roberto's avatar materialized, dressed as he was in the yacht's lounge, and walked tentatively into the space. He looked in Jeff's direction but didn't see him.

Good to know, Jeff thought.

"What? Who said that?" 'Berto's image said, looking around.

Jeff watched as his host wandered around, but after seeing only a limitless gray horizon in all directions, he shrugged his shoulders and disappeared. Jeff's goal was 'Berto's hippocampus memories regarding June 26, and he moved into a passageway, thinking he would get to that destination, but snapped back into the host's gray room. *Strange.* Jeff tried it several times with a different visualized goal each time, and the result was the same, an instant return to the gray room. *This was a waste of time*, Jeff thought. He exited back into the lounge as a ghost and watched the man stir in his sleep, took flight and returned to his own body. He sat on his pillow wondering about the mechanics of Roberto's mind that wouldn't let him look around. Would he ever get an answer?

~

The next morning, as Mindi awoke, Jeff was sitting on the edge of the bed watching her.

"What? Anything wrong?" she asked.

"No, everything's okay, Beautiful. I love watching you sleep. Your dream must have been something, because your eyes were working overtime behind your eyelids."

"Not too interesting. I'll tell you all about it. Give me a minute."

"I'll meet you in the kitchen."

Mindi told him she had landed in Miranda Valencia's head without having targeted her. The woman was alone, flying to Long Beach from Bogotá.

"It was June 1, with a one-way ticket. I didn't stay long, but long enough to hear her talk on the phone with 'Berto, though I couldn't get much because they were talking so fast. I just got the vibe that everything is still a go, whatever 'everything' is. She was reading a Danielle Steele novel, but in Spanish. I tried to read along, but I'm not ready for that yet." She chuckled.

"Anything else?"

"No. What did you do?"

Jeff told her about his night and finished with, "I wish there was a manual for this stuff."

"That's it?"

"For the traveling, yes. But before I went, I did some research on the internet and calculated when the *HMM Aisling* would leave Cartagena and arrive Long Beach by the twenty-sixth. That's public information." He opened his laptop and went to the website with the schedules to show her. "So now we have the container number, arrival date, Roberto's phone number and that the *Miranda II* sails July 1."

"But what we *don't* know," Mindi said, "is where the container comes from in Colombia, how it gets to Cartagena, who drives that truck, who picks it up in Long Beach, and how the cargo is distributed. And . . . we don't know where the *Miranda II* is going after it leaves Long Beach. We know some but not all of the plan."

Jeff nodded. "Right. And I'd like to know why the DEA is watching the *Miranda II*. They must suspect something. Maybe 'Berto's a bad actor with priors, or something. We need to know more. Do you want to go on a 'fishing trip' to Moreno for more info? It might be useful if you could operate a computer. I tried at the marina but couldn't make it work. What do you say?"

~

By traveling out-of-body in the daytime, they had the freedom of not being on a clogged-up freeway and arrived immediately in the DEA's offices, which were bustling with activity. Jeff reminded Mindi to avoid letting anyone walk through them. First, they went to the receptionist area, hoping to find where Moreno's desk was, but saw no seating chart. They wandered around, looking at the names on the office doors and the name plaques on the dozens of cubicles.

Intent on speeding up the process, Jeff said, "Why don't we split up and look around? We can call to each other when we find him." If anyone could hear them, it would be lost in the buzz of ambient office noise,

But as Mindi turned to go, without warning, a woman came out of the restroom and walked right through her. The woman held her arms against the chill she felt. Jeff wondered if whenever he'd gotten a chill on a warm day, he had walked through a ghost. He looked at Mindi and pointed up as he lifted to fly above people's heads to avoid similar ghostly contact with others.

After a few minutes, he heard Mindi call and followed her voice to a cubicle where two men were talking with Moreno at his desk. They were arguing about who was the better team in LA, the Warriors or the Clippers.

Jeff said, "Let's try something new, see if we can both slip inside his mind," and vanished from her view as he entered the agent's head.

She jumped inside, too. *Where are you?* Mindi asked.

Moreno rolled his head around, as if trying to break the tight feeling he'd just felt in his neck and shoulders.

I'm here. I can sense you. I'm seeing through his eyes.

Yeah, me too. What do you want to do?

Let's look through his memories for the reason for the surveillance of the yacht.

Moreno said to the other agents, "Hey, guys, I'll catch up with you later. I've just remembered something I've got to check."

Jeff snapped back to seeing through Moreno's eyes to see what the agent was going to look at, leaving Mindi to snoop around in the agent's memory.

What was it I wanted to check? Moreno thought, rubbing his temples. He pinched the bridge of his nose, rubbed his eyes, then glanced at the ceiling before shaking his head. He stared at files on his desk. *Oh, yeah.* He pulled a thick file out of a pile, opened it, and scanned the standard government-style notes—brutally simple, written in third-person narrative.

Jeff read along with Moreno and, on the final page, was a mention of the delivery of boxes by the food service delivery driver. Jeff wondered, not being careful with his quiet thoughts, *Are those the packages that Alejandro unloaded from the plane at the farm in Bakersfield?*

Moreno looked around to see who was talking near his cubicle. He stood and looked around but, seeing no one, returned to his seat. Moreno tipped his head sideways as if trying to remember something, then Jeff heard him think, *There's that name again.* He wrote the name "Alejandro" on a notepad, followed by a question mark.

Jeff saw nothing new in that file that indicated why the DEA had put the yacht under their scrutiny. He wanted Moreno to hear him. *Do you know when the* Miranda II *is scheduled to depart?*

Moreno listened as if hearing something being whispered, gave his head a shake, and wrote on the notepad next to Alejandro's name, *When does* Miranda II *sail?*

Jeff felt satisfied and went in search of Mindi. He wandered around the agent's mind—lots of hallways and doors, like wandering in a huge office building. *Where's Mindi?*

He sensed her nearby when he heard her say, *Watch this.*

As if she'd pressed play on a DVD player, they watched a scene unfold from Moreno's point of view when he and his surveillance partner had watched the *Miranda II* at the marina. They saw the agent talk to the delivery driver, pocket the bills from the clipboard, then converse with his partner back at the van as Moreno smoked his cigarette.

Now this, Mindi said. They watched Moreno, when he got home the next morning, put the money in an envelope with a stack of other bills in his desk.

As soon as they finished watching that memory, they left Moreno's mind to talk and not be heard by him.

How did you find those memories? Jeff asked.

I sensed you had left, so I followed you back to his eyes and watched while he read the file, then wrote Alejandro's name. I just, well, kind of asked to see a recent memory of him at the marina, and that's what I found. It sure looks like he's been taking bribes. What do you think?

Jeff nodded. *Looks suspicious. But I have to say, I didn't feel any guilt wrapped around that memory. It seemed licit, unless that's the way a crooked cop feels about things like that. We should have asked what he knows about Roberto.*

Do you want to go back? Mindi asked.

If we do, do you think it will alert him with us going back in?

I don't care, Mindi replied. *I'd like to know. Let's go back and check.*

They slipped back into Moreno's mind and "asked" about Valencia but found nothing they didn't already know. They tried "Carlos Cordoba." Nothing. They tried "cocaine." The results that appeared were like searching the internet; there were hundreds of hits and numerous pathways that lit up. Jeff narrowed the search to "drugs and *Miranda II.*" They found his memory of a briefing with the LA Bureau chief and five other agents in a conference room.

The DEA had watched the yacht this year because it was registered in Colombia, which alone was enough to have created immediate suspicion, but they had no evidence that the *Miranda II* was actually involved in drug smuggling. At the beginning of the surveillance, the DEA had merely been keeping agents busy, hoping something would turn up. Their research uncovered information that the yacht was registered to a construction company in Cartagena with the CEO and CFO of the company. They were brothers, last name Diaz, who owned the yacht free and clear. During the meeting, they mentioned Roberto Valencia as being the current occupant and gave no information regarding the crew. When research showed the *Miranda II* had been in port twice in the last year and matched those dates with Caltrans trucking permits, they found those same dates, each with those being the only permits for that company visiting the container terminal in the last year. There was a single open permit for June 26 and 27 this year. That created enough suspicion to continue surveillance. A shell corporation owned the trucking company. There were no direct ties to the Diazes or Valencia.

Moreno now had a raging headache from his "visitors" doing their research. He took two aspirin and the headache abated. He thought it was the aspirin, but it was because Jeff and Mindi had finally left.

The couple discussed their findings.

"How could we learn if Roberto works for the Diaz brothers?" Mindi asked. "You had trouble negotiating 'Berto's mind, but a leap into his wife's head might give us something. What do you think?"

Jeff grinned. "I think you are really enjoying this detective work, that's what I think. This sleuthing might be a new calling for you. You have quite a knack for it."

~

180

They arrived above the apartment building, expecting to drop back into their bodies and continue the day in real-time. Instead, they saw a neighbor lying on the floor in her kitchen.

Mindi's eyes widened in alarm. "Mrs. Jackson! She lives alone. Jeff, what do we do?"

They hovered just below the ceiling, looking at Mrs. Jackson's prone body. A ghostly image of the woman, looking anxious, stood beside her refrigerator.

"Mindi," Jeff said, "go call 911, ambulance needed. Then call your building manager. Tell her you heard a sound and suggest a wellness check. I'll stay with her."

While Mindi floated through the wall to her apartment, rejoined her body, and made her phone calls, Jeff moved next to the image of Mrs. Jackson. She was terrified.

"Mrs. Jackson," Jeff said, "don't be alarmed. I'm a friend. Someone is calling for help."

Mrs. Jackson's image noticed him and, in a fearful tone, said, "What's wrong with me? What's happening?"

Jeff stood by her, held her hand, and told her everything would be okay. Within moments, they heard a sound at the front door. The apartment manager entered, called out and when she heard nothing, found Mrs. Jackson on the floor of the kitchen and gasped. Even before the manager could lean down and check her, a siren came to an abrupt stop out front and bleeped twice. Footsteps in the hallway drew closer, and two paramedics entered, guided by Mindi. The manager stepped aside, and they proceeded to their tasks.

Mrs. Jackson and Jeff watched them working on her unconscious form while Jeff continued to hold her hand to reassure her. After a few moments, she withdrew her hand and gently slid back into her body. Her eyes fluttered. She coughed, took a deep breath from the oxygen mask, and tried

181

to sit up, but the paramedic spoke in a soothing voice and placed his hand on her shoulder to encourage her to remain lying down.

Mindi looked around, as if looking for Jeff, but, of course, couldn't see him. Jeff left the apartment to get his body. He then joined Mindi watching from the doorway, standing with the apartment manager.

The manager, Mrs. Mackenzie, turned to the couple. "You said you heard her fall. How did you hear that in your apartment?" She didn't wait for an answer. "Anyway, I'm glad you did. Thank you for calling me." She looked at Mrs. Jackson, then back to Mindi. "But how could you hear her?"

Mindi shrugged. "I don't know."

"Does she have family we can notify?" one of the paramedics asked.

"It'd be in her file," Mrs. Mackenzie said. "I'll go check."

"She's conscious, and her BP is coming back up," the paramedic said. "Mrs. Jackson, do you have any medical conditions, diabetes, or heart condition might have made you faint?"

The woman shook her head, accompanied by a muffled, "No." She tried to sit up again.

"I think we should take you to a hospital for observation. Is that alright with you?"

Mrs. Jackson nodded. She lifted her head and her eyes settled on Jeff. Her brow knitted together for a moment. She blinked, looked directly into his eyes, and silently mouthed, *Thank you.*

A police officer knocked on the open apartment door, entered, and asked, "Who called 911?"

"I did," Mindi replied.

The officer took her statement, and Mrs. Mackenzie handed him a piece of paper. " Her daughter's name and number are there."

"Thank you, ma'am," one of the paramedics said. "Make way." They wheeled the woman into the waiting ambulance.

As the ambulance pulled away, sans siren, the landlady pulled the door to Mrs. Jackson's apartment shut and locked it. "Thank you for being a good neighbor."

Mindi and Jeff bid Mrs. Mackenzie a good day and returned to Mindi's apartment to debrief and write in their journals.

"Mrs. Jackson looked right at you and said thank you," Mindi said over lunch. "Did you talk to her after I left?"

"Yeah. She looked scared watching herself lying there on the floor. I told her not to be alarmed, that someone would be coming to help. When they gave her oxygen, she went back into her body and woke up. It was amazing to watch. This whole out-of-body stuff—I never imagined doing anything like this. Maybe *this* is our calling, instead of being detectives—helping others in distress."

Mindi shrugged. "Maybe. It feels good, doesn't it? I'm glad we could help. Do you think she'll remember you helped her?"

"I don't know. I hope she was still in a kind of twilight space when she looked at me and won't remember. We don't want our cover blown, do we?" Jeff said with a smile.

"No. We'd end up guinea pigs for sure."

"Ingrid inferred that there are others like us. So do you think they intervene like this? I wonder if this is where the stories of guardian angels come from."

~

Later that week, Mindi leaped into Miranda Valencia on board the yacht, while Jeff jumped into Moreno in the Suburban. They kept telepathic contact to a minimum to avoid detection.

They needed answers to important questions. Was Moreno on the take? If not, what was the cash about? Why was the yacht there, if the shipment might go from the container terminal to somewhere in the valley for distribution, and was it important to know what was in the boxes Alejandro flew in and had delivered to the yacht?

Miranda, with Mindi listening, heard 'Berto's side of a phone conversation with Carlos. Even with Mindi's expanding Spanish vocabulary, the speed at which they talked limited what she understood to just the truck driver's name who would claim the container when it arrived. 'Berto had repeated it—Manuel Alvarez.

After that telephone call, Miranda and 'Berto left the yacht to go to a restaurant there at the harbor. They walked in clear view of the DEA agents. Mindi, feeling playful, wanted to wave at Jeff, so she left Miranda's mind, returned to ghost phase, and followed behind the couple as they passed in front of the Suburban. The agents wouldn't see her, but she hoped Jeff would be watching.

Jeff was watching through Moreno's eyes and saw as Mindi emerged from Miranda and waved at him. The other agent's digital camera, set on burst mode, took a rapid series of stills of Roberto and Miranda. When they entered the restaurant, he reviewed the photos on the camera's digital screen. All the shots were fine, except the ones when the couple walked past the SUV. Those photos showed a foggy blur trailing the couple. The camera had captured Mindi's ghost image.

He showed the photos to his partner. "Has that ever

happened to you? All the rest are good."

Moreno shrugged. "Get rid of them. Looks like the street-light screwed them up."

With a dozen clicks, the pictures of a real-life poltergeist were deleted.

Jeff had tried to find Moreno's memories about the bribe money but came up with nothing. Had Jeff's "requisition for information" from the universe failed him? Was there nothing to find? Or was the guy just a crooked cop?

Back at the apartment, Mindi shared the truck driver's name, and Jeff told her how the camera had captured her ghost image—two more data points that might come in handy.

～

Two nights later, while asleep, Jeff and Mindi went to the gray room to check on whether Alejandro had been there. Jeff hadn't protected access because they wanted to know if Alejandro would come back to check on the note, or maybe leave another.

They weren't disappointed. Once again, Jeff saw the apparent serendipity of the timing of their visits. While standing there looking at the note, they saw a doorway open. They instantly turned invisible and watched Alejandro walk in. Jeff moved behind the intruder and momentarily became visible for Mindi to see, pointed at Alejandro, and then grabbed his wrist to communicate to her he wanted to trap the intruder, then disappeared.

How to do it? Jeff imagined a cage with just enough room for the chair around Alejandro.

As soon as the captive saw the bars, he stood and shook them and shouted in Spanish, "What's happening? Let me out. Let me out!"

Mindi telepathed to Jeff, *You know, this could be serious. Remember what Ingrid said.*

Jeff answered, *Yeah. We won't keep him long. Let's find where he's sleeping, see if he's okay.*

Instantly, they were looking down on a condominium building on Lake Washington.

"Is this his condo?" Mindi asked.

"I guess so," Jeff replied. "The universe takes us where we want to go."

They found Alejandro and Charlene asleep. Alejandro's body twitched and jerked slightly. His eyes moved wildly behind closed lids. Sleep paralysis, the body's safety system to prevent self-harm during a violent or terrifying dream, was working overtime.

Mindi frowned. "What should we do?"

They looked at each other, and without speaking, he knew he needed to set Alejandro free. Charlene remained asleep, but if the body's movement increased, she might awaken.

"Jeff, leap into his mind right away, right here!" Mindi suggested. "Set him free. I'll stay here and watch out for him. I hope Charlene doesn't wake up." She saw Jeff's image dissolve into the sleeping man's head.

Jeff was back in the gray room, now seeing through Alejandro's eyes and feeling the panic of confinement. Alejandro froze for a moment at Jeff's arrival, then again struggled, pushing and shaking the bars. He sat in the chair and kicked with his feet, reached up at the bars on top and pulled down, but to no avail.

Jeff tried to soothe the captive, but Alejandro's panic was so great he didn't hear Jeff's voice. Then, with intent, Jeff tried to dissolve the bars to free him. He failed.

Jeff, I'm in here with you. What can I do? Jeff heard Mindi's voice in his mind while he was in Alejandro's mind.

Mindi, what are you doing here?

Charlene's still asleep, and I felt powerless. Maybe I can help.

This isn't working, Jeff said. *I've got to get out of his head!* But he couldn't exit the man's mind or remove the cage.

Alejandro crossed himself, and Jeff heard him think, *This is a dream. I should be able to control it. I should be able to wake up. What is wrong?*

Jeff again tried to reassure the man, but this time all that Alejandro heard was a low groan that increased his terror.

We've got to set him free, Mindi said.

We've got to get ourselves free first, Jeff replied.

The captive heard that exchange clearly. He said aloud, "Yes, set me free. Get out of my head and let me go!"

Jeff felt Alejandro's panic, and that panic transferred to Mindi.

What do we do? Her voice was laden with fear.

I don't know. Just a minute, I have to concentrate. He visualized meditation breaths and wished the bars to disappear. They shuddered and shimmered with a blue light, then returned to solid black. He visualized them gone. They remained solid.

Jeff! Mindi shouted. *It's getting tighter in here.*

Alejandro shook the bars. Jeff imagined them evaporating. Instead, they contracted, tightening down around the man's virtual body.

Mindi gasped. ·

Jeff conjured a switch set in the "on" position. His hand, within his captive's mind, reached for the switch and, with much effort, pulled it to "off."

The bars turned to shimmering columns of glitter

and evaporated.

The captive stumbled forward, away from the chair. He turned and with wild eyes looked to where he'd been trapped. He staggered to the other chair, grabbed the note, crushed it in his hand and ran, his arms flailing wildly. Unable to keep his balance, he tripped over tangled feet and fell. He tried to get up but his legs would not obey.

Jeff and Mindi were still trapped in the man's mind. The man on the floor writhed as if in pain, attempted again to stand, but collapsed, his face slamming into the floor with a resounding slap.

Ow! The couple felt the pain of the impact.

This is not good, Mindi said, her voice rising with panic.

Mindi, you've got to go! Jeff said urgently. *I've tried to leave, but you're anchoring us here. You pull me back.*

I'll try!

Jeff imagined her folded arms and the head shake, but she remained with him.

Jeff. I'm stuck. I'm still here.

Jeff forced himself to sound calm. *Okay. We go together.*

Alejandro's writhing had stopped. He lay as if unconscious, his breathing shallow.

Jeff said, *His eyes are closed. I can't see. He isn't moving. We've got to get out. Ciao!*

No change. A long quiet pause passed while Jeff took meditation breaths.

Ciao! Mindi shouted *Jeannie!* . . . *I'm still here, Jeff. We're both still here. What if we can't get out?* Terror laced her voice.

Jeff felt her fear and worked to be calm.

Okay, this is like a computer reset. Let me think.

Bands tightened around their minds.

Jeff! What's happening?

Deep breaths, Mindi. We'll wake up. Okay?

Okay. Mindi's voice still had an edge to it.

Jeannie. He waited. *Jeannie!* Jeff repeated with greater firmness. *That didn't work.* Then again, with stronger intention, *Ciao!*

Nothing, Jeff. What's wrong?

I can't see.

Mindi took a deep breath and took charge. *I know. I know! I know what to do! I'm going to scream—very loud. Right now. Ready?*

What?

Wake up! Mindi's yell reverberated through their minds like a cannon.

Alejandro's body shook violently.

Suddenly Jeff, with Mindi still in his mind, stood next to the prone Alejandro in the gray room. His image dissolved, leaving a residue of glitter on the floor before it too was gone. Without thinking of a destination, Jeff instantly was standing next to the bed, looking at the couple asleep in Seattle.

Mindi? Jeff said, *where are you?*

I'm here with you. Jeff heard in his mind.

In another instant, he awoke in Mindi's apartment. He looked at Mindi's body asleep next to him. Her breathing was shallow.

He heard her voice again. *Jeff, I'm still in your mind. I can feel your worry.*

"Mindi, you need to wake up. Please!"

Jeannie! he heard her say in his mind. A few moments passed. *I'm still here, aren't I?*

He frowned. "Yes."

Jeannie, she said again.

Jeff reached to feel her pulse. As he touched her neck, he

felt her leave his mind.

She inhaled sharply, opened her eyes, and looked toward him.

Jeff helped her to a sitting position, wrapped her in his arms, and rocked her. "Oh, thank God."

They were drenched in sweat.

She returned the hug, then they leaned against the headboard and stared at the wall opposite them.

"Jeff? I thought you didn't believe in God. But you just thanked him." She let out a brief, humorless chuckle.

Jeff looked at her and smiled. "Yeah, yeah. I know. In war, they say there are no atheists in a foxhole." He laughed with relief.

They sat in silence for quite a while before Jeff's fear dissipated enough for him to say, "That was a pretty stiff price to pay to see if the trapping thing works."

Mindi still felt in charge. "Okay. Let's analyze this. We went to the gray room in my mind, on a standard sleep-leap. You trapped him in the gray room, and then we transitioned to OBE directly to Seattle. Then you leaped into his mind in his bedroom there and were back in the gray room but in his mind, which is really inside my mind. Right?"

Jeff nodded. "I follow. I looped back to the gray room in his mind without going back to my body first. I must have tied myself in a kind of knot . . . Go on."

"So he was in my mind, in the gray room, and then you were in his mind, in my mind, in the gray room. My mind was OBE in Charlene's bedroom. Then I leaped into your mind, through his brain in Seattle to end up in his mind, with your mind in the gray room—in my mind." Mindi looked at Jeff, who returned the look without reacting. "Jeff, we got all knotted together when I joined you. It was my fault, right?"

190

She looked at him for confirmation.

He shrugged. "Yeah, that's the sequence, but you're not to blame. *We* reacted rather than thinking it through." He gave her a hug. "In computer talk, we locked up the program in sort of a do-loop when we got into his mind, and I think we maxed out the RAM." He tried to laugh, but it wasn't funny. Then, under his breath, he added, "If the program had crashed, it could've been bad."

"Ingrid said it could be dangerous," Mindi replied. "I didn't think it could be dangerous for us, just for the captive. I'm sorry we did that to him, even though he's a creep. And I bet he's sorry. He won't come back"

"Yeah. I do hope he's alright, that there's no permanent damage. Before we bounced back here, I saw them in Seattle. They were still asleep."

Mindi nodded. "I know. I was there with you." She paused a moment. "If we hadn't gotten out of his head, what would have happened?"

"Dunno. Glad we didn't find out. It's best we keep things simple from now on and not combine our tricks. A ghost plus a leap or from a leap to a ghost and back again is as far as I want to go. Okay?" Jeff looked back at Mindi. "That was scary."

Mindi held his arm to her body. "I love you, Jeff. I don't want . . ." She left the sentence unfinished.

Jeff kissed her. "I love you too."

They cuddled and fell into a welcome, dreamless sleep.

~

Alejandro awoke and jerked upright, pulling the covers off Charlene and startling her awake.

"What? What's going on?" Charlene said. "Alejo, are you okay? What's the matter?"

He sat on the edge of the bed, drenched with sweat. Every muscle in his body was tense.

"Did you have a dream?" Charlene put her hand on his back. He flinched and she pulled her arm away.

He stood, looked around, and made his way to the bathroom on unsteady legs.

When he returned, Charlene asked him if he wanted to talk about it.

Alejandro sat on the edge of the bed, shoulders slumped, swaying back and forth. The dream had not faded. The terror still enveloped him. He shook his head slowly.

Charlene sat quietly.

After a few minutes, he turned toward her and asked, "Have you ever had a dream, were trapped, and could not escape?"

The question was rhetorical. He didn't expect an answer. She reached out her hand, but he didn't take it. She put her hands in her lap and showed no anger or attitude at his refusal.

"*Estaba en una carcel.* I was trapped . . ."

"What does '*carcel*' mean?"

"*Carcel. Una jaula.* How to say it? A jail. A cage. I was in a cage in the middle of a room with no walls. I was alone. A large empty room except for chairs. Everything was gray—even those chairs. I had been there before. This time, I was put in a cage with no door. I could not move it, could not get away. There were voices in my head. I was trapped."

He looked at her and saw confusion on her face.

"*Por favor.* Forgive me. *Una pesadilla;* a bad dream. You must return to sleep. Think nothing of it." He touched her face. "Please. I am sorry to have awakened you."

For Alejandro, the nightmare in the gray room replayed: the bars, the voices, his struggle. His mind raced . . . *It was those demons . . . those same demons!* Exhausted, the veil of sleep finally descended.

⁓

Charlene stared at the ceiling. *A huge gray room? No walls? Gray chairs? Was he . . . ? How could he . . . ? No, it's not possible.* She shook her head and the comfort of denial shrouded her imagination. When she felt Alejo relax into his sleep, she too slept.

CHAPTER 13

Jeff was determined to ensure that Agent Moreno had the information necessary to seize the shipment coming into Long Beach in June. But there were doubts regarding the money taken from the delivery driver. Jeff assumed the driver had delivered, besides groceries, the five boxes unloaded from the airplane outside of Bakersfield. Was that money associated with the delivery? Did guests who visited the yacht ever leave with anything?

It was time to get into Moreno's head and find out—first, could he be trusted? And second, could Jeff plant enough information for Moreno to pull off a successful raid on the container of drugs? How could he do it?

Jeff talked it over with Mindi, and they decided he'd get into Moreno's head while he was asleep and create an REM dream sequence in order to feed him the information. But only if he could be trusted. The only way to know was to pay another visit to Moreno to search around in his memory for an explanation for the money accumulating in his desk drawer.

Jeff hoped that kismet would put him exactly where

he needed to be to get the much-needed information to go forward with their plan. He meditated, went out-of-body, and when he got to the Federal Building, eased into Moreno's mind. With a little searching, he found a memory of a private lunch conversation between Moreno and his section chief. The senior agent asked Moreno if he was sure that Valencia trusted him to look the other way during his surveillance and screening of visitors at the marina. Although not confirmation that Moreno was or was not on the take, that conversation gave Jeff clues to where other memories of this arrangement with the section chief could be found. He discovered Moreno had gained the trust of the smugglers by having them believe he was on the take for insultingly small bribes. Moreno's act as a double agent was off the record, which was why it was not noted in Moreno's files. The section chief kept the original surveillance order active, particularly because of the bribes, which were known only to Moreno's superiors.

With the validation that Moreno wasn't a bad cop, Jeff felt it would be safe to plant the information regarding the container ship, its estimated time of arrival, the container number, and truck driver's name into Moreno's mind. The DEA already had the trucking company and warehouse in the Central Valley in their sights.

Jeff described his plan to Mindi. He'd disguise himself so that the agent would never recognize the real Jeff. He'd talk to him and give him the information. Mindi approved.

That evening, Jeff's dream-self donned a longshoreman disguise and stepped into Moreno's mind. While Jeff waited for the agent's REM sleep to begin, he wandered, poking into his memories here and there. He watched a couple of drug busts Moreno had been involved in at both LAX and the Port of Long Beach. When Moreno's breathing ramped up, Jeff watched from a distance as the agent's family, and a pet dinosaur, were camping at an ocean filled with icebergs, talking whales, and bundles of marijuana washing up on the beach. The whales discussed local politics with Moreno's teenage sons and daughter.

Jeff, as Dan the Longshoreman, quietly walked up to dream-Moreno, tapped him on the shoulder, and in a very businesslike tone asked, "What if I told you something that I think you'd like to know about . . ." Then he told Moreno everything he knew about the upcoming shipment.

"Who are you?" dream-Moreno asked.

"I'm your confidential informant. You must remember this dream, so when you wake up, you are to write down the details." Then the location of the dream changed to an interrogation room with yellow daisy and pink butterfly wallpaper, where "Dan" gave Moreno the information again to be sure the agent got it all. "If you need to, tell your boss that you paid me from the drug dealer's bribe money."

Jeff reminded the agent, "Write everything down when you wake up. You got that, Agent Moreno? You got that?"

Dream-Marino nodded, said, "Sure." The interrogation room melted around them into a puddle of lime gelatin. "Dan" shouted, *Wake up!*

Moreno awoke with a start, the dream still fresh in his mind. He looked at the clock, at his wife asleep next to him, and frantically fumbled for the notepad and pen in his nightstand drawer, struggling to remember the names and numbers the longshoreman in his dream had given him before the dream faded.

Jeff remained in his mind and repeated the details. Moreno fell asleep questioning the source and validity of the information.

The next morning, Mindi asked how the dream went and complemented Jeff's efforts, but she wondered if Moreno got all the information correctly.

"Yes, I stayed while he wrote it down. He got it all right."

"But will he be able to use it?"

"What do you mean?"

"Would anyone trust a weird dream? For that matter, would an experienced government agent trust an anonymous text message? But what if he had both? Metaphysics is questionable, but something grounded in reality would cinch it."

"Okay, what's on your mind?"

They bought a burner cell phone, texted the same information to Moreno's phone, and signed it, Dan the Longshoreman. Jeff removed the SIM card and imagined that Moreno would be totally mystified how the information had gotten into his dream before the anonymous real-world text message.

For good measure, the night after Moreno's dream, Mindi dropped into Mrs. Moreno's dreams and gave her the name of the cargo ship and date of arrival and told her to tell her husband at breakfast the following morning. Jeff and Mindi could only imagine the look that would be on Agent Moreno's face.

~

When Mrs. Moreno told Tony about her dream, he crossed himself and looked upward. On his way to the office, he stopped at his church to say a prayer and light a candle for Saint Michael, the patron saint of law enforcement.

Jeff returned to Moreno's mind the next day and found the information had been put in a report about a confidential informant's text message. What wasn't in the report, of course, was how his and his wife's dreams had duplicated the information.

After the exercise, Jeff and Mindi discussed the impact and consequences of planting information this way—especially with extremely religious or highly suggestible people. They enjoyed using their psychic skills and laughed about the effect it would have on civilians. They would have liked to think of themselves as self-appointed guardian angels, but admitted they were, in fact, vigilante drug enforcement agents. They decided they had to be methodical and businesslike and not be tempted to treat their actions as practical jokes.

The DEA-LA passed the information to their agents in Cartagena, Colombia, who began an investigation in Colombia of one Alejandro Sarís as a person of interest. They determined that he regularly traveled and was currently out of the country, having left in his private jet. The agents reported back that Sarís was a respectable businessman with no known ties to the cartels. Nevertheless, his home and local office were put under quiet observation by the Colombian National Police until further notice or July 1, whichever came first.

Jeff uncovered this information while checking again on the status of the investigation in Moreno's mind. Although there was no reason for concern right now, Jeff realized there might be unintended consequences of alerting the authorities to Sarís. If agents felt a need to track him to Seattle, Charlene could get entangled in the investigation. They had been seen in public together and at her office. Jeff wished, now, that he hadn't been so free with the information on Alejandro.

When he and Mindi discussed it, they tried to develop a contingency plan to inform Charlene of the potential danger. But what would Charlene's reaction be if they did? Would she be angry and resentful, thinking they were meddling in her new relationship?

Mindi grimaced. "Even with good intentions, we're amateurs at this private detective stuff. We could screw things up."

She held his eyes for a long moment. The look on his face indicated his agreement.

He said with a sigh, "Yeah. It could destroy her career, or worse, she could get hurt or killed. And if we did tell her, well, who's to say she wouldn't go back on her word about talking about what we can do?"

Mindi nodded as she studied the cream swirling in her coffee. She looked up. "You know, she may already suspect something. I've been in her mind, and I know she's heard me thinking and talking to you. We've messed around with Alejandro's head, in his dreams, when they were together. What if he described the gray room to her—told her he's seen us in his dream? What if she suspects it's you who's been in her head? She knows how all this works."

"I've thought of that too. I've tried to imagine what I could say to her if she were to bring it up. Or what I'll say to her if things get dicey and she's in danger." He paused a long moment and took a long drink of his coffee. "You know, when this is over, I think I'd rather just help unconscious people we find on the floor of their kitchen. This is getting more serious than the hobby I envisioned last year. I, well, we didn't ask for all this, but I don't think we can stop now."

Jeff put his arms around Mindi. "It'll be fine. From now

on, though, I think we should plan more, rather than making it up as we go along like we've done so far. This is like writing a computer program. We should flowchart the choices and actions to avoid foreseeable problems. Make sure we don't miss anything; keep the bugs to a minimum."

~

Jeff and Mindi had become well practiced in going out-of-body and had eliminated the need to fly to be somewhere. They could just imagine their destination and be there. But once they arrived, they could fly and walk on water or up the side of a building. They didn't have to make reservations for air travel and hotels or make allowances for the traditional laws of nature. The downside was they couldn't enjoy dining in fancy restaurants or experience the excitement of being part of a crowd.

Mindi had never been to New York City. They flew in and around the Empire State Building and the Statue of Liberty, and watched a show on Broadway in the best "seats" in the house. They went to Niagara Falls, flew through the mist, watched the tourists on the boats, pretended they were in a barrel going over the falls.

As they cruised along, Mindi said, "When we get married, let's have our honeymoon here!"

Jeff was so surprised he lost his balance and tumbled in the air, spinning out of control.

When he straightened out, Mindi said, "Oh, Jeff! Are you alright? I'm so sorry. I just blurted that out. We haven't talked about it . . . Oh, Jeff! I'm sorry. We've had such a good time being together, been so good together, I should have been more considerate—eased into it . . . Maybe that isn't really what you want." Feeling off-balance, Mindi talked steadily without taking a breath. "I'm sorry. I-I just proposed to you. That's was so wrong . . . So, so untraditional. Jeff . . . Help me out here. I'm in over my head." She had so much more she wanted to say but needed to stop and give him a chance to reply.

Jeff finally said, "Oh, Mindi. I'd be lying if I told you it hasn't crossed my mind—us getting married. Please don't apologize. You know that, well, that I couldn't bring it up unless you did first. You know my story. So it's all good. I've been afraid of . . . Well, of saying anything. I'm glad you said it!"

They hung in the air above the rushing water of the falls. Mindi took his hands in hers, her eyes full of love.

Jeff continued, "Sure, I like tradition as much as the next guy, but I'm not hung up on it. I'm grateful. You just took the burden from me of getting down on one knee." He smiled.

They coasted side by side, holding hands, and he looked at her with such an expression of affection on his face that tears formed in her eyes. His eyes swept the view. "A honeymoon here at the falls would be wonderful."

She grinned and hugged him.

They flew on together, enjoying the glow of the moment, then remembered that they'd left their bodies sitting in her apartment, and they needed to get back and take care of them. Almost instantaneously, Mindi was back in her own head, no longer a spirit cavorting as an ethereal being. She took a deep breath, opened her eyes, and smiled at Jeff, who met her gaze with a smile of his own. They stretched, then stood and embraced, communicating with a real-world hug as they'd done as spirits, over two thousand miles away, just a few moments ago.

"We've been here since last night and most of today, and though I'm not as stiff and sore as I expected, if we plan on being gone for another day like this, we need to prepare ourselves better. I'm so thirsty," Mindi said. "But first, I've got to go to the bathroom."

"I was fine until you said that." Jeff held out a fist and gave it a shake.

She looked at his outstretched arm, then into his eyes. "What is that?"

He grinned. "Rock, paper, scissors. Who gets the bathroom first?"

~

Jeff and Mindi analyzed all foreseeable angles, consequences, and rewards of what they planned to do next. Because Charlene knew about Jeff's abilities, if they told her that Alejandro was married to Karina, had two kids in Colombia, and was at the apex of a major drug-smuggling operation into the United States, she might succumb to the temptation to betray Jeff to Alejandro. She could be dangerous if she became suspicious of Jeff's motives.

The pair could think of no way to get the information to Charlene safely. If she confronted Alejandro with what she learned from them, would he harm her? Maybe Alejandro had already told her about his wife. She might already know he was married and didn't care.

His imagination worked overtime. Charlene had kept Jeff's loyalty because she'd been so gracious in how she'd broken off their relationship and taken responsibility for advancing Mindi's career and now his own. They were still friends. He didn't want anything bad to happen to a friend.

"If we do nothing," Jeff said, "and she's with him when he gets arrested . . . or there's shooting . . . or some kind of retaliation on Alejandro and his girlfriend when millions of dollars of drugs get seized . . ." He paused, looking at Mindi. "I've already implicated him to the DEA. I wish I hadn't told Moreno about Alejandro and kept the information only to Carlos, Roberto, and the truck driver. This is so tangled. What should we do?"

Mindi nodded to show she understood his concern. "Jeff, I know you care what happens to her, but you're not responsible for what's going on in her life. She's made choices and, like all of us, will have to live with them. No, we don't want her to get hurt. So that's what I think we should focus on. I don't think it's our place to snitch that she's carrying on with a married man. She might even like it that way. It's safer to have the kind of relationship that won't go any further than a good time. You know she can take care of herself, right?"

"Right. But we've watched movies where the girlfriend is collateral damage. I don't know how I'd live with myself if I could have prevented it and didn't."

"Sure," Mindi said. "But if we didn't have these powers to know what we do, we wouldn't be responsible if she got caught in the crossfire. It would be unfortunate and tragic."

"You're right, but we *do* know."

"Okay. What if we knew more? What if we knew the future? Could we jump into the future and see how it all turns out? Can we change the future without affecting our now?"

"Good question. From what I've read, physicists haven't addressed time travel to the future much, and what changing the present will do to the future's past." Jeff made some notes. When he finished, he looked back at Mindi and said, "If Mary hadn't found the letter Rick wrote, could I have stopped Rick from writing it, or gotten him to shred it when I traveled back into his mind? If it had never been put in the book in his library, Mary wouldn't have found it." Jeff continued, thinking out loud, "If we go forward in time and see what might happen in the future, can we interfere in our real-time and set it up so those circumstances never occur in the future? And can we do it without messing with the timeline or creating a paradox? Last time, I was trying to fix things from my past; now, we're trying to control the future, which we try to do every time we brush our teeth to prevent cavities. So it's different from stopping Rick from writing a letter he's already written. Do you see what I mean?"

Mindi nodded. "Yes. But there's this. Remember my second email to you from 2015? It didn't show up in your inbox until the day after you visited me. It should've been there for two years already in 2017. How did that happen? You said yourself that was less psychic phenomenon than it was truly magic. There's a lot that makes little sense and may never make sense. We've accepted that."

"You're right," Jeff said. " Regardless, we change the future every time we come to a crossroad where we choose one path over another. If we can foresee a possible outcome, can we change someone's choice at one of their crossroads and change or prevent that outcome? Okay, here's a question. Let's see if we get an answer. I want to know where Alejandro will be when the container reaches Long Beach. You and I were in his and Charlene's head on April 21. We were there two times during the same trip when they went to Friday Harbor for dinner. Each time was a little different. The first time, I wasn't even in the plane and you bailed early. The second time, we were both there for just the return trip. That's one of those twists, and I feel those weren't accidents—the universe planned for us to witness something. It had its own plans. Maybe that was to prepare us to do what we might try to do tonight. We go forward in time, into Charlene and Alejandro, around the time of the shipment, to see if she'll be in any danger, and then come back to the present where we can guide or change things to avoid a catastrophe. If it doesn't work, we repeat it, come back, and do it again. Like the movie, *Groundhog Day*. Just keep doing it until we get it right."

Mindi thought for a moment, then said, "Okay. Just don't let them know it's us. And stay out of our gray room. You go first, scout it out, then come back and tell me what you found."

"Roger that."

Jeff settled down to meditate. He got comfortable, closed his eyes, did his deep-breathing exercises, and he soon entered the desired alpha state that had become routine the last few months.

When Jeff thought of Alejandro, his field of vision opened onto the familiar view from the deck of Charlene's apartment. Alejandro was talking on the phone in Spanish. Jeff couldn't make out any of the conversation, but neither party conveyed any sense of urgency. It ended with none of the traditional politeness between friends; it was a business call. And the information exchange left Alejandro feeling satisfied.

The time and date had been on the phone screen, but Jeff didn't get a chance to see it. Alejandro turned the phone off, looked back over his shoulder, and saw Charlene dressed in matching panties and bra, covered by a short, open, diaphanous robe. She handed him a cocktail in a frosted glass.

This reactivated Jeff's memory of his times with Charlene. Though not jealous, he still appreciated her beauty, but he worked to cancel those feelings because he was committed to . . . Jeff stopped himself before he could think Mindi's name so his host wouldn't hear it. He needed to set aside all thoughts not related to the present mission. The first thing was to get Alejandro to reawaken the phone to get the date.

Alejandro took the glass from Charlene. After taking a drink, Alejandro rubbed his forehead with his free hand and pressed his thumb and forefinger into the corners of his eyes, squinting as if trying to prevent a headache.

"What's wrong? Is the drink okay?" Charlene asked.

He took another generous swallow, turned his head to look at her face, then let his eyes caress the loveliness he saw all the way to her feet. "It is perfect, as are you."

Jeff made a serious effort not to appreciate her beauty while he tried to get her new boyfriend to open his phone to get a look at the screen.

It worked. Alejandro picked the phone off the table, thumbed it awake, and looked at the screen. That gave Jeff what he needed: June 15. Their future.

Jeff worked his way gently back down the optic nerve, cutting off the splendid view of Puget Sound and his ex-girlfriend, and mentally asked to see recent memories of the drug shipment from Cartagena. The recent phone conversation reactivated. Jeff left that memory and found other conversations, including a phone call with Roberto, but again their Spanish made it impossible to understand what they were saying. He was about to give up that line of investigation when he stumbled upon the memory of the night Alejandro was trapped in the cage in the gray room.

A surge of adrenaline raced through Alejandro's body as the memory reactivated in the man's subconscious. Jeff felt it too, reliving both his and his host's terror. Jeff fought to endure it, because he wanted to see the end, to find out what may have transpired between Alejandro and Charlene after they awoke. His patience was rewarded. He saw what Alejandro had told Charlene about the gray room, the chairs, and the cage.

Damn, Jeff thought. *She knows about him being in the gray room.*

Jeff suddenly knew that he was being watched, right there in his adversary's mind. Alejandro's subconscious knew Jeff was there and recognized him. His cover might've been blown. *Time to go.* He raced toward the cerebral cortex, the center of consciousness in the brain, planning to see what was happening in Alejandro's real-time and find out if that watcher could follow him.

In real-time, Alejandro's consciousness had focused on the reactivated fear of being trapped—the elevated heart rate, the sweat, the fight-or-flight feelings that had come up from the depths of his mind.

Does he consciously know I'm here? thought Jeff.

Jeff was about to "Jeannie" himself out when he heard a mental shout: *I know you're here!* Because of conscious Alejandro's preoccupation with the bad feelings, Jeff knew the shout would've come from the cerebellum, the center of the subconscious's manifestation of Alejandro's avatar's voice.

Suddenly, Jeff was swept into Alejandro's gray room with an enraged copy of Alejandro advancing on him, arms outstretched. The monster version of Alejandro bellowed, *It is you, demon Jeff! I have finally caught you!*

You won't catch me, Jeff yelled back at him, his mental adrenaline flowing. *You're the one who'll be caught.* Jeff forgot the remorse he had felt at uncovering the punishment by the man's father as a boy. *You will be caught again, as you got caught and beaten by your father.* He yelled *Ciao!* as loud as he could, adding *Jeannie* for good measure to assure escape from the foul image's impending clutches.

~

In Charlene's apartment, Alejandro dropped his cell phone as Jeff's shouts to escape reverberated through his mind. He slumped into a chair, grabbing his head in both hands, sweat beaded on his brow.

"Alejandro, what's wrong?" Charlene's concern was palpable.

The feeling passed as if a switch had been thrown. Alejandro opened his eyes and looked at Charlene. He'd quit sweating and the pain in his head had instantly vanished. He finished his drink in one swallow. "It's nothing. It was a sharp pain, but it is gone." He rubbed the back of his neck and looked up at her with an apology in his eyes. "I am sorry. Yes, I'm fine." He handed her the glass. "May I have another? Let us continue the evening."

Charlene searched his face for validation that whatever had happened had passed. "Alejo, I was afraid you were having a stroke, an aneurysm or something. You are sure you're okay, now?"

He stood and encircled her with his arms and kissed her passionately. They both became distracted and forgot the passing event.

~

"Well, how did it go? Did you see him? What did you find?"

Jeff explained the substance of the leap, including

monster Alejandro's attempt to trap him, but did not include Charlene's lack of clothing.

Jeff wanted—no, he *needed* to be sure that the chase through Alejandro's mind had remained in Alejandro's subconscious and hadn't worked its way up to the conscious. Did he know Jeff was in his head, and would he tell Charlene? Jeff was concerned and he craved assurance.

"Would you—could you—try to leap into Charlene and find out what he may have told her? Now that we know the date, location, and the people, you should be able to target her with some accuracy. Please. We need to know what she knows."

Mindi nodded. "Sure, I'll give it a try."

Jeff felt unsettled with what now seemed an impulsive request, and momentarily considered canceling it, but he discounted the feeling as residual emotion from his leap. "Good, thanks." He gave her a quick kiss.

~

Mindi's leap started with meditation, and she accurately met the target of Charlene's mind. The timing, though, was wrong. So very wrong. Charlene and Alejandro were in bed together and not sleeping.

Mindi's realization they were making love enforced that she had to exit *right now!* In her haste to end the encounter, without any consideration of possible consequences, in her mind she screamed, *Jeannie, Jeannie, Jeannie!*

She left Charlene's head instantly. Mindi's eyes snapped open back in her living room. In one quick motion, she stood, looked for Jeff, and collapsed onto him, sobbing and shaking.

He held her. "What's wrong? What happened?"

She caught her breath, but still trembled. "Oh, Jeff. It was so bad. I panicked. I screamed to escape."

Jeff helped her onto the sofa and sat beside her, an arm around her shoulder. "What happened? What did you see?"

"They were making love when I got there. I felt what she felt. I couldn't control myself. I just screamed to escape. I had to get out of there. As I left, I saw the look on Alejandro's face and felt the terror I'd sent through her mind. It wasn't right. I didn't think . . . and I don't care. Oh, Jeff." She closed her eyes. "It was so unexpected. Right then I felt trapped, just like . . ." She gave a shallow sigh, her shoulders slumped.

Jeff wrapped his arms around her and rocked her while she clung to him. They sat quietly for a long time until finally, she relaxed.

She let go and sat back. His eyes contained a question. Was she okay? She nodded but didn't speak.

~

"I'm so sorry that happened," Jeff said. "It must have been terrible. I would never have put you in a situation like that had I known." But he should've known. He'd had a premonition but didn't examine it. If he'd considered Charlene's state of undress . . . *That* was the feeling of unease, the intuition he'd felt earlier that the timing was wrong. He should have asked her to target for another day, and this wouldn't have happened. There'd been no urgency for him to know right then if Alejandro had said something to Charlene. *I was being selfish.*

"Do you want a glass of water, maybe a drink?" He didn't want to patronize her by telling her everything would be okay. The experience had resurrected bad memories, and he didn't want to do more harm.

"I'll be fine. It was such a shock. I know I wasn't being raped. I've worked through worse than that. But it was . . ." She took a deep breath and let it out slowly. ". . . such a surprise. We've never had a leap like that. I'm sorry I blurted out what happened. She was your girlfriend before we met. This must be difficult for you."

"No. No, it's fine. This isn't about me. Really. No, don't worry about that. I worry about you." He looked into her eyes. "Minn, I should have anticipated that. And I didn't. I'm so sorry. They were drinking when I was there. She was dressed, well, let's say, way too comfortably. I feel responsible for sending you there to . . . that. I can't even imagine what it was like. I'm sorry."

"Yes. I felt trapped. But I got out of there quickly. Poor Charlene. I think I might have messed up her having a good time." Mindi chuckled.

"This is about us right now," Jeff said. "We've had some tough lessons lately around this stuff. We got stuck in the gray room with him. And now this." They remained quiet while they drank their drinks, then Jeff said, "I know this will sound insensitive, but I *would* like to be a fly on the wall after you left to see how *he* handled it. It had to be distracting for him. I can only imagine." It was Jeff's turn to laugh, but the laugh was without humor.

Mindi considered for a moment, and then said, "I want to be really careful before I leap into her head again. Not because I might catch her doing something like that but because she's got to be wondering what was going on in her mind. I've been in her situation. If I were her, I would probably call someone and ask questions about people in my head. To her, I'm the expert, so she might call me. What do I tell her? I bet she's wondering if someone else is doing to her what you did with me, and it's probably scaring her something fierce. What do you think?"

"We should go back through our journals to see how many times you've been in her head and what you were thinking and saying. She's a creative thinker. I bet she's tried to remember things like this, and I bet the Frisbee incident in her April has come to mind."

Jeff stopped abruptly. "Wait! We're still in March, and the Frisbee shout hasn't happened to them yet. That's next month, April. And tonight's leaps won't happen for them until June. She won't call you now; it hasn't happened to them yet."

"But it happened to me. To us, tonight. But what does that mean?" Mindi answered her own question with, "So the butterfly isn't dead, right?" A reference to a sci-fi short story Jeff had told her about time travel.

"No, it isn't. We saw their future. They haven't lived it yet. It only exists in *our* present."

"Okay, does this become another scenario where we break up another couple? You got Rick and Carolyn to break up. Did I, or will I, interfere with Alejandro and Charlene?"

"Yeah, we can only hope. It could work to our advantage. What happened might cause them to break up. Alejandro is a good-time Charlie, a Casanova. He only wants temporary companionship and good sex. He has a wife and kids at home. Karina's a good woman, and he won't leave them for Charlene. Charlene isn't looking to settle down anyway, so that's okay. Maybe what happened will make Charlene look crazy to him, and nobody wants to be with a psycho. There's no sense trying to fix it. There's nothing to gain in keeping them together after it happens. And with luck, they'll break it off if we leave it alone. It just didn't happen to them *tonight*."

Mindi frowned. "So what you're saying is that we shouldn't change the future we saw tonight, because the night of June 15, 2018, will end in disaster for them."

Jeff shrugged. "We can hope, right? It's all good." He turned serious. "Except that it was bad for you. It scared you. I'm sorry I let that happen."

"What's done is done. You're trying to take responsibility, and that's another reason I love you—you're honest. Now, if *you* want the truth, I think the episode left me just a little, well . . ." She did the coy head movement with which Jeff had become familiar—dipping her chin down and looking up at him under her eyebrows with a twinkle in her eyes. "Let's put it this way. I can think of a great way to help me forget what I felt then by . . ." She flashed Jeff a look with a toss of her hair that told him that if he didn't agree, he'd be a fool.

~

They slept until noon, and after brunch, sat at the table, ready to write in their journals. Mindi said to Jeff, "So just to be sure, when we write last night's leaps, it will lock in the future, correct?"

"Maybe. We don't know that if we don't write it down their future will still change, but it won't hurt, and we may need the documentation. We need everything we can think of to ensure Charlene doesn't get hurt. You know, I'm thinking that whatever or whoever is in control set that up, *made* that happen, to get the result we want: her to not be around if the drug bust happens. We'll have to wait and see."

They wrote in their journals.

"What's next?" Mindi asked.

Jeff pulled the yellow legal pad in front of him and looked

at it with his pen in hand. Boxes, diamonds, and arrows of a decision tree flow chart covered the top half of the page. He sketched in an arrow leading down from the box with Charlene's name and ended it in a decision diamond into which he wrote, *Out of Danger?* His choices were a *Yes* and a *No.* He drew a line ending in an arrow from the *Yes* down to a box labeled *Maybe.*

He then followed a line down from *'Berto* which intersected with *Miranda Valencia* and a dotted line to *Carlos Cordoba.*

"I guess we're here." He turned the pad around for Mindi to see.

She pointed to the group of boxes and diamonds labeled *Moreno,* then looked at Jeff and said, "What do you see for this one?"

"Well . . . How about this? I leap into Moreno's head and talk to him again to validate I'm a real, although disembodied, confidential informant who wants to help the DEA and thousands of suffering drug addicts—my excuse being to guarantee things go smoothly."

"Could he ever find out who you really are?"

"No, don't think so. He won't ever see my real face like Alejandro has. And on that subject, if—no, *when* Alejandro gets apprehended, nobody will believe him if he says I was in his mind and in his dreams. If he tries to expose us, it won't work."

Mindi fixed herself a mimosa and brought him a bottle of beer. "Yeah, okay." She stood behind Jeff and looked over his shoulder at the flow chart. Her hand caressed the back of Jeff's neck.

"What information could we give Moreno that he doesn't have already?" She continued to scan the chart. "What about him?" She put her finger on the box labeled *Roberto.*

214

"Hmm," Jeff said. "We still don't know what his role is, besides living large. He's got to be critical to the operation. If we could give Moreno more details about where the stuff is going and why 'Berto's yacht is here, it would be good. How do we get around his brain-barrier and the language problem?"

"Well, I've been practicing my Spanish," Mindi replied. "What if I try searching Miranda's mind for more information? She seems to be as involved as the rest of them. I've already been in there, so it might be easier to strike up a 'conversation' with her and maybe play on some guilt and shame."

"Sure, worth a try." Jeff looked back at the flow chart. Put his finger on Carlos's name, then followed a line to a connected box: *Sofia*. "His daughter's in Boston. There might be some leverage there. Why don't I get into his head and see if I can find where she is? Failing that, maybe I can find her at Harvard, or through the BMW dealerships."

"You're starting to think like a detective, Mr. Marlen. *Detective* Marlen. I like that."

Jeff said, looking at her with a smile, "We can name our detective agency Dewey, Ketchem, and Howe." The reference to her and her relatives' names.

The blank look on Mindi's face told Jeff the joke had fallen flat.

He tried to recover. "Do-we-catch-them-and-how? The joke was Craig's."

"Oh. Yeah. Funny." Her tone told Jeff it wasn't.

"Your cousin said if you have to explain a joke, it isn't that funny."

"He was right." Mindi patted him on the head. "That's okay, Detective Marlen. Don't quit your day job. You know, a comedian shouldn't steal other people's material." She finished up with a big smile and gave him a kiss.

Jeff shrugged. "Point taken. Do you want to get going? We've got nothing else scheduled for the day."

They closed the curtains and put on their meditation music.

~

Mindi wondered if she'd arrived in the right place. She could see nothing but heard the soft sound of water slapping against the side of a boat and felt the warmth of the sun on her host's skin. Miranda took off her sunglasses and rubbed her eyes. Mindi knew what Miranda was feeling at having someone in her mind; she'd felt it dozens of times herself.

Miranda was alone on the deck, a drink with ice at her side. She wore a two-piece swimsuit and a short, plush beach robe pulled across her body.

What time is it? Mindi asked her host.

Absently, Miranda picked up her cell phone and thumbed it awake: *5 de junio de 2018, 10:45 a.m.*

Good, Mindi thought.

Miranda looked around. A couple walked by on the dock, and she thought the voice in her head came from them. Miranda put on her sunglasses and sat on the lounge chair.

Miranda? Mindy. What are you doing? Mindi said in English.

The woman sat up and looked again. She was on the top deck of the sleek yacht with a clear view all around.

"Who said that?" she asked in Spanish.

Also in Spanish, Mindi replied, *I did. Here, in your mind.*

Alarmed, Miranda stood. Her book fell to the deck. She pushed her sunglasses to the top of her head.

In English now, Mindi said, *Try to relax, Miranda.*

"Who are you? How do you know my name?"

216

That's not important. You wouldn't understand. But what you and your husband are involved in causes pain to thousands of people. You do not seem to care. You used to care. Why not now? What if you are caught? You know you will be caught eventually.

Miranda said nothing and kept looking around.

Sit down, Miranda, Mindi ordered.

Miranda obeyed, but she shivered, despite the warm sun and her robe.

You can't see me. I'm in your heart. You mustn't allow your heart to grow colder. Mindi hoped that she'd brought the subject of the shipment to the front of Miranda's mind. It should make it easier to find information about what was planned in June. She quit talking to the woman and went looking in her mind, but as she moved toward the center of her mind, down Miranda's optic nerve, she heard a male voice talking to her host in Spanish.

"Miranda, there you are."

"Hello, 'Berto." Miranda's answer sounded distracted to Mindi. Did it sound the same to Roberto? Mindi returned to seeing through the woman's eyes, and she watched him watch her. Then, still in Spanish, Roberto said, "Remember. Carlos will be coming in tonight, and he'll stay here until all arrangements have been made. Do you want to have dinner here or eat at a restaurant?"

Mindi understood most of what he said.

Miranda didn't reply to 'Berto's question. She was still distracted by the voice in her head.

Roberto continued to study Miranda closely, his expression indicating that he sensed something was off.

Miranda, you must answer your husband, Mindi said. *Tell him you'd prefer to eat here tonight. Reassure 'Berto that you're okay, that you just have a headache. Do you understand?*

"Sí," Miranda replied under her breath to the voice. Then she told her husband exactly what Mindi had told her.

The man tipped his head sideways, confused with the way Miranda was acting, but he stepped over to her, bent down, and kissed her gently on the top of the head, then said in Spanish, "I'll have the caterers deliver dinner for three. You want the salad you like?"

She nodded, still distracted.

Roberto continued, "We should eat in the salon; there may be a chill out on the deck. Don't you agree you should lie down for a while before you get ready for tonight?"

He spoke quickly, and Mindi only understood *comer en el salón*, eating in the salon, and that it would be *frío*, cold, outside. Though businesslike, his voice showed concern.

"Sí, 'Berto."

Miranda stood and picked up her book and cell phone. 'Berto embraced her gently, gave her a kiss on the cheek, and then steered her toward the short stairway leading down to the main deck. He followed her with his hand touching the middle of her back to guide her. They went below deck, along the hallway, then entered the main stateroom. When Miranda lay on the bed to take a nap, Mindi would go on a tour of the woman's mind.

During her search, Mindi found nothing of value regarding the shipment. She found the memory of the dinner with Carlos in Cartagena, and that she'd felt Carlos's desire for her but had no desire for him. Memories of extravagant shopping trips, cocktails, and dinners with wealthy and boorish friends back in Colombia filled Miranda's mind. It seemed that she'd been nothing more than a messenger that night to give the information to Carlos. She was singularly Roberto's arm candy, but she felt he loved her.

When Mindi returned to her body, Jeff was still seated, breathing slowly and rhythmically. She wrote in her journal, left a note for Jeff on a sticky note, mischievously putting it on his nose so he would find it, and returned to rejoin Miranda in time for their dinner party. She considered she might meet Jeff there, riding in Carlos's mind. She'd slip the word Frisbee into the conversation to see if Carlos did have a stowaway. At the very least, she'd be able to drink and dine in luxury. Except for a Frisbee message, she had no intentions of again letting Miranda know she was there. The seed had been planted to create guilt and fear. Would it grow?

When Mindi returned, Miranda was putting on makeup. A wet towel lay over the back of a chair in the stateroom, and a rosary sat on the dressing table next to the makeup. With the training Mindi'd had, she found it difficult to watch Miranda and not say something. She at first tried to direct Miranda's hands but couldn't. But neither could she not help the woman do a better job with her makeup. In a gentle mind voice, she said, *Miranda, dear. May I show you something with your makeup that would make your face look so much more natural?*

Miranda's eyes widened, startled. She stared into her own eyes, trying to see who or what was talking to her.

"What do you want?" Miranda whispered in Spanish to her reflection.

Oh, Miranda, my dear. You should practice your English, Mindi replied. *Now, I want what you want, to look as beautiful as the Lord intends you to be . . . and as 'Berto desires. May I help?*

Still confused, Miranda said, "What do I do?"

Just do what I suggest. You have good makeup here. Some of it, to Mindi's pleasure, was LaDormeur.

The next fifteen minutes were fun for both. They fell into a rhythm of doing what both women enjoyed.

When satisfied, Mindi said, *Now sit back and look. Turn your head sideways, both sides, and look at what you've done. Do you like it?*

In a conversational voice, because she had become comfortable with the voice in her head, she said, "Oh, yes. That is better than I have ever done."

"My dear, who are you talking to?"

Miranda jumped. She turned to see Roberto standing in the doorway watching her.

Surprised, Miranda froze.

Though also startled, Mindi waited to see what would transpire.

Mindi said to her, *Repeat what I say. You startled me. I was talking to myself. I tried some things I saw on YouTube with my makeup. Do you like it?*

Miranda regained her composure and repeated what Mindi had said, but in Spanish. She stood, approached Roberto, and modeled for him, twisting and turning, then she leaned in for a quick Hollywood kiss.

Her husband reached for her, trying to draw her close.

"No, no, no. Do not mess up my makeup. At least, not until much later, my darling." The confident woman that Mindi had first met in the restaurant months ago had returned.

Roberto, properly admonished, but with good nature, smiled at his wife. "Carlos's airplane has arrived. He should be here within the hour. When you are ready, come; let's have a drink."

Miranda nodded and returned to the mirror as Roberto turned to leave.

He's quite fond of you, Mindi said. *Are you as fond of him?*

Softly, Miranda whispered, "Why do you ask? If you are in my heart, you should know."

This caught Mindi off guard, but she quickly regained control of the situation. *My dear, my duty is to ensure that you're honest with yourself. Your answer to me was a deflection, which means you either don't know how you feel, or you don't want to admit that you're being dishonest with your feelings.*

Mindi felt Miranda's reacquired confidence wane.

Miranda, again at the dressing table, picked up the rosary and mindlessly thumbed the beads one by one as she studied her face in the mirror.

They heard Roberto call to her from the hallway.

"I'll be right there," she called back.

~

Jeff's leap into his host found Carlos in first class, flirting with the flight attendant who'd just brought him a drink.

Where are we going? What time is it? How long is the flight? Jeff thought quietly.

Carlos obliged automatically by taking his ticket out of his breast pocket and looking at it: *CTG to LAX, Arr. 5:40 p.m.* Then Carlos looked at his Rolex: *5:45 p.m.*

Cartagena was two hours ahead of LA with Standard Time, but daylight saving time had already gone into effect, so unless the flight was seriously delayed, he hadn't yet changed his watch to LA time.

Carlos looked at his watch again, took it off his wrist and turned the time back an hour to match the local arrival time. If they were on time, they would land in less than an hour.

Jeff was glad this leap wouldn't be long. He wanted to establish a telepathic link with . . . He stopped short of thinking her name. Could he do it without calling her name?

Hey. You there? he called to Mindi.

Carlos looked around to see who was talking so close to him. He was in an aisle seat, and the couple on the other side were reading. The guy sitting next to him was dozing. When he turned around, he saw that the other passengers were either watching a movie or reading. Carlos shook his head. He was sure he'd heard someone.

Jeff decided to wait and "give her a call" later.

Carlos pulled a shipping magazine from the seat pocket. He unfolded it and pulled out a photocopied shipping schedule for the *HMM Aisling*. As Carlos scanned the page, Jeff recognized it was from the website he'd found. If Carlos was arrested with this in his possession, it might be circumstantial evidence.

I'm here. Jeff heard Mindi answering in his mind, quite clear, but not loud. Their system had improved. At the beginning, they'd needed to be close. Now, six or seven hundred miles wasn't too far.

He answered with a quick, *Good. See you soon. No more talk.*

A thought flashed through Carlos's mind that someone was making a phone call using the plane's wi-fi and it had somehow come over the PA system.

Jeff decided that even though Carlos was "in tune" with his thoughts, he could quietly go exploring and see if he could pick up any other intel. Jeff focused on the shipping schedule, hoping that would send out a beacon for him to follow to Carlos's memories.

Sure enough, there was a text message—luckily in English—Carlos had sent to someone named Jaime. Carlos had typed the encrypted text message to a cell number in area code 213. He memorized the number. The text confirmed the driver would pick up the truck at a warehouse at 15669 Sepulveda Boulevard in Van Nuys and arrive at Terminal Five at 07:00, and wait in the queue with the rest of the trucks. Customs paperwork would be in the cab. There would be a cell phone to be used solely to contact "Speed Dial #1" confirming possession of the container. Then the SIM was to be removed and burned with a cigarette lighter found in the glove compartment. The phone was to be driven over by the truck and left on the pavement. Instructions for the route and subsequent delivery would be in the "Notes" app on the phone, to be read and memorized prior to the destruction of the phone.

Jeff concealed his joy at this bit of intelligence for fear that it would sound an alarm in Carlos's mind. Soon after the memory ran, he realized that as he'd watched the memory play out, Carlos had remembered it too. It didn't set off an alarm, but it did trigger Carlos to confirm with Jaime after he deplaned.

Jeff hoped he'd be able to stay in Carlos's mind to get Jaime's phone number to give it to . . . He stopped his planning. The old saying came back to him, "The walls have ears." When his host's mind was open to him, his own thoughts were often available to his host, just like today when he tried to contact . . . He stopped himself again from saying her name.

CHAPTER 14

Jeff watched as Carlos texted 'Berto that he'd landed. A text came back immediately, telling him the evening meal would be served soon after he arrived. During the rest of the trip, Jeff listened to Carlos's thoughts of resentment of smoking laws in California which forbade smoking in the airport area, in the limousine waiting area, and in public vehicles. He kept tapping his coat pocket to reassure himself that the cigarettes were still there.

A quick text to Jaime received no reply, but Carlos resolved to follow up later. Jeff noted the phone number, then decided to have some fun with Carlos, trusting it would be harmless. He thought about Carlos's dog. *How is Max? Has he been fed?*

Carlos's response was to wonder if he should call the employee taking care of the dog while he was away. Carlos fidgeted with the phone, then finally called him under the pretense that he wanted to make sure he'd left enough food for Max and the phone number for the veterinarian. The call took place entirely in Spanish. Jeff was sure that Max in Colombia and Sofia in Boston were the entirety of Carlos's family.

The minute Jeff thought of Sofia, Carlos took out his phone and texted her he was in California—a reminder of how sensitive Carlos was to his thoughts.

A few minutes later, a text arrived: *Papá, can I come see you? I'll be done with finals tomorrow and I miss you.*

Carlos texted back: *I'll call when I get to Tío 'Berto's yacht.*

Sofia replied: *Please say I can come visit!*

Jeff got the vibe that Carlos wouldn't deny his daughter's request.

The limo dropped Carlos, with Jeff still with him, at the marina. The black Chevrolet Suburban with heavily tinted windows sat in its spot in the parking lot with a full view of the marina. After initial greetings, Carlos mentioned the Suburban to 'Berto.

"Please use *inglés*," Roberto said. "The crew is from Colombia, and they speak very little English. I wish to keep to a minimum what they may understand of our conversations, *¿Sí?* And yes, we know about the agents. They watch us day and night. But we have one of them in our, how you say, confidence. He is willing, for a small fee, to tell us what the American *gusanos* are planning. They are as *codiciosas* as our *policía*."

Frisbee, Jeff telepathed to Mindi.

In Carlos? she replied.

Yes.

Carlos was too busy with his drink, enjoying his cigarette, and admiring the lovely Miranda to notice their quick conversation.

Two Mirandas in one? How delightful, Jeff said.

Mindi giggled.

Carlos heard that exchange and turned a questioning gaze toward Roberto.

"*¿Qué?*" Roberto said. What?

Carlos frowned and gave his head a shake. "*No paso nada.*" It's nothing.

Miranda walked up to him, and he turned toward her. They exchanged a quick hug and a peck on each cheek. "Miranda, my dear. You look lovelier every time we meet."

Jeff felt the flash of lust in Carlos's mind and a stirring in his loins. *This guy has it bad*, Jeff thought. Then he stifled his judgment of Carlos's morals and, possibly, his lack of loyalty to his friends and team.

"Carlos," Miranda said. "So good to see you."

And how are you? Mindi telepathed to Jeff.

Just fine. This is fun. At least for now. Meet me outside.

Carlos looked around again but wasn't on alert. He did, however, put his hand to his ear as if trying to hear the voices in his head more clearly.

~

The transition to being out-of-body had become easy for Jeff—now most pleasing to be out of Carlos's body because of the cigarette smoke. He was even more pleased when he saw Mindi's image appear next to him.

"I had to be so careful not to say or think your name. Carlos is very in tune with me inside his head. How did it go with Miranda?"

"I could sense Carlos's interest in her. That whole thing with him lusting after Miranda is disgusting," Mindi said. She told Jeff how she'd presented herself as Miranda's conscience and then as her friend. "She's probably thinking she has a split personality. I gave her a makeup lesson, and she liked it, but it almost got her into trouble with dear 'Berto. He caught her talking to herself." Mindi smiled.

"Did she have anything to share?"

"Not much. She's smart in her own way, and I'm sure she knows what's going on, but she's not directly involved. She's obedient and subservient to her man—and loves the luxury. He's devoted to her, though. After all, it looks like he named two boats after her. They've been together a while. How about you?"

"Oh, yeah. Got some good stuff. But I wanted to be clear of them for a while. I want Carlos to forget he has voices in his head. Come with me. Let's see who's in the Feds' rig."

They slipped into the backseat of the Suburban. Jeff had stopped believing in coincidence and was now certain that the universe was in control because Moreno was there, right when he needed him to be. The agents had each been reading. Their scanner, set to the DEA channel, crackled with static, and infrequently a quick announcement made it come alive. Nothing much was happening within the agency today.

Be right back, Jeff told Mindi as he dissolved into Moreno's head.

Moreno shook his head as if a fly had buzzed his ear, but he quickly went back to his book.

Jeff said, *Tony. Don't let your partner know I'm talking to you. Don't move.*

Moreno looked up and out the window.

You can communicate with me, but not out loud, Jeff continued in Moreno's head. *Just think what you want to say, and I'll hear it.*

Moreno didn't move. Just kept staring out the windshield.

Tell me you understand, but don't move your head.

Y-y-yes. I understand.

Good.

Who are you?

Do you remember your dream? I'm Dan, the longshoreman.

I'm going crazy, aren't I? Someone from my dreams is now a voice in my head?

No. You're fine. Think of this as new technology out of HQ. No worries. Just listen. The agent fidgeted as if uncomfortable. Jeff used a stern voice. *Don't panic! This is important. I will ask you to remember what I'm going to tell you. Do not write it down now, or your partner will wonder what's up. Okay?*

Okay. I'll try.

Make it look like you're reading.

Moreno lowered his head and looked at the book.

Okay. Get this. Jeff relayed the information about the truck in Van Nuys. *Important contact names are Carlos Cordoba and Jaime, no last name.* He gave him the phone number. *Got that? No, don't nod your head.* Jeff repeated the information. *Tell me, yes or no: do you have it?*

Yes.

Repeat it back to me.

Moreno repeated the information word for word.

Excellent. I'll see you in your dreams. Goodbye, Tony.

Jeff appeared next to Mindi. He signaled for her to get out of the Suburban, and they stood outside while Jeff filled her in on how he got the information from Carlos and that he'd told Moreno. Then he started laughing. "This part is so much fun. They'll put the warehouse under surveillance. They'll get a fix on this Jaime's phone. I wonder if they'll apprehend the driver then substitute an agent and pick up the load themselves. I don't care. That's their job; they'll figure it out. We've done ours."

"How will they be able to tie Roberto, Alejandro, and Carlos directly to the operation?" Mindi asked. "They probably won't be anywhere around the container when it's intercepted. There has to be a boatload of money involved." She smiled. "Pun intended. But how will it change hands? A briefcase of money is only in the movies. For a load like this, it would be a lot of briefcases, right? Bank transfers to the Caymans or Switzerland for some kind of money laundering, right?"

Jeff shrugged. "Those are good questions, Detective Madisen. Looks like they'd need to know more if DEA wanted shut these folks down, rather than just the inconvenience of an intercepted load. We'd better get back to Gardena. I bet when we get back, nature calls."

Mindi laughed. "What would happen if we did have to go to the bathroom, and we didn't get back in time?"

Jeff just looked at her with a smile. "Depends."

She frowned, puzzled, and urged him to continue.

"Think about it. You'll get the joke. Let's get back so we won't have to find out."

~

Time was growing short, and they still didn't know who was in charge of this cartel or who controlled the money. Jeff and Mindi had poked around in the smugglers' heads and confirmed that each of them had two phones: their high-end iPhones for innocuous personal use and burner phones, changed regularly, for their nefarious business. Jeff had tried to harass Alejandro's string of phones, but he'd blocked anything not in his address book on his personal phone, and after he'd changed his burner a few times, it wasn't worth it for Jeff and Mindi to keep up. That idea had seemed like a good one, but they couldn't tell if it created the internal mistrust they wanted.

Jeff and Mindi went to the yacht and snooped around as ghosts and found quite a few boxes marked with the grocery-chain logo, but could not, in spirit form, open them. So the contents remained a mystery.

Jeff examined reports Moreno had filed and found nothing concerning overt activity of any drug-dealing operation at the yacht at the marina. Moreno and his partner, cooperating with Long Beach police, had investigated a drug party attended by underaged rich kids on a lawyer's yacht two docks away. The investigation showed that the drugs, mostly ecstasy, a little cocaine, marijuana, and alcohol, were completely unrelated to the *Miranda II*. But it had given the DEA a chance to question Roberto and his crew. Moreno spoke Spanish and had interviewed, with Roberto's assent, the two crew that were needed for routine maintenance and piloting the vessel when underway.

Separately, the DEA had found out that domestic duties on the yacht were provided by local services for housekeeping, laundry, and catering. Expenses were paid for using an American Express Black Card in Valencia's name. Cash was used sparingly, except to grease Moreno's palm.

The report concluded that Roberto Valencia, and now his wife Miranda, were merely wealthy residents of a luxury yacht, visited occasionally by a few wealthy friends, primarily Colombian. They neither leased or owned any vehicles in California, and when they left the yacht to attend the theater, go to dinner, or go shopping, they used a limousine service.

The DEA Regional Chief in Bogotá had drawn a complete blank on answering the question of if or how Valencia was tied to any illegal activities. The Valencia family had a history in Colombia for five generations. Roberto was the only surviving son of Arturo and Michele Valencia, successful cattle ranchers in Antioquia. His two older brothers had been killed in an automobile accident when they were in college. Roberto had no criminal record, had a business degree from Stanford, maintained a luxury home in Cartagena, and had no children. They looked squeaky clean.

The DEA had previously found that the legal owner of the *Miranda II* was the publicly traded Colombian construction company listed on the Colombian Securities Exchange. Roberto wasn't one of the company's officers, neither were his parents, although the Valencias did own a substantial amount of their stock. But that did not solve the mystery of how the company-owned yacht came to be named after the younger Valencia's wife, or why it had not been moored at its leased dock at the yacht club in Cartagena for over two years.

Carlos Cordoba had no locatable history before the mid-1990s. He appeared on the tax rolls in Medellín when he purchased a leather tanning company and associated luggage factory, along with a home in an upscale part of the town, for which he paid cash. He held a Colombian driver's license, but there was no record of him on any voter registration rolls anywhere in Colombia. And like the Valencias, he had no police record or reported relationship with crime. Not even a traffic ticket. His wife, Carlota Rosario Cordoba, died in 2004. Their one child, daughter Sofia Angelina Cordoba, was a law student at Harvard, in Boston.

These reports on the Valencias and Cordobas had originated from the US-DEA in Colombia, and Jeff read them during a leap into Agent Moreno after he'd quietly planted a seed in Moreno's mind to again review the files in case they'd missed something. Jeff had done research on the history of the cocaine industry in Colombia. Although no mention was made in the report, Jeff noticed that Carlos's seeming magical appearance as a factory owner, a homeowner, and holder of a new driver's license happened, coincidentally, at roughly the same time as the fall of the Medellín Cartel and the death of Pablo Escobar in 1993. No one, not the DEA or the Colombian Police, had noted this coincidence. After some later research, Jeff noticed another coincidence. The name "Cordoba" was possibly a transliteration from Arabic, meaning "hub," the center of a wheel, which appeared to be Carlos's role in the shipment of drugs from Colombia.

Jeff explained all this to Mindi, and she asked Jeff where Antioquia was located.

Jeff looked it up. "That's the area where Medellín is located, more or less, in the northwest, between Cartagena and Bogotá."

"Okay. Just a hunch. Please Google where cocaine is manufactured in Colombia."

The answer came up right away. "It doesn't say where it's made," Jeff said, "but it does say this . . ." He read, "The great majority of coca cultivation takes place in the departments of Putumayo, Caquetá, Meta, Guaviare, Nariño, Antioquia, and Vichada."

"What are departments?"

"Municipal subdivisions. Like a state or county here."

"So that's where we assume they make it, near where the coca is grown?"

"That's a good guess. What are you getting at?"

Mindi pulled Jeff's journal toward her on the table and scanned his notes on the Valencias and Carlos. She looked up and, in a quiet voice, said, "I'll bet here's the link between 'Berto and Carlos."

"What?"

"Medellín is in Antioquia. So are the Valencias' cattle ranch, leather tanning, coca, Carlos, and his luggage and bags. They're there in one place."

Jeff clicked on the map of Colombia on his laptop, looked back at his notes, and then at the smile on Mindi's face. "Ms. Mindi Sherlock Holmes, that is brilliant. I bet the DEA missed it. Hell, I missed it. And 'Berto lives mainly on the yacht, but has a house in Cartagena. The shipment goes out of there. But what was Carlos doing in Cartagena? It's a"—Jeff searched on his laptop—"twelve-hour drive from Medellín to Cartagena."

"How long is a flight?"

"Yup, good thinking." Jeff opened another window on his browser. "Just a little over an hour, and there's a dozen flights a day. I bet they have a warehouse and major contacts there."

Mindi grinned. "That's it. Get this to your friend Tony. Let's see if this closes the loop somehow. He'll be a hero."

Jeff sat back in his chair with a sigh. "I hope this helps their investigation. Even though this is fun, it's time to wrap it up. We need a vacation . . ."

~

Mindi had headed to bed. Jeff prepared to meditate and was going to find Moreno and give him the latest information they'd found. But as soon as Jeff lifted toward the ceiling, his cell phone rang.

Dang it. Jeff dropped back into his body and opened his eyes. The caller ID said *Charlene.* What could she want?

"Hello?"

"Jeff. Charlene. Hope I didn't call too late."

"Just getting ready to turn in. What's up?"

"I was going over the schedule for the next set of photo shoots and saw that our agreement with you will expire soon. We've notified your agent, but I wanted to give you the courtesy of telling you that we want to activate our option." When it came to business, Charlene always got right to the point.

"You want me for the next part of the campaign?"

"Yes. Both of you. We've run several focus groups' reactions on all models from the beginning of the campaign last fall to now. You and Mindi scored the highest in three segments. Mindi as young female brunette; you, as white male, and both of you together as the 'LaDormeur couple.' The last shoot you did at the beach was fantastic. When we measured the physiological response with both the videos and the stills, you two were off the chart." She let that sink in before she went on.

"That's great. You want more?" Jeff said.

"*They* want more. And we're willing to pay for it. I know you enjoy your computer work in Seattle, but we hope to lure you away with a full-year contract this time. And we're going to sweeten the pot for Mindi too. I hope I'm not assuming too much. You two are still together, right?"

"Yeah," Jeff replied absently, thinking about what Charlene had said, then he added, "Oh, yes! Things are good. Thanks for asking. What kind of money are we talking about?"

"It's in the paperwork. It'll be sweet. And—they're willing to pay for an option of another year if we don't see market fatigue. You get the option money even if we don't renew the year after." She paused again, waiting for a response.

"You've sent it to my agent?"

"It should be in your email too."

"Okay. It sounds attractive . . ."

"Good. We'd like to move on this. My top management at the agency, the head of LaDormeur, and I would like to meet with you and Mindi as soon as possible for dinner and drinks. You all met at Halloween last year. I'm sure you remember."

"Yeah. Sure. I'll talk to Mindi—"

Charlene cut him off. "She and her agent have her paperwork too. Thanks. This is looking good for all of us."

"Great. Thanks for calling."

"Bye, Jeff. Good talking with you. Oh, one more thing on the company dinner. All husbands, wives, and significant others will be there. This is more of a social, family-building meeting, not a negotiation. There shouldn't be a need to negotiate. We've anticipated objections and hope to have covered them all. We want you two as part of the family— you two are the face of LaDormeur. I'll send you information on the reservations."

"Great, Charlene. Thanks again. Bye."

She disconnected.

Jeff had been wondering how things would work out when his contract ended. He and Mindi were getting along so well and were engaged to be engaged. He'd figured he'd stay in LA and get a job with a software firm there—his reputation should get him in. But this might be another answer to their dream come true. He smiled at the double meaning.

Charlene had mentioned that "significant others" would be there. Would she be there with Alejandro?

Jeff muted the ringer on his phone and continued what he'd started before the call.

~

Tony Moreno was sleeping next to his wife at home. Jeff morphed from his out-of-body spirit into the agent's sleeping mind. Moreno wasn't yet in REM sleep, so Jeff searched around in his mind, hoping to find the spot that would get things moving. Jeff found himself alone in Moreno's gray room as Dan the Longshoreman. Moreno appeared soon after. He wore full SWAT gear, complete with helmet, tactical vest, baton, sidearm, a plexiglass shield, and an AR-15.

He looked around. "Where is this? What are we doing here?"

"Whoa," Dan the Longshoreman said. "Were you expecting an army?"

Moreno frowned. "What?"

"You're a bit overdressed for a meeting with your CI, aren't you?"

Moreno looked down at his gear, then set down the equipment and took off his helmet. As soon as he put them on the floor, they disappeared in a silent flutter. He now only wore his black jumpsuit, marked with a large *DEA* on the front and back. He repeated, "What is this about?"

"I just said, this is a meeting with your CI. Are you interested in more information?

"You were in my head last week, weren't you?"

"You know I was."

"Am I crazy?"

"I told you this was the latest tech. How it works, that it even works, is need to know only. You don't need to know more than that it works. Got it?"

"I got it, but I'm going to request an agency psych eval."

"I don't think that's a good idea. Not yet, anyway. Now, the information I've given you has been useful." It was a statement, not a question.

"Yes. Everything has checked out. How do you know?"

Deflecting the question, Jeff asked, "Do you have the warehouse in Van Nuys under surveillance?"

"I shouldn't tell my CI anything. Agency rules."

"I take that as a yes. Don't you think I already knew it? I merely asked rhetorically to show you you're not crazy. You're blessed with information you don't have to work or pay for that has been worth the effort for you to follow up on. Okay?"

With hesitance, "Yes."

"Now, ready for some more?"

"Sure."

"Want to sit down?"

Moreno looked around, then back at Jeff—as Dan—as a folding chair appeared behind him. Jeff motioned for Moreno to look behind him at the chair that had appeared there. Moreno put his hand on the seat to confirm its reality. He glanced at Jeff sitting, hands folded in his lap with a relaxed posture, and then sat.

"Correct me if I'm wrong, but I think you and the agency have missed the connection between the Valencias and Carlos Cordoba, correct?"

"I'm listening."

"You feel confident, at least so far, that you'll be able to intercept the container of drugs coming from Cartagena next month aboard the *Aisling*. Right?"

"Well, if it doesn't happen, I've got some explaining to do, but so far, things look straight up. We've got a trace on the phone numbers, and we're watching the warehouse where we think the container will be delivered. We've contacted the shipping company and confirmed the load position of the container number you gave me. I have to say, if you'd approached me on the street instead of the way you have, I would've been even more suspicious than I am now, but you seem to know things."

"Yes, and I know about the money in your desk drawer in your office at home." Jeff looked directly into Moreno's eyes as the color drained from the agent's dream face.

He didn't blink for what seemed like a long time, then he crossed himself and lowered his eyes.

"Are you a demon? No one else knows where the money is. Only my superior knows I'm acting as a double agent, and money's involved, but the location and amount . . ."

"Tony. Have you wondered if you're being set up by the cartel for failure?"

"Yes."

"Sure, you could end up with egg on your face. But how would the cartel be able to send me to you in your head and in your dreams and in your mind? They'd do it with contact on the street. Right?"

Moreno looked around. "This place looks so real. This *is* a dream, isn't it?"

"Yes. This place is inside your head. It's a meeting place for you with others like me."

"What's this all about?"

"The information is in your files. You just haven't connected the dots. That's how you can bring this into the open without betraying that you may be going batshit crazy."

Jeff smiled, but Moreno didn't. Jeff continued, "The Valencia family owns a large cattle ranch. They provide quality beef for export. Where do the hides go? Could they go to Carlos Cordoba's tanning operation in Medellín, then the leather goes to his luggage and bag manufacturing operation? The department of Antioquia, among others of course, is a major coca growing region. We know that manufacture is usually

238

near the supply of the coca leaf, right? Then the laboratories can be anywhere, but better they be close by to minimize transport. Okay? Where do they store the product until they can put it in a container? How do they ship a container full of cocaine? They cannot put the product description on a bill of lading as 'Thirty tons of cocaine,' can they? No. So they ship meat, luggage, maybe raw leather hides, cleverly packed with their specialty product of choice among it. Cartagena is only a twelve-hour drive from Medellín, and truck traffic is routine." Jeff stopped and watched Moreno's face. "And then fifteen or more days in transit at sea. Once out of the terminal in Long Beach, the drugs disperse like dandelion seeds in the wind—up the noses of American citizens."

Moreno nodded.

"The key point for Valencia and Cordoba," Jeff continued, "is to keep their hands clean, and have loyal enough workers, packers, and transporters to get the job done without risking an information leak. But even so, I bet the DEA or Colombian police could get to someone inside the luggage factory, right? I don't know. That's their job. This is a completely different style of operation from Escobar's network of sicarios, their bloodshed, stress, and bad press."

Jeff waited for what he had said to sink in, then said, "As much as is likely to be in the container, this is probably a small operation. One spoke in one wheel of possibly many. And it's repeated several times a year, that you now suspect into Long Beach. What other cities do loads go to?"

Moreno nodded again, a thoughtful expression on his face.

"So this is probably multiplied many times over by these and other players. That's how a franchise operates. Find a system that works and duplicate it. We just don't know the full extent. But if you take out these key individuals, it may stop the wheels from spinning, or at least slow them way down." Jeff paused, maintained eye contact, and then added, "Good luck." He and his chair dissolved into glitter, settling to the floor like candy from a burst piñata.

Antonio Moreno awoke in his bedroom and lay there listening to his wife breathe softly in her sleep beside him. He arose, went to his office, and wrote a synopsis of the information he'd gleaned from his meeting with his demon. He crossed himself again and went back to sleep and awoke refreshed in the morning. On his way into the Federal Building, he stopped at his church, lit another candle, and said another prayer.

Jeff, after returning to his body in Gardena, continued to contemplate how Alejandro fit into the picture. He had a lot of money, much of which Jeff assumed was laundered through real estate and investments in various businesses. Which spoke in the wheel was he? They'd have to wait and see.

CHAPTER 15

Jeff went to sleep and immediately was falling in the traditional gray cloud space. He consciously relaxed, began to float, and ended up in Alejandro's mind as the man brushed his teeth while watching himself in the mirror.

When is this? The "where" he recognized was the bathroom in Charlene's apartment, but Jeff hadn't asked to be there. Nevertheless, he was resigned to watch. Alejandro finished brushing his teeth, turned, and opened the door. Charlene stood a few feet away, taking off the same diaphanous robe she'd been wearing during the earlier, near disastrous leap.

If it was June 15 again, immediately before Mindi leaped into Charlene, he had made a mistake wishing to be a fly on the wall—because now he was sure they're going to have sex! He had to leave. Jeff visualized the Jeannie move, with crossed arms and a nod. But he didn't leave Alejandro's head. He visualized the escape word, "ciao." And again, nothing. He was stuck in Alejandro, who was clad only in a pair of boxer shorts. He couldn't let himself be trapped. Alejandro took a few steps toward Charlene—now clad only in her bra and panties—and embraced her.

I'm not interested! Jeff shouted, *Ciao! Jeannie!* Again. Neither escape word worked. *Trapped! Why?*

Alejandro heard the voice in his head, stopped a moment, and looked over his shoulder, but he was preoccupied with, committed to, and seriously prepared for having sex with Charlene. He shook his head and continued the embrace while unclasping Charlene's bra. She put her arms around his neck and kissed him with desire.

This triggered memories Jeff had long forgotten of being with Charlene, and as attractive as she was, he wasn't interested, even though his host certainly was. He was, in fact, angry that the universe had put him here now.

Why this? Jeff felt everything Alejandro felt, but unlike his host, he wasn't enjoying it. Jeff thought about disgusting things—cleaning a toilet, a dead skunk in the road and the memory of being raging drunk in college, puking his guts out in a parking lot. Those thoughts intruded into his host's mind but only created a brief problem with his concentration. Charlene held Alejandro close and caressed him, which distracted him from the images Jeff was trying to plant in his mind.

Jeff neared panic, something he hadn't felt in a dream for almost a year—but for different reasons now. He had no desire, even through a surrogate, to have sex with Charlene again. The panic started to take hold. *Is this how Mindi felt?* He thought of his escape word again but to no avail. He remembered Mindi telling him what would happen, and the scene unfolded just as she described, and when it did . . .

Charlene's hands went sides of her head. She shouted, "What? *Oww!*"

Jeff recognized this as the point where Mindi's story had

242

ended, but it wasn't finished for him.

Alejandro froze. "*¿Qué?* What's wrong?"

Alejandro was no longer aroused. Jeff gratefully felt no more discomfort at being a participant, yet he continued to see the world through this guy's eyes.

Charlene still held her head. "A scream! In my head. It hurts!"

Alejandro held himself up by his arms.

"Get off me!" Charlene screamed as she pushed at Alejandro, who rolled off to the side.

He reached for her. "*Chiquita,* what is wrong? Are you alright?"

"No, I'm not!" Charlene was off the bed and had grabbed a bathrobe on her way to the bathroom. She turned on the light. Squinting, she looked in the mirror as she massaged her temples.

Alejandro stood behind her and put his hands on her waist. "What happened? What did I do?"

Charlene turned around.

He looked her in the eyes, "*¿Paso algo malo?* Please tell me, what is wrong?"

"Alejo, you did nothing. Something in my head. I heard a voice, a loud scream in my head." She leaned into him, and he put his arms around her. She wriggled free. "Alejo, you should go. Tonight is not a good night." She left the bedroom and walked into the living room, holding the robe tight around her.

Alejandro followed her. She sat in the dark, holding her head.

"Did I hurt you?"

Her mood hadn't changed. "No, you're fine. Please, let yourself out."

He looked at her, but she didn't meet his eyes, so he dressed quickly and shut the door behind him.

Jeff heard Alejandro's confused thoughts as he replayed the event. *The pain in* my *head. A pain in her head. Ever since I met this woman, things have been bad. Crazy dreams—dinosaurs, snakes, cages, running. She is beautiful, but there are other women not possessed as she. She is poison. I must go. Esto se acabó.* It's finished.

Alejandro gave his head a shake as he pressed the keyless ignition. Jeff returned to the all-encompassing grayness and in a moment gratefully awoke in his bed next to Mindi, who was still sleeping.

This was the first time he mentally spoke directly with whatever was controlling their dreams. "Damn you, universe. Putting me through that, making me watch you terrify Mindi, scare Charlene. It's unfair, so unfair!" He shook his fist at the ceiling.

As he transcribed the dream event, Jeff's anger dissolved and transformed into compassion for Mindi's pain. He calmed enough to reflect that Mindi had been there for the first part of what he'd seen. When he'd heard her description before, he'd felt her pain. But now that he'd been in Alejandro's mind at the instant Mindi leaped into Charlene, Jeff felt the close bond between himself and Mindi grow even stronger. He wrote it all down in his journal, and as he reread the entry, he understood why he'd needed to see that scene tonight. Alejandro's role in Charlene's life after the evening of June 15 would be over. He and Mindi had witnessed the couple's breakup.

Jeff closed the notebook, went back to bed, and went to sleep. He fell again. *Another leap? Relax. Float.* Wait for the lights to go on, the sound to come up, and start experiencing whoever his host was this time. He just didn't want it to be Alejandro again. But here was another unplanned leap into . . .

Who is this?

He got no answer, only the feel of a warm summer day and bright sunshine. The view was a coin-operated newspaper box on the sidewalk, the front page just visible through the scratched and sun-fogged window. The headline read, *DEA Busts Cocaine Smuggling Ring in Long Beach.* The view changed, robbing Jeff of the opportunity to see the newspaper's masthead or the date. His host fumbled in his pocket for some change. Jeff saw the pinstriped sleeve of a suit jacket, the white cuff of a shirt, a watchband half covered by the shirt cuff, and in the palm, two nickels, a dime, and two pennies. Jeff felt the guy's frustration at not having change for the paper. Then Jeff was whisked back into his gray envelope, falling and awakening again next to the still-sleeping Mindi.

This latest time travel leaps had given him information that comforted him. Alejandro would leave Charlene alone. And sometime, when the weather was warm, there'd be a major drug bust. Was that a past bust or theirs? He wished he knew more.

Jeff searched the internet for a history of major drug busts in Long Beach and found nothing and concluded that had been a future leap. As he finished the latest journal entry, Mindi came into the kitchen, gave him a kiss, and asked, "What are you working on?"

"Had unsolicited dreams last night. Two of them. Here, sit and get started. I'll get you a cup—you want tea or coffee?"

Jeff turned the page back to the start where he'd leaped into Alejandro in Charlene's bedroom. She began to read.

Jeff brought her coffee, set it down in front of her, and

watched her face.

She paused a moment, reached for the cup, and noticed he was watching her.

There were tears in her eyes.

Jeff nodded, then looked at the notebook to guide her gaze back to it.

When she had finished reading, she looked at him with such compassion. "Jeff, what can I say? This has been a roller coaster. I know what you said after I got back from this before, that it didn't bother you about Charlene. But it had to at some level. She's our friend." She motioned at the page. "I'm so sorry you had to go through it and see it for yourself."

Jeff tried to maintain a stoic look on his face, but tears welled up in his eyes too.

"Yeah, I do feel bad for Charlene. Even though it hasn't happened yet, it will, and she'll have grieving to go through. Then she'll be happy he's gone. Especially after she sees this . . ." Jeff turned to the next page and urged her to read the entry with the newspaper headline.

Mindi's head jerked up after reading it.

"Yeah, right?" Jeff said. "I didn't get to read it, but if his name is in that article, she'll see it. As will everybody at LaDormeur and her agency. We don't know what the financial impact will be on her ad agency if the DEA busts him, and his bankroll is pulled out of the budget, but . . ."

"What do we do now, Jeff? Have we done everything on the flow chart?"

"Well . . ." He thought about what he wanted to say. "There's still Sofia. There might be a leap into her to see what she knows. What do you think?"

Mindi nodded. "Yes. At least to satisfy our curiosity. If Carlos gets busted, he might have trained her to move into his role while he's in prison, and the band plays on."

"Do you think there could be a shootout? Or have we been watching too many episodes of *Narcos?*"

Jeff shrugged. "Moreno and Carlos both carry guns."

~

Another dream. Jeff recognized Carlos's Rolex and rings. He unfolded a note on which was written, *Paquetito, el 25 de junio en el puerto pequeño.* A cell phone beeped next to him on the table. He pressed the home button and the screen revealed—overlaying a picture of Max with Sofia—the date and time: *20 de junio de 2018.* Carlos sat in the main salon of the *Miranda II*, eyes alight with desire, watching the lovely Miranda Valencia in a skimpy two-piece bathing suit as she walked toward the stern deck doors. Carlos punched a speed dial number and put the phone up to his ear, and the speaker announced the sound of call going through, but before anyone answered, Jeff's view went gray. The leap was over.

He awoke with a jolt, feeling nauseous, and it didn't pass while he sat documenting the short dream. He pulled out the flow chart and timelines they'd created from their dream books, including what could happen into the future. Today was May 31. This leap contained information for three weeks from now. Jeff couldn't translate the full contents of the note, but he had memorized it and written it down.

Mindi walked into the room, and Jeff smiled up at her.

"You're up early." She looked down at the journal and their planning paperwork. "You had another dream?"

"Yeah, a leap—it was really short, though. What does this say?" He still felt queasy.

"Let's see. Small package, June 25, at the small port.

Small port? Hmm." She checked the translate app on her phone. "*Puerto pequeño* is idiomatic. It can mean 'marina.' Small package, June 25, at the marina."

"It'll be delivered the day before the container gets in, right?" Jeff said. "So what's in it won't come from the container contents, because the container won't be unloaded yet. It's singular, so no boxes from Bogotá by way of Bakersfield, right? Just one package."

"Yes. A small package."

Jeff sat with his elbows on the table, chin resting in his hands, frowning as he thought.

"Are you okay? What's the matter?"

"I feel a little nauseous. It started right after the leap. That's never happened before." He gestured toward the notebook. "You know, we still don't have control over whether we go into the future or the past when we leap while we're asleep."

Mindi sat across from him. "What about a leap from a meditation? An out-of-body experience?"

"That's mostly been done in our real-time, except those leaps into the June 15 debacle at Charlene's. I don't know how we managed it that day. Going ghost, out-of-body into real-time, is the only time we've been able to control a leap."

"Well, yeah, but we've still gotten things done."

"But not being able to control our dreams distracts from us being able to follow a fixed plan, that I'm sure it's controlled by someone. We have no free will, then, but still have to make it up as we go along." He paused and rubbed his stomach. "You know, I still feel a little sick. I'm going to go take something."

"I'm sorry. I hope you feel better. You know, you said yourself the dream-thing is evolving. We're doing better than when this all started."

Jeff looked at her. "You always seem to say the right thing at the right time in a most uncomplicated way." He smiled. "You're right. But you know, this has become like a three-hour movie that could have been cut to an hour and a half. I'm antsy to get it over with."

~

Carlos ordered a car to pick up Sofia at the airport. Jeff and Mindi, in ghost form, sat in the back of Moreno's Suburban while the two agents watched the arriving limousine. Moreno snapped pictures of Sofia as she got out of the limo and collected her luggage from the driver.

Mindi telepathed quietly to Jeff, *Look at those bags. Are they Carlos's product? Wow. There must be a couple thousand dollars' worth there. How long is she planning to stay?*

See if you can leap into her now, Jeff telepathed back. *Catch her off guard. She'll think it's jet lag if she's as sensitive as her father. And find out how long she's going to stay.*

Moreno pulled the camera down from his face, turned around, and looked into the back seat but saw nothing. Jeff smiled. He figured Moreno had heard them talking, but Jeff didn't care now. Moreno was going to need a long vacation after this investigation anyway. Maybe he'd get a promotion— or a desk job.

~

The ship was due to arrive the day after tomorrow, the twenty-sixth. Mindi and Jeff had to attend to real-time business today. Jeff would meet with his agent to finalize the new contract Charlene's agency had sent over. His agent had confided on

249

the phone that this contract was unusual because so many models, especially new ones, were contracted on a one-off basis. The agent was pleased; this would be a lucrative deal for both of them.

Mindi wouldn't be joining him. She had a pre-shoot meeting to go over the mood board. Jeff drove Mindi's Honda, dropped her off in front of the studio, and confirmed they'd stay in touch when each was done. Jeff watched her as she walked to the entrance of the building, until an impatient driver leaned on the horn behind him to demand he move on.

It was close to noon when Jeff finished his meeting and texted Mindi that he'd wait for her text in the parking garage.

He felt they had done everything they could to set up the DEA for the bust. The universe had had nothing else for them to do of late, and he was looking forward to them living like normal people. So, to stave off boredom while he sat in his car waiting for Mindi, Jeff meditated and rose out of his body and headed to the *Miranda II*. Sofia, wearing a swimsuit, lay on the bow deck, on a lawn chair, reading a magazine, enjoying the Southern California weather. Two young men on an adjacent dock walked over to strike up a conversation with this pretty young woman. Miranda was, as usual, lounging in her swimsuit in the covered area in the stern. Roberto sat at the table nearby, working on his laptop, and Carlos was watching a soccer game on ESPN inside.

Jeff hovered nearby, deciding what to do next as he watched the lifestyle of the rich and, if things worked out, soon-to-be famous as felons on a luxury yacht in Southern California. In a couple of days, things should be more exciting.

The DEA agents had temporarily left their post and were not present when a late-model Jaguar sedan arrived. Jeff was surprised to see Alejandro punch in the gate code and walk down the dock and onto the *Miranda II*. Roberto and Miranda greeted him with a smile and a quick *hola* in Spanish and then went back to what they'd been doing. By the way the three acted, Jeff figured he was either staying on the yacht or was a regular visitor of late.

Alejandro walked into the salon. Carlos looked up, muted the TV, and motioned for him to sit down. Alejandro gestured to the bar.

"*¿Quieres una cerveza?*" Carlos said. You want a beer?

Alejandro helped himself, then sat down opposite Carlos, twisted the cap, and took a long, slow drink.

"Everything is arranged," Alejandro said. "The package should be delivered tomorrow, which will assure everything will go smoothly if the *federales* have something planned. You have everything arranged?"

"*Sí.* It is arranged."

"*Bueno.*"

They turned toward the soccer game and Carlos unmuted the TV.

What is this package, and what is it supposed to assure? Jeff wondered as he felt another wave of nausea, but it passed. He hadn't told Moreno about the package. He was sure the agent had his hands full with the bust. Jeff and Mindi had done everything they could to feed information to the DEA. He was disappointed that they still had no information to tie these people to the arriving shipment. But even so, he felt Charlene had been made safe.

Jeff looked at the clock and would head back to the car soon—and his body—currently in the front seat in a back corner of the fourth-level of a parking garage in downtown LA. But first, he wanted to see what Roberto was working on.

A peek over the man's shoulder revealed a spreadsheet

open on the laptop with no title on the heading. There were columns headed by an alphameric code across the top. Down the sides were additional codes, none of which made sense to Jeff.

Jeff slipped into Roberto's mind easily, hoping to see what he could learn. 'Berto switched back and forth between two pages. The second page listed the western states and major cities that used some of the same codes.

Roberto's using the database function to apportion the shipment for distribution!

Roberto looked up and around.

He heard me! Jeff quieted his mind.

Jeff asked where the key to the codes were, and unlike the night when he kept getting kicked out of 'Berto's memory and into his gray room, in this leap he was pleased, as he was guided directly to the answer to his request.

The list was neatly laid out in the man's mind.

A1011—cocaína.

B1012.a—tabletas de fentanilo

B1012.b—fentanilo en polvo

C1013—heroína

Holy crap! The surprise coursed through Jeff's consciousness like fireworks, and he shut his loud thinking down right away, but not before Roberto grabbed his face as if he'd been slapped.

Jeff left Roberto's mind and returned to his out-of-body ghost form, hovering nearby as he watched Roberto rub his closed eyes, massage the back of his neck, and stretch his shoulders.

Miranda watched him for a moment, then said, "'Berto, are you alright?"

"I'm fine. It's nothing." But it *was* something. Roberto

went into the main salon, passing by the two men watching the soccer game, yet did not glance at them as he went toward the staterooms.

Carlos shouted after him, "'Berto, come join us!" But the man disappeared beyond the doorway without looking back.

Jeff glided off the boat and saw that the Suburban had returned and hoped that one of the two agents inside, eating hamburgers, was Tony Moreno. He knew that the drug dealers were so nonchalant because they thought the DEA agent was protecting their interests rather than being a threat to their operation. The Latino agent had taken their insultingly small bribes, and they felt protected within their expensive clubhouse.

Jeff entered the Suburban and was happy to see Moreno there. He was finishing up the last few bits of his fries as Jeff slipped into his head and said, *Hey Tony, Dan here.*

"Huh?" Moreno said out loud.

"I didn't say anything," Tony's partner for that day, Carl, said, glancing at Tony, who stared out the window, trying to distract Carl from his spontaneous reaction to the voice in his head. Carl looked to see what Moreno was looking at just as Miranda stood and took off her beach robe, showcasing the too-small swimsuit top trying to hold everything in. "Yeah, I know, right? Must be nice."

Tony kept his focus out the window, even as she sat down and removed herself from view.

Inside his head, he asked Dan the Longshoreman, *What do you want? You're not real. Leave me alone.*

Oh, I'm real. Believe it. Everything I've given you has been good, right? Do you want more?

Silence from Moreno.

The shipment on Tuesday has more than cocaine in it. There's fentanyl and heroin, too. These folks are serious. It's an important load, and that's probably why the movers and shakers of this operation are right there on that boat, sitting directly across the water from where the container will be off-loaded. The evidence is on a laptop on the boat. I repeat, the evidence is on Valencia's laptop on the Miranda II.

Moreno didn't move, just kept staring through the windshield.

"Tony, down boy," Carl said. "She sat down a while ago. You won't be able to see her again for a while. Besides, your missus wouldn't appreciate knowing you were lusting after that rich woman. She's way out of your league."

Jeff had stayed to see what Moreno's response to his partner would be to the distraction.

Moreno snapped out of it. "Yeah, Carl. I know. I just got to thinking. We've been watching these swinging dicks for a couple of months now. All we have to show for it are hemorrhoids. HQ told us to be here, and my CI has given us enough to grab the shipment, but we still got nothing linking these guys to that shipment, except a strong suspicion on the CI's part. We got nothing when I checked on them for that kid's party bust a little while back. This is frustrating. Been trying to figure out how to get them to slip up."

Carl nodded. "Well, maybe they'll make that slip when we grab the container."

"Sure, but they may just go to ground. They're scheduled to leave July 1, anyway. If they left early, we'd have nothing on them. They've been stocking up with provisions, getting a few hand trucks every couple of days like they're getting ready to leave. I bet that boat can do thirty or forty knots, easy. At that rate, they'd make it beyond the two-hundred-mile limit in a morning. Then we can't touch them, even if we had proof."

"Sure, but remember, the Coasties have a fast response boat. It can do up to sixty-seven miles per hour. Should we notify them to be on alert?"

"Good idea. No harm in at least letting Williams know. Have them ask the Coast Guard to be on alert. Get it started through channels."

Dan? Dan? What about the laptop? Moreno asked of Jeff.

Jeff was satisfied Moreno was taking the tip seriously, but said as he left the agent's mind, *There's evidence on the laptop.* Jeff made it back to his car in the garage and woke up just as his cell phone announced a text from Mindi.

How about lunch? You done?

He texted back: *Be right there.*

Mindi returned a thumbs-up emoji, and Jeff pulled out of the garage.

At lunch, Jeff filled Mindi in on his morning's spy activities.

She told him that all she knew about fentanyl was it was alleged to be involved in Michael Jackson, Prince, and Tom Petty's deaths by overdose. Petty just last October.

"We might be saving lives with what we're doing."

"Sure. But I'll still be glad when it's all done with."

"Me too. Want some good news? They told me at the studio they want us to go to Jamaica for the next series of shoots with another couple. They're waiting for your new contract. You got that done today, right?"

"Yep. My agent's got it."

"Then they'll be getting in touch with you too. It's scheduled for the second week in July. I've got to go back for another short meeting tomorrow morning."

"You want me to come along? Or drive you?"

"No, love. I'll just take the bus. Less hassle. I assume you're going to want to keep watch and figure out what the big deal is with the package delivery to the yacht, right? It'll be easier to do if you're at home rather than sitting in a musty garage."

"Okay. If you're sure."

"Yes. I'm also sure I'd like to spend the rest of this afternoon over at the beach. What do you think?"

They walked in the surf, sat on a blanket, people watched, read escapist novels, and later chose a restaurant close to the beach. It was a glorious afternoon.

~

The next morning, Mindi told Jeff she'd text him when she was on her way home from the photographer's planning meeting, gave him a kiss, and headed for the bus stop.

Jeff finished his breakfast, closed the curtains, turned off his phone, and settled down to meditate. He went out-of-body and headed for the Cabrillo Marina in Long Beach.

The Suburban was parked there, but there were two DEA agents that Jeff hadn't seen before. He slipped into the back of the rig and listened to the two agents talk baseball and doze—one sleeping, then the other. One of them walked over to the marina restaurant and returned with two coffees.

"Jeez," said the officer, "I paid five dollars apiece for these coffees, and they aren't even full to the top. Can you believe that?"

The other replied, "Only two creams? Last time we buy there."

You're probably right, Jeff thought to himself. This duty would be shut down after they busted the container.

Jeff sat there, bored. The agents' notes on the clipboard noted a Jaguar and its single male occupant had arrived at 09:15 and left at 09:35. Jeff assumed it was Alejandro, but there were no notations about a delivery.

It wasn't Alejandro that delivered the small package, unless it'd fit in his pocket. After a while Jeff returned to the apartment to give his body a break, check to see if Mindi had sent a text or left a voice mail, and have a light snack for lunch. Since she hadn't yet tried to contact him, he'd wait for her call.

He sat and read his book on the deck, and at one-thirty, not having heard from her, he sent her a text, figuring if the meeting was running long, she wouldn't text back. At two-thirty, Jeff decided to call, but it went straight to voice mail. She should have been in touch by now, so he called the photographer.

He drummed his fingers impatiently, waiting for the recorded voice to get over the choices, and after pressing the right selection, he talked to the photographer with whom Mindi had the meeting.

"No, Jeff. We got done a little after twelve. Sorry I didn't call you. I found her cell phone on the floor under the table. I'm always frantic when I can't find mine. Just a sec. Yes, the screen shows a text and a missed call."

Concern rising, Jeff said, "She's not home yet. You said she left right after you were done?"

"Yes."

Working to control the rising panic, Jeff said, "We'll come by later and get the phone." Jeff thanked him and disconnected.

She'd dropped her cell phone. It'd been well over two hours, and it was only a forty-five-minute bus ride. Something was wrong.

Jeff reached out telepathically.

Nothing.

Shit! What's happened?

He contacted the transit company, asking if there'd been any accidents on the Metro J-Line. No accidents. This wasn't like her. She should be home by now.

An intuitive flash hit him. He wanted to deny it, but the thought pestered him.

Alejandro! Could it be his doing?

He had to investigate. But he had trouble centering himself enough to meditate and couldn't focus enough to go out-of-body.

Relax. Breathe. Relax. Breathe. Be by a gentle stream watching the water flow by. Breathe. Relax. Breathe. He couldn't concentrate.

His phone announced a text message from a blocked number:

We have her. If you want to see her again, call off the federales. Do not wait! It was unsigned.

Jeff felt a surge of panic. His intuition had been right. It was Alejandro! *But how could they know about us? How did they find her, get this number?* How could he know about the bust? If they knew, why were they so nonchalant on the boat? So many questions, but this was critical. He sat back on the pillow and began his breathing exercises, but his mind raced with thoughts. First of fear, then guilt that he hadn't driven her to the appointment. He pushed those thoughts back to deal with the problem at hand.

She was the small package, and if they sailed, he'd never see her again.

Damn. What do I do? Relax and take a breath.

It took every bit of discipline that Jeff could muster, but he centered himself by breathing deep and long to achieve the alpha state required to leave his body. He hovered over the apartment building, feeling powerless, looking down through the now transparent roof, ceiling, and floor into Mindi's apartment, and suddenly he was at the marina. The Suburban remained parked in the same place with the same agents from the morning. He checked their surveillance log. It read: *Delivery, 13:42, white unmarked van. One driver, large cardboard moving box hand trucked to boat. Loaded by crew.*

The entire group, three men and two women, was in the salon eating and drinking wine and beer like nothing was going to happen. Jeff flew down the passageway, down the short stairway to the staterooms, and looked in each room. Nothing. The last door on the left toward the bow was the storeroom. He slid through the wall, but it was too dark to see, and quiet. Frustrated with his lack of vision, his anxiety built. *Don't think of the consequences. Think of the solutions.* He repeated his breathing exercises in his mind. *Light switch. Think. Light switch. Breathe. Switch on. Breathe. Switch on.*

The switch clicked, and the single light in the storeroom came on. Boxes with grocery store markings were stacked against the bulkhead, and right in front of him sat a box marked *Extra-large box.* It was sealed. He reached to open it, but his hands went right through.

Damn.

He kneeled and put his head through the side of the box. He couldn't see, but he could hear soft breathing. Breathing he recognized, from sleeping beside her for the last six months, as that of his friend and lover.

Mindi. Mindi. Wake up.

Soft breathing.

They've drugged her.

He knew where she was, and she was safe—for now. They wouldn't know that he knew. What to do? He didn't want

259

to leave her, but she'd be fine until she woke up. Would she panic? He'd figure something out before then. He stood up.

What could he do? His mind worked like a disk drive, searching for the DOS command to activate a program. Then it clicked: *Charlene!*

Immediately he was in her apartment, watching her talking on the phone, a conversation about the LaDormeur account and her plans to attend the next photo shoot.

Jeff didn't wait. He concentrated and slipped into her mind without effort.

Charlene. Charlie! I need to talk. It's an emergency.

Charlene stood, taking the phone down from her ear and looking around.

"What? Who's there?" Jeff was the only one who had ever called her Charlie. "Jeff, that's you? What the . . ?"

Charlene lifted the phone back up to her ear. "Phil, I've got to call you back. Sorry." She clicked off and dropped the phone on the chair and put her hands to her temples.

"Jeff, are you in my mind?" She gave her head a shake. "What are you doing here? I don't like this. You've done this before, haven't you? Get out!"

No, Charlie. Listen, I've got a lot to explain. I will. I wouldn't be here if it wasn't an emergency. Please. Will you please listen?

"Now I know what Mindi must have felt like." She took a deep breath, looked around the room like there'd be an answer there, then said, "This better be good."

Thank you. Are you and Alejandro still seeing each other?

"How did you know? And why do you want to know? Are you jealous?"

No. No, nothing like that. No. Please answer me. It's important. Are you still together?

"Something happened about a week ago and he hasn't

called me. Why? Get to the point!" She wanted to be in charge.

Alejandro is a drug dealer, he told her. *A major drug dealer. A bad actor. There's a shipment from Colombia tomorrow into Long Beach.*

"I don't care what he is or what he's doing now. I'm sure it's over between us, and I think I'm glad."

Charlene, they've taken Mindi hostage. She's been kidnapped. And drugged. They'll kill her if I don't stop the DEA from interfering. There's a container of drugs arriving in Long Beach tomorrow.

"Jeff, you're mad. This is so . . . What do—"

I . . . we . . . We've got to act fast. Please . . . I'll explain later, but . . . we've got to save Mindi. You're the only one with credibility that can get through to the DEA, or the FBI, to raid the yacht where she's being held before they do something to her.

"Jeff, I'm getting a horrible headache."

Charlie, please. I could phone you, but it would take longer for me to do that . . . I need you to call the DEA right away. Write down this number.

She looked around. "Just a minute, I'll get a pen. Okay."

Ready? He gave her Moreno's name and phone number. *Tell him you know Alejandro Sarís, and you found out he's involved in something illegal. You'll have his attention. If he hesitates, tell him you know about Dan the Longshoreman. He'll understand.*

"Jeff, this doesn't make sense. You'll tell me what this is all about?"

I will, but not now. Okay, here's the rest of it. Tell him Mindi's been kidnapped and threatened with murder if the drug bust isn't called off. Give them Mindi's name. Tell them she works for you. That's important. Tell them she's being held hostage on board a yacht, the Miranda II *. . . slip 186 . . . at the Cabrillo*

Marina, Long Beach.
"Who's Dan the Longshoreman?"
Me. But don't tell him that. Don't. It's important that you don't tell them that! It's complicated. Charlene, you've got questions, but there's no time. You'll get answers later, I promise. Listen, we know that a full container of cocaine, fentanyl, and heroin is on a ship to be unloaded tomorrow. If the DEA intercepts that load before Mindi is free, they'll kill her and dump her in the ocean after they leave the harbor. These people are evil.

"I want to believe you. I know you well enough . . ."
Charlene, thank you. I'll explain it all later. Forgive me if I've scared you. We've got to rescue Mindi. Please?

"Okay, okay. I'll call. What if I can't talk to him right away?"
I'll stay here with you and help. Call Moreno now. If we can't get him, we'll do something else. Only you, a real person who knows Mindi and Sarís, can get this done. It's the only way.

The woman who answered at the DEA told Charlene that the agent was on duty and would return the call at his earliest opportunity.

"This can't wait," she said, her voice full of authority. "This is extremely urgent. It's about the drug shipment from Colombia tomorrow at Long Beach terminal."

"Who's calling, please?"

"Charlene Thomsen."

"One moment. Please hold."

After a few moments, with a background of static, "This is Agent Moreno. What is this regarding?"

"Agent, this is urgent. I am calling about the case you're on, about the drugs being shipped from Colombia arriving tomorrow in Long Beach."

"I'm listening."

She gave Moreno the details that Jeff had told her, including that Mindi worked for her agency, and that she knew Alejandro and that he somehow knew the DEA might intercept the drugs. That Ms. Madisen was a hostage until the bust was called off.

"Ms. Thomsen, how do you know about this shipment?"

Tell him about Dan the Longshoreman, Jeff whispered in her mind.

"From Dan. He's a longshoreman."

There was a very long pause and a sigh. "Okay. Say I believe you. What else do you know?"

"She's been drugged and is being held onboard a yacht."

"Which yacht? And you know this from Dan?"

"Yes. The *Miranda II*. Cabrillo Marina, Long Beach. Agent Moreno, I know Alejandro, better than I want to admit. He's holding Ms. Madisen on . . ."

In her mind, she said, *Jeff, whose yacht is it?*

Roberto Valencia's.

"Robert Valencia's yacht. He told me it's a large yacht, and they're going to leave soon. They'll kill her and dump her body overboard if they don't get their way. Can you help?"

Moreno asked for her full name, phone number, and address, and told her that agents from the Seattle office would be in touch soon to get a full statement.

Charlene said, "Oh, Agent Moreno, Ms. Madisen's boyfriend is living at her apartment in Gardena. Do you want her address? His phone number? Just a moment."

"Yes. Thank you, Ms. Thomsen."

Jeff let out a sob of relief. *Charlene, thank you. You did so well. I'm going to go check on her. When the agents ask about Dan, tell him he's Moreno's CI, and they can ask him. I'll be in touch. We'll be in touch. Thank you, Charlene, thank you.*

"CI?"

Confidential Informant. It's cop-talk.

"How are you doing all this?" Charlene asked. "This is more than just dreams for you now, isn't it?"

Yes, but no time to explain. If you want to know more now, and I know you're curious, go to the Metaphysical Bookstore on Yesler Avenue. Talk to Ingrid; tell her you know Jeff and Mindi.

"What about?"

I'm sure she'll know. Mention our names. She can give you enough until this is all over. Go take some aspirin. I'll call you. Thanks. Bye.

"Bye, Jeff. I hope this does it."

Me too. He left.

Charlene poured herself a stiff drink, took some aspirin, and found the Cabrillo Marina on Google Earth. She stared at the image and replayed the conversation with Jeff as the alcohol took effect.

CHAPTER 16

Jeff went back into his body, checked his phone, and saw another text:

Time is running out.

Jeff felt much better since Charlene's call to Moreno. He decided not to answer the text, but it ramped up his anxiety even more. He returned to his out-of-body state and found Moreno at the Federal Building during a briefing on tomorrow's activities.

Moreno, several other agents, and Jeff listened to the recording of Charlene's phone call, and then they talked with the team leader assigned to the warehouse in Van Nuys.

Jeff took a deep virtual breath to control his anxiety. *Agent Moreno, it's Dan. You believe Charlene Thomsen, right? Don't react. Just tell me.*

Yes. Who are *you? How are you doing this?*

Another time. This is real. Ms. Madisen is being held in a storeroom on board the yacht. She's unconscious, probably drugged. Her fiancé has received two text messages warning they'll kill her if you don't call off the bust. I know you can't stop the operation, but she must be rescued. What are you doing about that?

The FBI has been called. Kidnapping's their gig. We verified that Ms. Thomsen is credible. I don't know what they're doing. That's their jurisdiction.

And the Coast Guard has been notified?

Yes. Dan, how do you know all this?

Agent Moreno.

What?

Good luck.

Jeff left Moreno's head and shot back to the apartment in Gardena, arriving just as the entrance buzzer announced a visitor. Jeff shot back into his body and stumbled to the intercom. It was the FBI. He pushed the buzzer, letting them in. Soon after, a knock sounded at the door.

Two agents flashed their badges and asked if he was Mindi Madisen's friend.

"Yes, she's my fiancée."

He told them he'd taken a nap and didn't know what was going on. He was expecting her home, and had woken up and saw the texts on his phone advising she'd been kidnapped. "I was just about to call the police."

They peppered him with questions, to which he intentionally had few answers.

"Do you know Charlene Thomsen?"

"Yes."

"How?"

"We used to date in Seattle."

"Do you know Alejandro Sarís?"

"Who? No."

"Does Ms. Madisen know Charlene Thomsen?"

"Yes."

"How?"

"She's a model for Charlene's ad agency."

"Does Ms. Madisen know Alejandro Sarís?"

"I don't think so, no."

"Are any of these names familiar? Carlos Cordoba?"

"No."

"Roberto Valencia?"

"No."

"Miranda Valencia?"

"No."

"Have you ever visited the Cabrillo Marina in Long Beach?"

"No. What is this all about, agent? Why all these questions? Are these the people that kidnapped Mindi? Do you know where she is? How can we get her? All these questions are scaring me. I answered your questions. Please tell me."

"Mr. Marlen, we have word that Alejandro Sarís is alleged to be involved in the kidnapping of your fiancé and she may be held hostage at that marina. There are other agencies involved, but I'm not permitted to share any details. I can tell you that the Long Beach Police Department has been dispatched, as well as our agency. All care will be taken to assure the safety of the hostage, which at this time, is presumed to be Ms. Madisen."

"What can I do?"

"We'll need your phone so we can determine where the texts originated from."

Jeff gave them his phone.

"Password?"

The agent opened the phone.

The FBI agent said, "I see that the caller ID is blocked, but we may be able to unlock the information and ID the sender."

"Okay. But I'll be without a phone, so how will they contact me, and how can I contact you?"

"We'll return the phone to you as soon as possible. I suggest you purchase a prepaid phone. Here's my card. Call this number as soon as you get a new number. We'll monitor incoming calls and texts and have the technician forward phone calls and texts to the new phone. It's the best I can do, but it should be sufficient. Our job is to capture the kidnappers and release your fiancé. Thank you, Mr. Marlen. We'll keep you informed."

The other agent, who'd been surveying the apartment, presumably for clues, turned and said to Jeff, "Mr. Marlen, as much as you may be tempted, please do not go to the marina. It could put your fiancée in greater danger."

"I understand."

"Please, do not go to the marina."

Jeff nodded.

As soon as the FBI left, he grabbed his keys and wallet, went to the nearby big-box store, and bought prepaid sim cards and minutes for his burner phone. He activated it and called the FBI agent with the new phone number. Then he called Charlene, told her what he knew about the DEA and FBI, and gave her his temporary phone number. "Charlene, please let me know when the FBI or the DEA contact you, okay?"

She agreed and told him she'd rather talk with him on the phone than in her head. He forced a laugh, saying he understood, but that he couldn't have done it otherwise.

"Jeff, I'm worried about Mindi."

Jeff headed back to his apartment and took up the meditation pose.

He arrived back at the marina and hovered to survey

the scene. He saw that the Suburban was gone and what he thought were unmarked police cars were parked out of sight from the yacht. He saw a man and a woman setting up a camera on the dock with a clear view of the yacht about sixty yards away.

He glided over to them and confirmed that they were watching the yacht.

Jeff hovered beside the team to get a look at their arrangement—an infrared, thermal-imaging camera with a long zoom lens. However, when he got close, he created interference. The small monitor on the back of the camera pixelated. He backed off, and it cleared. He tested it again, the static returned when he got close.

He slid into the female officer's mind and watched through her eyes. Once sure of her observation, she picked up a radio, keyed the mike, and said, "This is Eagle-Eye. Do you read?"

"Copy."

"We've got five subjects in the main cabin. There's one heat signature toward the bow on the port side on the floor, about the size of a large dog."

"Copy. Continue observations. Report changes."

"Roger."

Jeff was satisfied they had an eye on the locations of the group. He exited the officer, causing a short burst of static in the camera, flew toward the yacht, dropped down through the bow deck, and into the storeroom. The light was still on, and the top of the box had been opened. Someone had been in there and checked on her.

Mindi lay in a ball at the bottom of the box, still unconscious. He saw a small drop of dried blood on her neck and guessed they'd given her a shot to knock her out. As he backed away from the box, he went through the wall into the passageway. He saw on the outside of the door that a length of pipe had been stretched from jamb to jamb with a bungie tight around it and the doorknob. The crude arrangement secured it from the outside, so if Mindi awoke, she couldn't open the door from the inside and escape.

Now what?

Mindi had said that Sofia didn't know about the drugs, or at least, she couldn't find any complicity on Sofia's part in the drug dealings. She worshipped her father. Sofia seemed to be innocent. She got along well with the others, having known them since she was a girl, so Jeff probably couldn't convince her to be his ally, even if he explained that her father and the other three were dealing in deadly drugs.

He dared not leap into Alejandro, as he'd know something was up because he'd guessed his and Mindi's involvement. Carlos knew about the kidnapping, since he got the note, and he had a gun. He felt sure the group on the boat hadn't grabbed Mindi, so who was it that had done the kidnapping, and where were they?

Miranda Valencia had been merely a messenger. She was there to satisfy Roberto's ego. Roberto was the business end in the States; the accounting on the laptop confirmed that.

Jeff jumped back to the apartment to see if he had any calls or messages. Nothing.

Jeff felt he needed to pay a visit to Moreno again to maybe see if Roberto had contacted him, thinking he was still working on their behalf, to press him for information regarding Alejandro's suspicion of a bust.

Moreno was in his cubicle waiting for word from the surveillance team in Van Nuys when Dan the Longshoreman announced his presence.

I was wondering if I'd hear from you again, the agent said with no humor. *We have to stop meeting like this.*

This ain't my idea of a good time, Moreno. Tell me, have you heard from the people on the yacht?

Yes.

Who?

Valencia.

Does he still think you're still on the take to betray the agency?

I think so.

What did he say?

He asked if the agency had any information on what he was doing in the United States. I told him what I told him before, that my superiors were merely suspicious because of the Colombian registry of the boat and his country's history of drugs, that my surveillance was because the agency didn't have anything else going on.

Jeff said, *So he didn't sound like they knew a bust was imminent?*

No.

He was satisfied? Confident?

Sounded like it. Yes.

Good. So you are going to apprehend the driver and container tomorrow?

I thought you knew all about this. I told you I'm not supposed to tell a CI anything.

Come on, Moreno. Don't be cranky. I know stuff, but not what you're planning to do.

Sure. Okay. I will tell you, based on what you've told me, the Colombian authorities flipped one of Cordoba's employees in Medellín. Tomorrow is definitely a go.

Okay. Now, what can you tell me about Miranda Madisen, the hostage?

271

FBI told us they may have her as a heat signature in a compartment in the port bow. Say, I've given you lots of information. Now it's time for you to tell me, who are you, and what are this Thomsen and Madisen to you? How are they involved?

Jeff told him that he thought that Alejandro Saris was only acting on a hunch that there was going to be a bust, and didn't think he knew for sure. He was heavily invested in Thomsen's client's company, so he knew that Madisen worked for Thomsen's agency as a model. She was just a pawn.

As far as you're concerned, I'm just an unpaid CI who has watched all the episodes of Narcos *and* Narcos Mexico, *and I happen to know the players in this drama. I'm sure that Saris is bluffing; that he doesn't really know what you've got planned; that he's operating on nothing but a hunch. But Ms. Madisen is still in danger. I believe they're all complicit in the kidnapping, except maybe Cordoba's daughter. Back to Valencia. Did he say anything about you pulling surveillance off the boat?*

Yes.

What did you tell him?

I told him that whatever the DEA in Colombia had, which had caused Washington to have us surveil them, had been withdrawn. They were clean.

What did he say?

He thanked me and told me he'd compensate me well if I had anything to share with him when they return next year. He'll be in touch. I told him it was nice doing business with him.

Okay. They've been reassured. Yeah, Saris is bluffing. But the hostage would be discarded even if you weren't going to bust the container. She's a witness. Tell me, does the DEA have enough on Valencia, Cordoba or Saris to arrest them tomorrow?

Frankly, no. Unless we can find a connection in the paperwork at the warehouse, or someone flips to make a deal that implicates them. But by then, they'll be out of reach. You said they're getting ready to sail?

Yes, Jeff replied. *You need to get the laptop on the yacht— that might be enough to nail Valencia.*

Don't tell me how to do my job.

Jeff ignored him and continued, *And Cordoba has some paperwork showing he's interested in the* Aisling. *You said you checked with the ship regarding the container. Did you notice the name of the company that shipped the container?*

Yeah, we tried to track it down, but there's no company registered by that name in Colombia or here. What do you know?

AR&C? It's the initials of the first names of the three key players. Alejandro, Roberto, and Carlos.

How do you have access to all of this information?

It's my job. You do yours. Save the girl.

We'll get the drugs.

The FBI will get them on kidnapping, right?

Maybe. Hope it's not murder.

Not if you all do your jobs.

If you want a report on how it went, check with me tomorrow night.

Oh, I'll know. Thanks, Tony. I can call you Tony, can't I?

I haven't stopped you yet, have I?

⁓

The kidnapping was an unintended consequence of Jeff and Mindi working to make Alejandro paranoid with the antics in the gray room and the phone harassment. Mindi and he had been more successful than they thought and had caused the man to become unstable. It looked like he'd panicked. An overreaction that had put Mindi, and possibly the smugglers themselves, in jeopardy. Jeff was scared.

He arrived at the Long Beach marina to do something. But what? He wasn't sure.

Mindi was still unconscious.

He telepathed, *Mindi? Mindi?*

Nothing. She was out deeper than a dream sleep. Whatever they'd given her was strong.

What can I do?

He slipped into her mind.

Jeff? Jeff, is that you?

Relief. *Mindi? Where are you?*

It's dark. I can't see you.

I'm here with you. In your mind. Do you know what happened? Why can't I see you?

Can you go to the gray room, find me there?

I don't know. Why can't I see you?

Can you wake up?

I'm asleep? Where am I? Jeff, what's happening? I don't feel so good. Where are you?

I'm right here. Take a deep breath. Think meditation breaths. In through your nose, hold it, then exhale.

Jeff wandered around inside her mind, but it was darkened. Suddenly, he stumbled into the gray room. It was dark gray.

"Mindi, I found the gray room. Follow my voice."

"What are you doing here?" a husky female voice asked from behind him. A familiar voice; one Jeff hadn't heard for months.

He spun around. Shirley had her hands on her hips.

"Shirley! I'm looking for Mindi. She's here somewhere. Can you help me find her?"

"Why are you here?" Despite her initial bravado, her words were slurred by the drugs. "You're not supposed to be here."

"Neither are you. Why are you here?"

Shirley stared at him with glazed eyes. "I'm here to protect Mindi."

"I'm here for that too. Can you find her and bring her here? She's in danger."

"She's in danger?"

"I need your help. If you want to help her, find her. Bring her here. You'll know where to find her. Please, go. Now!"

Shirley turned and shuffled toward the horizon. Her image disappeared into the dark gray space.

He called out again. "Mindi?" He waited.

There was the sound of labored footsteps from the gloom. He peered in their direction and saw Shirley carrying Mindi, her head hanging to the side, eyes closed.

"Chairs!" Jeff said, and they appeared.

Shirley lowered Mindi into the chair's softness. Jeff sat opposite and took her hands in his. "Mindi, I'm here. I'm here. You're safe. Wake up. I'm here." He rubbed her forehead and put his hand behind her head to hold it up.

She stirred. Her eyes fluttered open, then closed.

"Jeff," Shirley said. "I know you *are* supposed to be here."

Jeff looked up. Shirley still stood guard. "Yes, I am. Thank you for finding her. If you want to stay, you can, but I'll take care of her."

"She loves you, Jeff. You take care of her. I'll always be here if she needs me. Thank you, Jeff."

Mindi groaned. He saw her eyes were still closed. He looked to where Shirley had stood, but she was gone.

Mindi's eyes fluttered open, searching. The lighting in the

room increased.

"Jeff?"

"Yes, Mindi, I'm here."

Her focus found him. "Someone grabbed me. Put me in a van. They were rough. Right on the street. No one helped. I screamed. No one helped. My alarm, my spray . . . They took my alarm. They stuck something in my neck." She touched her neck. "It hurts. Where am I?"

"We're in the gray room. My body's at the apartment. Your body is in a cardboard box in a storeroom on the yacht. You were kidnapped and drugged."

"We have to leave."

"You can't right now. First you must wake up. When you do, be quiet. Pretend to be asleep, or they might hurt you. The FBI is watching the boat. The DEA will get the container tomorrow. We have to get you out of there, past five people who are armed and bigger than you."

"You'll stay with me, Jeff?"

"I'm with you. The door to the room is locked. You can't open it from the inside."

"Ohhh. I don't feel so good," she said, letting out a deep sigh.

"I understand. If you wake up, I'll be close by, but I have things to do to get you out. Do you understand? You need to be quiet. Pretend you're asleep if they check on you."

"Okay. Pretend to be asleep."

"Yes. Good. You stay here, and if you wake up, stay in the bottom of the box. Do not move. Do not make a sound."

"Okay. I'll . . . be . . . quiet . . ." She let out another sigh and was back asleep.

Jeff left Mindi's mind and returned to out-of-body in his ghost form. The sun was going down. He flew over to the FBI agents with the thermal camera and entered the operator's head.

In her mind, he said, *Agent, can you hear me?*

The agent looked down at her radio, which remained silent. She looked over at the other agent.

"Did you say something to me, Jamison?"

"No, Alice. I did not."

It's me. I'm in your head, Jeff said. *The other agent can't hear me. If you tell him you're hearing voices in your head, you'll be relieved of duty. Only talk to me in your mind. Please. I have questions for you. Even if you think you're going crazy, the life of the woman you're watching on that monitor is in danger, and I can help you get her out. Okay?*

"I—"

"What?" asked her partner.

Alice, say "never mind!"

She stared at the camera's monitor.

With force, Jeff repeated, *Say it!*

"Never mind."

Now, don't speak out loud again, agent. Alice, is it?

She answered silently. *Yes.*

Alice, you're FBI, right?

Yes.

Who's the lead agency? Do they have a search warrant?

The Long Beach Police. Yes. But our hostage negotiator is on the way.

Okay. The woman on the monitor, on the floor in the bow of the boat, was drugged. She'll be waking up soon. You'll see her image stand up. She'll signal she's in danger.

Who are you? How do you know this? Why are you here?

To help you help her. When that happens, you need to have the police serve the warrant. These people are armed and dangerous. We don't want them to hurt her or any agents. Understand?

Silence.

Alice! You're not crazy. I know you think you are. I am a voice in your head, but I am a real person who can talk to you like this. My job, like yours, is to save that woman. Do you understand?

The agent kept her hands busy adjusting the camera. *Yes. Yes. Okay! What am I supposed to do?*

Good. In a few minutes, you'll see her stand up and wave her arms. You call on the radio and tell the police that she's signaling distress. That should give probable cause to raid the boat. We want them to serve the search warrant. Do you have that?

Yes.

I'm going to leave now. Watch the screen. When she waves, she's saying she's in danger. Radio for the warrant. The radio and the camera are being recorded, right?

Yes.

Okay. Keep watching. Please repeat what you need to do.

The woman will signal, and I'll tell them she's signaling distress.

Good. Thank you, Alice. Do good work.

Jeff returned to the storeroom. She stirred. "Mindi, I'm here."

"Jeff?" she mumbled out loud.

He slipped into her mind and called for her to wake up.

Shhh. You're locked in the yacht's storeroom. Don't make a sound. But I need you to stand up.

Mindi squirmed, almost got her legs under her, but they were made of rubber.

Jeff imagined himself taking control of her muscles. He felt the interruptions of the drug in her nerves. Slowly, using the sides of the box to steady themselves, he guided her. She stood but wavered, stumbled, and caught herself.

Now wave your arms, honey. Wave your arms.

Her eyes fluttered open and closed, making it difficult for Jeff to see, but he gained some control of her arms and they waved them back and forth over her head a few times before they dropped to her side. He tried to ease her to a sitting position. Mindi staggered. He eased her back into the box. Her head lolled to the side.

Mindi. Don't go back to sleep. I'll be right back.

Okaaay, Jeffff. I love youuuuu.

I love you too.

Jeff left her mind, went ghost again, then went to find Sofia. She was playing backgammon with her Tío 'Berto.

He snapped into her mind so fast that she sat up straight, her eyes widened as she tried to focus.

"Are you okay, Sofia?" Roberto said.

Jeff swept around in her brain, creating havoc.

"It's a migraine." Sofia said with a whine, covering her eyes to block the light. As she stood, she caught the corner of the backgammon board, sending the pieces flying. She stumbled into the passageway, found the head, and splashed water on her face. She searched the drawers in the vanity for anything for the pain in her head.

Jeff spoke. He was stern. *Sofia!*

She froze at the voice in her head.

Sofia. Alejandro has kidnapped a woman and put her in the storage room down the stairs to your right.

"What?"

Alejandro has kidnapped a woman, drugged her, and put her in a box in the storage room. Down the stairs to your right. Let her out!

Jeff and Sofia heard scrambling and voices in the lounge. She looked that way.

Never mind them. Go to her now! Go! The pain in your head will stop when she's free. Go. Now! He moved through her brainstem like a tornado, continuing the migraine attack.

Sofia stumbled out of the bathroom, turned right, tripped, caught herself before she fell down the stairway.

When she saw the pipe and bungee cord holding the door shut, she said, "What the . . . ?"

The voices were loud but indistinct, from the aft of the yacht. Then there were sounds of scuffling. She turned toward the sounds.

Don't, Sofia! It's dangerous there! Open the door!

She fumbled with the cord.

Get it loose. Now! Open the door. Keep the woman safe. Stay with her.

Sofia rubbed her head. *What's wrong with me? This pain, it's . . .*

Sofia! He was patient, but said with firmness, *The pain will stop when you open the door. Do it!*

She struggled. It snapped and came free. The hook cut the back of her hand. "Ow!"

The pipe fell to the floor with a clatter.

Sofia! Jeff yelled. *Open the door!*

The door pushed open, revealing Mindi trying to stand, wavering back and forth. Jeff stopped sweeping Sofia's brain, ending her pain. Sofia let go of her head and steadied Mindi as she tried to stand up in the box, but she stumbled to the side and both fell over. A gunshot. Sofia ducked. A woman screamed. More shouting and scuffling.

The sound of sirens filled the air. Flashing red and blue lights came in through every window in the yacht, and the whop-whop-whop of a helicopter was deafening.

Before Jeff left Sofia's head, he shouted, *Stay down. Keep her down!* He looked at the two women in a heap, satisfied that Sofia wouldn't run into the passageway.

Jeff went aft, past the staterooms, as two officers with

pistols at the ready moved from stateroom to stateroom checking for threats, each shouting "Clear" as they searched.

They reached the storeroom. "Show your hands. Stand up—slowly."

One officer lead Sofia out, her hands on her head. The other officer checked Mindi's pulse as she lay crumpled on the floor. He radioed, "Need medical assistance. Forward, lower deck, port side."

Jeff was grateful Mindi would get care. He was curious to see what was happening and lifted out above the boat and saw the parking lot swarmed with law enforcement: vehicles, flashing lights, blue windbreakers with large letters marking FBI and DEA and Long Beach police in SWAT gear.

Officers, two to a prisoner, hustled Sofia, Roberto, Miranda, and Carlos into the back of a police van. Where was Alejandro? He spotted him, dripping wet, being frog-marched by two officers toward the van. He had tried to escape.

Jeff flew back to Mindi and found paramedics with her. Satisfied she'd be fine, he returned to the apartment to check his phone. The FBI had left a voice mail a couple of minutes old asking him to call.

"I have word that your fiancée is fine," the agent said, "and being cared for. She'll be transported to Long Beach Medical Center."

He returned the call.

The agent asked, "Are you still at your apartment?"

"Yes."

"Thank you for your cooperation in not being near the marina. We'll need to get a written statement from you. We'll be in touch."

After traveling at the speed of a spirit all evening, driving the car to the Medical Center where Mindi had been admitted seemed to take an eternity.

The duty nurse gave him her room number. As he turned to go, she commented that she'd seen both Mindi and him on the TV commercials for that new makeup company. "Before you leave, can I have your autograph?"

Jeff pushed aside the curtain that had been drawn across the open doorway to Mindi's room. She had an IV and a nasal cannula, and was wired to several monitors. She was awake, watching the lights of the city.

At the sound of the curtain rings scraping the railing, she turned to see Jeff's worried face.

As she reached with her hand for him, the tubing and wires stretched tight.

Jeff took her hand and leaned down to kiss her. He drew back, searched her eyes, then leaned in again.

"The nurse told me you'd called to be sure I was here," she said. "Do you want to know what she said?" Jeff's blank look cued her to continue. "The nurse said, 'Your fiancé just called. He's coming now.'"

Jeff's blank look didn't change. "Yes, I called."

With humor in her tone, Mindi said, "Was it you that was drugged or me?"

Tears pooled in his eyes. "I'm so glad you're safe. So glad." He stroked her hair.

"Jeff," she said with emphasis, "the nurse said 'Your *fiancé* will be right here.' *Fiancé*. You called me your fiancée."

Now Jeff understood. "Yes." Pause. "I guess I did." He leaned in and kissed her again. "Yes, I did. We need to shop for a ring."

For a few minutes without talking, they held hands, enjoying being together and safe. Jeff broke the silence. "Wait until you hear about the crazy dream I had."

CHAPTER 17

The crowds on the Fourth of July holiday were dense, but Jeff and Mindi found Charlene at the base of the Space Needle, and they rode the crowded elevator to the restaurant to enjoy lunch and the view—spectacular on this clear summer day.

Jeff wanted to thank Charlene again for her role in helping rescue Mindi, and for trusting him without lengthy explanations. They planned to tell her the rest of the story and how things had developed to where they needed her help. They owed her that.

After being seated, Jeff began by asking Charlene if she'd talked with Ingrid.

"I went to the shop, but it was closed, and I never went back," she replied.

Jeff started by telling her about the workers in the jungle making cocaine, then meeting with Carlos and Miranda in Cartagena. He told her about the leap into Alejandro in April, in his new Audi, when he picked her up to fly to Friday Harbor for dinner.

Charlene froze, her wineglass an inch from her still open

mouth. Her eyes were wide in disbelief. She lowered her wineglass with a shake of her head and said, "You were where?"

"In his head—in his car—with you."

She kept eye contact and took a drink of her wine. "How did you know him? How did you choose him?"

"I didn't choose him. Like before, with Mindi, it just happened. And no, we didn't know him until that night. And he never knew me, even toward the end."

Charlene set her glass down and looked from one to the other. "You said *we* didn't know him." She looked at Mindi. "You, uh, you were there too?"

She doesn't miss a beat, Jeff thought.

Mindi glanced at Jeff, and he nodded for her to go ahead. "Yes, I was in your mind that night, going to dinner at Friday Harbor."

Charlene, usually poised and professional, put her hand to her mouth and inhaled so quickly it made a sound that all could hear. Her eyes widened again as she looked from Mindi to Jeff and back again. She said, "You said 'Frisbee' in my mind." She looked at Jeff and asked, "You said it in his mind, too?"

Jeff and Mindi nodded.

Charlene took a large swallow of wine, then said, "You couldn't do that last year, at . . ." She thought a minute. ". . . Halloween, could you?"

"No. That night was the first time."

"That was in April."

"For you, it was April," Mindi replied. "For us, it was November, just before Thanksgiving."

"You traveled forward in time, both of you?" Her gaze darted between the two.

Jeff nodded. "Yes. Without trying."

"So how many times . . . ?"

"Mindi and I talked about how much to tell you." Jeff looked at Mindi. She tipped her head sideways in a movement that told him it was his decision.

Looking back at Charlene, directly into her eyes, Jeff said, "As you know from my journal, none of the leaps were planned. Something or someone is controlling the leaps—past, now present and future. Sometimes I'm able to make some choices where to go, like when I came to you and asked you to call the DEA."

Impatient, Charlene said, "Get to the point."

"Okay. When we found out Alejandro was married—"

"What?" Charlene said loud enough to be heard at the next table.

"You didn't know?" Jeff meant it as a statement, but it came out a question.

"No. This is the first. Oh, hell. If I'd known . . ."

"We discussed that," Mindi said, "and tried to figure out how to tell you without doing it in a leap. We didn't know how you'd react. You didn't know about the drugs either, did you?"

"Oh, heavens, no. Damnit! It seemed like such a good relationship. Until that last night." She looked from one to the other and back. They said nothing. Mindi put her hand to her mouth and looked away.

Charlene frowned as she looked from one to the other. She focused on Mindi. "You were there then, weren't you? That was you, you were . . ."

Jeff's hesitation to speak, and the look on Mindi's face gave Charlene the answer.

"Both of you? How dare you?"

"Charlene, we never planned that. Not with you. With

Alejandro, I leaped into him on purpose because we were trying to figure out how to intervene in the drug shipment. It was an accident, what happened with you that night." Jeff looked at Mindi, indicating for her to take the story on.

Mindi reached across the table and took Charlene's hand. Charlene didn't flinch, maintaining eye contact as Mindi explained. "When I leaped into you, it scared the hell out of me. It reminded me of when . . . Well, I used my escape word right away. I mean, *right* away. Besides being uncomfortable for me, I knew it was no place for me. It was wrong."

Charlene didn't blink. "'Jeannie' was your escape word, wasn't it? I'd heard it before." She released her hand from Mindi's and put both hands on her face, then lowered them to look at Jeff.

His heart swelled with compassion.

"That was a bad day." Charlene said.

Jeff nodded. "When we realized Sarís's role in the drugs, our first priority was to protect you." He repeated, holding her gaze and saying it with authority, "Our priority was to protect *you*. Then, if we could interrupt the drug shipment, we would. We helped the DEA do that. We didn't plan the way it got him to break it off with you. Charlie, I would *never* interfere with your life. Never. But we could foresee that if you were with him when the DEA busted them, you'd have been deeply entangled, maybe even hurt. This is where we think that fate, the universe, or whatever's watching out for all of us, put Mindi there in your head to break up the relationship. We couldn't have predicted what would've happened. We could never have planned it, and if we could've, we would *never* have done it that way. It terrified her." He looked at Mindi, then back to Charlene. "It terrified you. I'm so sorry. So very sorry."

Jeff waited another moment, then said, "But it proved to be the wedge that put enough distance between you and him to protect you when the shit hit the fan in Long Beach. It feels like it was planned and put into effect, but not by us. Then, when Alejandro had Mindi kidnapped, you were there to help. For that, we're grateful."

Charlene said, with tears in her eyes. "I'm grateful too. For all of it. How could I not be?"

~

Mindi's window seat in first class on the Airbus A380 afforded a fabulous view of the fall colors of the trees thirty thousand feet below. This delighted Mindi, who in her corporeal state had never been to the eastern US. Jeff held her hand until they touched down at the airport. The weather was perfect for early October, the temperature somewhere in the mid-eighties.

A thirty-minute limousine ride delivered them to their hotel where, from the balcony of their honeymoon suite, they had a magnificent view of Niagara Falls—another dream come true.

~

Alejandro Saris was arrested and convicted of resisting arrest, conspiracy to inflict bodily harm, kidnapping, and malicious harassment on the strength of evidence in his cell phone and, ultimately, the full testimony of Carlos Cordoba. The judge administered the maximum sentence of five years at San Quentin and extradition to Colombia at the end of his sentence.

Jeff leaped into Alejandro's mind while he awaited trial so

he could satisfy his curiosity about how Alejandro knew how to find Mindi and him. Jeff found Alejandro experiencing the same sense of shame and punishment as when his father had physically disciplined him. Jeff didn't let Alejandro know he was there. Alejandro had found their names, address, and phone numbers in Charlene's cell phone address book and had them followed by three Colombian nationals, men who had overstayed their visas. They kidnapped her outside the photography studio building and used stolen animal tranquilizer to subdue her.

The Los Angeles Police investigators identified the kidnappers and their van using surveillance and traffic cameras. They were convicted, served their sentences in a federal prison, and were deported.

Karina was heartbroken at Alejandro's admitted infidelity and his secret involvement in drugs, but the Catholic Church wouldn't sanction a divorce. Even with all of that, she was still in love with him and told him she'd wait for him, on the condition that she had complete control over his entire financial empire. Karina continued support for the LaDormeur line of cosmetics, and while in LA for the trial, she contacted the cosmetic company and asked to meet with Miranda Madisen. Mindi and Jeff had dinner with her in Los Angeles, where the couple acted as if they were meeting for the first time. Karina became a spokesperson in Latin America for the LaDormeur line.

Carlos's plea bargain, in exchange for his extensive testimony against Alejandro Sarís and Roberto Valencia, resulted in all charges against him being dropped, including the illegal discharge of a firearm within city limits, on the condition that he immediately leave the US. Upon arrival in Colombia, he transferred a substantial part of his financial, business, and real estate holdings to his daughter, then dropped out of sight. Sofia Cordoba remained in the United States, completed her law degree, applied for citizenship, got married, and now practices corporate law in California.

Roberto Valencia was charged with conspiracy to distribute narcotics in the United States, based on evidence found in his computer and the detailed testimony of Carlos Cordoba. Despite the evidence, because he wasn't in direct possession of illegal drugs, the penalty was six months in a United States federal penitentiary, then deportation to Colombia.

Roberto's wife, Miranda (Mindy) Valencia, was acquitted on drug and kidnapping conspiracy charges, primarily based on Carlos Cordoba's testimony. She immediately divorced 'Berto and received a generous divorce settlement. She applied for and received permanent resident status in the United States and is now a film makeup artist in Hollywood. She and Mindi became close friends.

Senior DEA Agent Antonio Moreno received a Drug Enforcement Administration commendation for his leadership in the operation that intercepted 45,677 pounds of Schedule I and II drugs. He took a six-month leave of absence during which he requested and received extensive psychological counseling. With the permission of his superior, he anonymously donated the bribe money received from Roberto Valencia to Catholic Relief Services, an international charity serving 110 countries around the world, including countries in Central and South America.

The semitruck and trailer, and approximately fourteen thousand pounds of dried Colombian beef, leather luggage, and quality cow hides, were impounded by the DEA in the operation and were sold to support drug-abuse treatment programs, drug-crime education and prevention, drug recovery housing, and jobs for ex-offenders.

After a thorough search, no illegal drugs were found aboard the *Miranda II*. As a result, it was not subject to forfeiture and was released to the registered owners in Cartagena, Colombia, and was subsequently renamed.

Dan the Longshoreman was listed in official reports of the operation as an unpaid confidential informant, a member of the public, whose identity remains unknown and who has not aided the DEA since.

COMING IN 2024

∎ ∎ ∎

The third book in *The Between State* series,
From Beyond where more lucid dreaming and
paranormal adventures reveal the source of Jeff and
Mindi's 'dream magic' to answer the question,

'Where have they been getting their help and guidance?'

A NOTE FROM THE AUTHOR

If you enjoyed this book, I would be very grateful if you could write a review and publish it at your point of purchase. Your review, even a brief one, will help other readers to decide whether they'll enjoy my work.

If you want to be notified of new releases from myself and other AIA Publishing authors, please sign up to the AIA Publishing email list. You'll find the sign-up button on the right-hand side under the photo at www.aiapublishing.com. Of course, your information will never be shared, and the publisher won't inundate you with emails, just let you know of new releases.

ABOUT THE AUTHOR

Born to a military family, Joe has lived and traveled worldwide, earned a Business/Psychology degree, and chose the Pacific Northwest of the United States to settle, raise his family, and pursue his careers—first in telecommunications, then environmental, health and safety education. His interest in science fiction blossomed in his teens while doing research for an essay for a class assignment. The mystery of what takes place in our minds while asleep, during meditation, and yoga provided the foundation for his *Between State* series.

Printed in the USA
CPSIA information can be obtained
at www.ICGtesting.com
CBHW031204160724
11666CB00030B/151

9 781922 329455